Officially Noted
Smudges on edge 10/14 DS

# COLD HANDS

# COLD HANDS

Clare Curzon

THOMAS DUNNE BOOKS
ST. MARTIN'S MINOTAUR   ✿   NEW YORK

Thomas Dunne Books.
An imprint of St. Martin's Press.

All situations in this publication are fictitious and any
resemblance to living persons is purely coincidental.

www.minotaurbooks.com

ISBN 0-312-20464-7

First published in Great Britain by
SEVERN HOUSE PUBLISHERS LTD

First U.S. Edition: March 2001

10 9 8 7 6 5 4 3 2 1

# Contents

# Cold Hands

S uperintendent Mike Yeadings paid off the taxi and strolled into the station. He had ten minutes in hand before the train was due.

Because Nan's Vauxhall was in for servicing, and she needed his Rover for the children's school jaunt to Legoland, he'd been obliged to make alternative arrangements. He intended breakfasting with an old London crony before his nine a.m. appointment at Scotland Yard, so he'd opted for the local Chiltern Line 06.03 out of Aylesbury, due to change at Amersham and reach Baker Street by 06.58.

Settled comfortably in a window seat, newspaper still folded on one knee, he savoured the freshness that would surely give way to another torrid day when he'd end cursing collars, ties and the teeming metropolis. But so far on that country-scented bright July morning all augured well in Thames Valley.

But the 06.03 was fated to get little farther than Great Missenden station. When a screeching halt was followed by an extended wait, a tide of tetchiness began to rise among the passengers. With no broadcast message received from the driver, an overweight workman in string vest and jeans started making aggressive noises into the doorway microphone of their compartment. Recognising it eventually as a monologue, he conceded, " 'Ere mate, you all right or what?"

He had already punched the door-button for automatic opening without result. "Bloody stupid!" he complained to his audience. "It's controlled from the cab. We're shut in like

1

a lotta bloody sheep and gawd knows what's 'appening up front."

Yeadings, with ingrained scepticism for modern automated technology, wondered how soon the outer world would become aware of their situation. Hopefully before the next train was due in behind?

Even as he groped for the new crisp timetable in his jacket pocket there was a crackle of static and the driver's voice came through apologising for the delay. There was – as anyone by then could have guessed – an incident on the line and he must ask for everyone's patience until he was given instructions to proceed.

Which implied, Yeadings noted, that he was already in touch with base and the problem was being dealt with. But the man's voice, too deliberately controlled, was higher pitched than when he'd announced the previous stop. It might be due to nothing more serious than a tree trunk across the rails, or yet another concrete slab dropped from a bridge by twisted kids. Nevertheless the man was on his own at present. Yeadings flipped a notional coin in his mind, and natural curiosity decided that it favoured his sticking his nose in. Unusual happenings were, after all, in his line of business.

He took over from the string-vested protester, spoke to the driver, identified himself, listened and offered to help.

"Perhaps," he suggested, "you could do with some back-up until your own Transport Police get here."

He was allowed out, with the proviso that no one else followed. He walked up front, his city shoes slithering on the flint clinkers, and found the driver hunched on the grassy embankment, his head in his hands. The reason was hideously obvious.

Yeadings, accustomed to the sight of sudden death but never immune to its horror, took one swift glance and looked away. His indrawn breath brought with it the nutty scent of warm gorse in full flower, and as he gulped upwards the tops of feathery birches moved gently against a sky of the purest, innocent eggshell blue.

But for one person this morning the bright, living world had savagely stopped.

There was nothing to be done but wait and offer what support he could to the shocked driver.

"I couldn't avoid him. Not as if I was going fast."

"You wouldn't have seen him in time. That's why he chose that corner. And it was his choice, not yours."

Even so early there came a continuous sea-sound of traffic from the hidden A413. Roughly parallel to the railway cutting, it couldn't be far off. It was where the British Transport Police would have to leave their cars. And the blood wagon. He'd strike off up through the trees and signal to them where to pull up.

"Did you ask for a doctor?" he asked the driver.

The man shook his head.

"But you told them it was a fatality?"

"Yes. I radioed in straight off. They'll know what to do."

Of course. Not the first time by any means. There would be an established routine for bodies on the line.

"How about your passengers?"

"I'll have another word with them." The man got unsteadily to his feet and turned back towards the cab.

"What are the options?" Yeadings asked.

"When the track's cleared they may let us go on. Otherwise I have to lead the passengers back to Great Missenden on foot, then get them coached on by road."

Good, so the man wasn't too badly in shock: he was applying his mind. "I'm going up to meet the cavalry," Yeadings told him and started off up the embankment.

First to arrive was the police surgeon, a fiftyish woman Yeadings had come across once before – Marlowe or Thurlow, something like that. "Just a formality," he assured her.

"Very dead, then?"

"Not for me to say, is it?" Medics could turn awkward if you poached on their preserves.

With a British Transport van pulling in at that moment he was free to take her down to the train, but she needed little help, tackling the undergrowth and brambles like a teenager. And she was good at her job, going in unsqueamishly, not satisfied with uttering the necessary words but really looking to see what was there.

She knelt back, rubbing at her latex-gloved fingers with a tissue. "Now if I'd been meaning to do this," she said simply, "I'd have gone about it a little differently."

Despite the warmth of the risen sun Yeadings felt the short hairs rise on the back of his neck.

"Imagine, Superintendent, if you can, getting yourself psyched up to the act, spreading yourself out and waiting to hear wheels ringing along the rails towards you. Once committed to the idea, wouldn't you want to make a sure thing of it? Having a horror of half measures? Put your whole body over the rails, with your head on the far one?"

She was thinking of the uncomfortable way the man must have lain on the track, head level with his wrists lying over the nearer rail. Inert, not rigidly gripping the metal as he waited for the violent end.

"Perhaps he changed his mind too late, started to crawl off and was just unlucky," Yeading suggested.

She was crouched again over the pulped jaw which crumbled between her fingers. There was a little silence then she withdrew her hands, sighed and said. "Well, *somebody's* been unlucky, that's certain."

So his earlier frisson had been no false alarm. "It isn't a suicide?" he queried stolidly.

"I'm almost sure it isn't." She rubbed gently at some lacerated flesh with a finger end, clearing away some of the blood and tissue.

"Look at that fine line, and there again. He never did that himself. Before the train got to him he was garrotted. With something like a cheese wire. The 'suicide' was meant to cover it up."

There was a deal of telephoning and a brief explanation for the transport officer in charge, because now the scene had to be preserved for the pathologist and a SOCO team to view the body *in situ*. Passengers from the train were being escorted back to Great Missenden.

Yeadings withdrew, accepting a lift to Amersham to keep his

appointment at Scotland Yard. But it seemed pretty certain to him that he hadn't heard the last of the body on the line because, if the doctor's theory proved correct, he would be picking up the active investigation, with DI Angus Mott, heading a reinforced murder squad.

As soon as he was through with the brass at the Met and had settled the obligatory three-course lunch with a stroll to the ducks in St James's Park, his mind returned to the day's grisly start. He contacted Mott on his mobile to check what earlier trains had gone through on the Aylesbury up-line. As the Chiltern timetable showed, there had been no passenger train since the 22.36 on the previous night. Mott had already inquired about goods trains and learnt that the route wasn't used for freight.

So, awaiting more precise findings from the post-mortem examination, they had time limits for the placing of the body, but not necessarily the time of death. It was seven and a half hours since the last train on the previous night, a wide margin which could almost certainly be cut as soon as the dead man was identified and his activities of the previous day established.

Back at the morgue, the body awaited autopsy in a refrigerated drawer – the routine bagging of head and hands carried out as comprehensively as possible under the difficult circumstances. All clothing had been removed for laboratory analysis. Dr Littlejohn the senior pathologist had booked the post mortem for ten thirty next morning. Saturday or not, DI Mott and DS Beaumont were to join the Coroner's Officer and other ghouls attending.

At the scene of the crime, while uniformed police were conducting a fingertip search of the track and surrounding area for clues, passengers from later trains were still being transported by coach between Great Missenden and Amersham stations. Their initial reactions of complaint or flippancy were quickly damped at news of what had actually occurred.

For the Thames Valley police force it was a case of solid, unspectacular routine swinging into action. Yet Yeadings had a distinct feeling that this wasn't going to prove a straightforward crime of the usual domestic, sex-and-hate-based boiling up of passions. There was something cold about its planning. Cold as his own hands on the body when he'd tested for rigor. A corpse chilled beyond that of any recently breathing man who had laid himself on the line just as the train was due.

Somewhere out in the unknown there had been a calculating mind setting about its intentions: consulting the railway time-table even as Yeadings himself had done; transporting the body; laying it out where – hopefully – the thundering wheels would sever the neck and destroy all signs of earlier lacerations.

Luck was with the investigation then, because the train driver had been alert and had applied his brakes the instant he saw something on the line. Had it been another train, a less respon-sive man or a misty morning, luck could have been with the killer. The body's destruction would have been more complete. Then, who would have questioned an apparent fresh case of rail suicide? Sad and regrettable, but with no great follow-up apart from extra paperwork and the need for family counselling.

The doctor's arrival had been prompt. Otherwise, by the time she had appeared and officially confirmed life extinct, would the body's external temperature under July sunshine have passed as normal for the circumstances? Would she then – Marlowe or Thurlow – have thought it necessary to take an instant rectal reading and record air temperature?

Wait and see what Littlejohn makes of it, he advised himself. Just thank our lucky stars this murder isn't one of those that slip through the net unnoticed. We know there's a killer out there, someone we have to get to before he makes a habit out of clearing people from his path.

Elbows on the bridge-rail at St James's Park, he opened a paper bag and pulled apart the two sticky buns he'd bought on the way. They were stodgy, possibly indigestible. But the coots and mallards looked a bright-eyed mob who could tackle most things in their relatively simple world. He attempted a fair division, but the mere rustle of paper had brought a vast crowd at speed, towing interlocking vees of ripples, beaks snapping equally at crumbs and uppity rivals.

Not so different from police canteen culture, he observed. And the tufted duck just upending below was a definite caricature of fat Sergeant Bellamy: same beady eyes and greasy slicked-back hair, with a wayward bit sticking up at the crown.

He dropped the empty bag in the water and watched it float off, turned and caught the offended expression on a woman's face. She clearly thought him an antisocial slob.

Biodegradable, he comforted himself: paper's wood, wood's organic. And anyway, since midday he'd been off-duty. There's many would have plumped for some more heinous occupation on their free half-day.

He beamed at the offended woman in passing, politely raised his squashed trilby and bowled off in the direction of the Underground.

"Sharp-eyed lady," was Littlejohn's appreciation of the police surgeon's neat casenotes. "She's right, of course. This gentleman never intended disrupting the Chiltern Line's punctuality record. Taken unawares from behind, I'd say. Maybe never got his hands up to defend himself."

Mott moved in to follow the detailed external examination. Later on he'd be less enthusiastic, the explorations, removals and weighings of organs having long ago put him off buying his own meat. And in any case the state of liver, kidneys, lungs and heart must be of only academic interest after what had happened.

But stomach contents were different. Their nature and the stage of digestion could give a more accurate estimate of the time of death.

Unlike many surgeons of living patients, Littlejohn never worked to an orchestral background, preferring to provide his own grunted version of seventies' musicals, punctuated by brief, staccato observations into the mike clipped to the top of his plastic apron. The clerical assistant who later transcribed these notes claimed he could match tune to organ, or alternatively, to the surgeon's progress towards a causal theory of death.

Today, however, the pathologist began basso profondo as he delved. "Full fathom five," Mott recognised. Then later a flighty soprano, "Over hill, over dale . . ." Nothing more significant, he reckoned, than that Littlejohn had recently unearthed an old recording of the Zwingle Singers.

"Roughly an hour to an hour and a half after taking a meal," Littlejohn declared suddenly. "Now that's encouraging. Do we know his eating schedules?"

"We haven't even a name for him," Mott confessed. "What kind of food was it?"

"Substantial, meaty. Most likely minced beef or lamb with sheet pasta. Some form of alcohol, definitely gassy. Quite a lot of some lumpy substance that could be pudding – cake maybe. Ah, here we have whole sultanas. That's nice. Analysis may show better, but I think either doughy buns or spotted dick."

He straightened under the bright lights and wiped his brow with a wad of tissue. "I know what you want next: was it a meal out or a domestic slap-up? Well, I can't say, because he didn't think to swallow the menu, but we're certainly not talking *nouvelle cuisine*. The condemned man ate a hearty whatever. Not breakfast, I'd say. Main meal of the day."

"And time of death, roughly?"

"Like you always ask, and I always have to say. We may know later. For the present you must be content with somewhere between when he was last seen alive and shortly before he was found." Whereon Littlejohn slopped a handful of offal into a steel dish and resumed his choral concert, now lugubriously in French. "*La nuit, le froid, la solitude . . .*"

The SOCO team weren't too happy. By the time the death scene had been made secure with bollards and police tape, any residual signs of the killer's presence would have been trampled by the helpers. On the sloping bank they were looking for deeper indentations in the peaty soil made by someone carrying a dead weight, but anything of the sort had been overlaid by later footprints. There was the same doubt about marks on trees and undergrowth. Their young twigs were most likely broken off by the stretcher carriers shouldering their way through.

A heterogeneous collection of samples painstakingly collected from the surrounding area included crushed beer cans, bottle tops, cigarette packets and chocolate wrappers which could have been as easily thrown from open windows of passing trains as left by adventurous kids playing on the embankment.

Only one find seemed to have promise – a beige thread of some shiny man-made fibre retrieved from a thorn bush, but later to be identified as coming from the victim's own rain-proofed jacket.

"At least it shows the point where the body was carried down to the line," DS Beaumont consoled the Serious Crime group.

"Or walked down, either freely or under pressure," Mott cautioned. 'Let's leave all options open at this point. I've had a fatal accident sign put up for passing motorists. Someone may have seen a car parked on the road above and either one or two persons leave it to go into the bushes. All we have on the car at present is a double track from Ceat 165 T 14 S tyres on the grass verge, which statistically isn't tremendously encouraging. There is, however, a promising enlargement from the forensic lab of an unusual scarring on the front nearside. Take a good look at it. Who knows: that may be the best lead we'll get."

"What hope of identifying the victim?" asked DS Rosemary Zyczynski.

"You're just back from leave," Mott growled, "or you'd have gathered from the shots of the body that there's nothing we can reproduce in the Press. Dr Littlejohn finds the bone formation consistent with an age of late-thirties to forty. We're scrolling through details of suitable male Missing Persons on the national computer and eliminating those with the wrong blood groups. Anyway it's early days and his absence may not have been reported yet.

"Unfortunately our man's group is O positive, same as over forty per cent of the population. Samples have been sent for DNA testing. He was five feet ten inches tall, muscular and hirsute. Dark hair and eyes; no operation scars. His clothing is undistinguished, high-street store stuff. No laundry marks. Empty pockets – which could imply robbery as the motive, or an intention to hide who he was. Any watch he may have worn is missing, which isn't surprising in view of the mutilated wrists, but so far no pieces have been found by the track."

It wasn't much to go on, but they'd had equally negative starts before and still come up with full answers. The frustration for them all, eager for the chase, was that time was ticking away and, as yet, nobody had reported a relative, neighbour or fellow-worker missing. Whatever trail existed – and they hadn't caught on to it yet – was growing colder by the day.

Angus Mott was visiting the DI at Amersham nick regarding an earlier case when Garvey from Traffic came in with a memo from the Met. "It's a wild chance, but we've heard you're looking for a car with these tyres. There's a new area request for a stolen Nissan Bluebird, six years old, Middlesex registration, last seen four days ago in Heston."

"What sort of person takes four days to notice his car's gone missing?" Mott demanded, his ears pricking at the coincidence in dates.

Garvey looked at his notes. "Bloke called Walter Merton, works at Heathrow. He reported it missing. Seems the car isn't his; belongs to a friend, but he'd borrowed it."

"Who's it registered to?"

"I haven't checked yet."

"Well, do that."

There was a funny smell to it. You usually borrowed a car to make use of; not to leave to go missing. And why hadn't the owner's name been given first? Mott wandered after Garvey and watched him key in the registration. The name that came back was Oliver Webb, with an address in Uxbridge.

"Get him on the blower. I want a full description of the car. Let me talk to him."

He made the call from Garvey's office; the voice at the other end was a woman's. "Thames Valley Police here," he told her. "Could I speak with Oliver Webb?"

"I'm sorry, he's not here at the moment. Can I help you at all?"

"Is he your husband?"

"No. My brother. Is something wrong?" Her voice was apprehensive.

"Not really," Mott answered carefully. "We've just received a report that his car has been stolen, so I need to confirm a few details. Would you know if Oliver had been in any accidents recently? Something that might – say, have scarred his tyres?"

"No. What do you mean? Has something happened to—"

"Please keep calm. There's nothing to alarm you. Do you know anyone called –" he glanced at Garvey's memo "– Walter Merton?"

"Walter? Yes, of course. He's my brother's boss."

"I see. Thank you. We're just checking since he was the one who reported the vehicle missing. Was it the firm's car?"

"What is this? Why are you asking so many questions? Of course it wasn't a firm's car. They use their own on a job. Oliver never lends his to anyone."

Mott paused. She'd said 'on a job' and that sounded familiar. Could Webb have been 'in the job'? "Is your brother CID, Miss Webb?"

"No, he's a Customs' Officer. Didn't you know that?"

Mott finished the call as tactfully as he could. Things didn't look good for Webb – or his boss. Merton must have been running an undercover operation without Thames Valley knowledge and back-up. Reporting the car as lost had been his way of fishing for information on his missing officer.

Mott left it to Superintendent Yeadings to make contact through the upper echelons at Heathrow.

"We had – we *have* – every intention of working in close cooperation," Walter Merton assured him fervently by phone. "It's just at such an early stage. We barely know what's involved ourselves. Webb's gone out on a limb on this. He was purely on obbo, and failed to report back. He wasn't authorised to make any contacts himself."

A lot of bluster. And it was back to the ancient rivalry between agencies. Despite the progress and recent successes with joint Police–Customs operations, Customs still wanted to bag the loot and scoop the glory. On our patch, dammit, Yeadings fumed.

11

Yet had Webb actually gone missing locally? The missing car report had been a general one. The only Thames Valley link, Yeadings had to admit, was a slim one: a suspicion that the missing Nissan Bluebird with the right Ceat tyres might have been the one parked above the railway line where the unknown's body was later found.

But it seemed now that the dead man might be identified through the car. He decided to chance his hand. "I think, Mr Merton, you should come and look at a body we've had for a few days. It could be someone you know."

# Out of the Game

W alter Merton accompanied DS Beaumont to the morgue and came straight back to a stiff interview with the Boss. "Yes," he said shortly. "It was my man. I couldn't be sure at first until I saw the clothes. Then I looked again, and yes, it was Olly Webb."

Merton was clearly shaken but had himself tightly in control, a hard, straight line between thin lips. He was tall and big-boned with a craggy face and fine sandy hair that fell over a square pale forehead. Pale blue eyes were set deep and close to a beaky nose. Too pale: not an outdoor man any more, Yeadings decided, whatever his track record might once have been. In his mid-forties, he too was doubtless condemned to an office chair, computer-dominated when he wasn't checking output from the surveillance screens.

At Heathrow, Yeadings knew, it was a high-pressure job in bursts, punctuated by demoralising gaps of waiting for results. And, like himself, Merton would be quietly envious of his juniors still out there in the proactive scrum, taking the risks, getting the full adrenalin rushes.

The two men sat facing each other across Yeadings's desk like adversaries instead of near-colleagues. And that's his fault, the Superintendent stubbornly insisted to himself. If he'd the remotest notion that there was contraband getting this far we should have been notified. Joint measures should have been taken.

He said as much. "In which case," he observed, driving it home, "your man would probably still be alive and able to act on what information had been gathered by us. I trust you will be informing his family yourself."

13

Merton looked grimmer still at the reminder of what lay ahead. That and the coming reprimand from his top brass should keep his department in line for a while.

Still, we all make mistakes, Yeadings granted silently. No call for *schadenfreude*. That just calls down bad luck on one's own head. Nevertheless . . .

"So I think I'm owed an explanation," he suggested. "What is it we should be looking for? And what's your source?"

"We had information from Amsterdam," Merton offered, relieved to be dealing with material facts. "Of a consignment recently passed through Schiphol, but by unknown agents."

Drugs, then, Yeadings supposed. Or it could be porn. A vile trade in either case.

But he was wrong. "A sizeable quantity of counterfeit notes in large denominations."

"Sterling?"

"What better at present? European currencies are wobbly by comparison. Our Netherlands colleagues suspect the printing's done in Rotterdam, but the centre hasn't been located yet. One of the unnamed suspects was due to fly back in ten days to contact his UK distributors, so the Dutch passed us the tip."

Yeadings considered the implications. If there were plates and printing equipment set up for the counterfeiting in Rotterdam, then they could certainly expect further consignments to be sent over later.

So Webb had been put on to tailing the suspect, he guessed. The Customs man had somehow slipped up, and, over-keen, had blown his cover and been summarily despatched, to keep identities hidden and ensure the safety of further supplies. Risking such final measures must mean that really big money was involved.

"We've seen no surge in circulation of counterfeit notes here," Yeadings said cautiously.

"It's early days. This killing puts their operation at new risk. They'll wait to see what happens when the body's identified. The stuff will be stashed away until they consider it's safe to start spreading it to other points for simultaneous release on the street.

They could be scared, unsure whether Olly got a chance to report back on them."

Yeadings nodded. It made sense that any distribution plans set up in advance must now be put on hold. However keen to get the money circulating, the dealers wouldn't risk the whole operation if they believed the sample consignment had been sussed. But they weren't necessarily convinced that their cover was blown: it depended on how soon they had become aware of Webb's interest in them. And what information they'd forced out of him before they finished him off.

"I'm surprised they didn't bury the body or sink it somewhere," Merton wondered aloud.

"No, they want it found. They're relying on the death being accepted as suicide," Yeadings gave as his opinion. "Are there circumstances to incline us to that theory? Had Webb any credible reason to kill himself while on this assignment?"

Merton stayed silent, biting at his thin lips until they disappeared from view. Yeadings was left wondering how well the man knew the officers working under him. Then, "He'd been under considerable strain lately, so we kept him on routine inquiries. I wouldn't have used him for this but we were sparse on the ground. There's a lot of high-powered stuff coming through Heathrow at present. And he was very keen to take on the obbo, so I let him."

Yeadings waited. Funny money being of less importance than big drug hauls. Yes, he could see that. But there was more to come.

"Olly was having money troubles. And domestic. Maybe the other way about: first the wife going off and then finding she'd left him with considerable debts."

"A liability to the service?"

"He'd always been reliable until then." Merton clearly didn't like the implication. But members of his department, as much as the police, were vulnerable under pressure, especially investigating operations where a great deal of money could be involved.

"There's a sister," Yeadings prompted. "Who else?"

"A son. Eight years old. Tom has cystic fibrosis and needs

constant care. That's possibly what finally got to Monica so that she felt she couldn't take any more. Very pretty woman and used to being made much of. Ran off to Limassol with a Greek-Cypriot café-owner. Left Webb and his sister to shoulder the hard stuff."

Yeadings eased the collar away from his neck. It seemed to have grown suddenly oppressive in his usually airy office. He didn't want to know any more about the dead man. Not a lucky one. There were some who seemed to attract misfortunes. If he'd smelled such a one in his own team, how would he have dealt with it?

"This suspect," he said, changing tack, "what do you know of him — him or her?"

"Little enough. The identity came through just half an hour before the KLM plane touched down. A Kurt Nederhuis, but there was no one of that name listed on the flight. The only ID detail available was that his cabin luggage — a navy blue grip — had a tiger printed on the side. He had no bags in the hold. We got him on film as he came through, and that's the point at which Webb picked him up. Here — I brought this enlargement of him."

It wasn't the clearest of photos. Nederhuis had contrived to get himself in the middle of a throng of tourists heavily loaded with gear. He appeared to be of medium height, lean, mid-thirties, mousey-haired with a drooping moustache which might or might not have been genuine, and round, dark-rimmed spectacles. Among so many people, halted in mid-queue, there was nothing distinctive about his stance. Nothing distinctive about him at all. If his travelling bag bore a logo with a tiger, it certainly seemed out of character.

Yeadings stared at the other man. "Now that we have a name for our body we shall have to release it to the Press. What I want to do next may be distressing for the family; for the sister anyway." He hesitated.

"Go on."

"A full disclosure of the unhappy circumstances of his life. We won't go so far as to say the police regard this as a straightforward suicide. Let the tabloids make that suggestion. As to the

16

man's occupation, 'a junior civil servant' covers the facts for the general public. Unfortunately we don't know how much his killers got to know about him, but we can take it they gathered he was from your department."

Merton was looking more wretched by the minute. He hadn't missed the Superintendent's use of the plural, implying a gang killing. "There is just a chance that he met his death through some other connection."

Yeadings suppressed a sudden rush of impatience. "I like to think we run a comparatively tight little ship in Thames Valley," he said tersely, "but of course we suffer from the odd sociopath let loose to 'care in the community'. Then again, we can't discount jealous husbands, female rapists or little green men from outer space. But no; if he was close on the tracks of a gang of counterfeit distributors, it's reasonable to suppose it was they who got to him."

There were beads of sweat on Merton's forehead. "Was there any – I mean, did it appear that they'd . . . ?"

"Tortured him for information? You saw the body. The train wheels could have covered up any traces of that. It was sheer chance that parts of the ligature marks survived. What information could he have given, supposing that he did talk, whether willingly or otherwise?"

"No more than I've told you. It was just the start of an operation. We were still waiting for the Dutch authorities to fill in the outlines."

"You'd nothing more than the report of counterfeit currency being brought in and that a Kurt Nederhuis, as contact for the UK distributors, would come off a named flight, carrying a navy-blue cabin bag with a tiger logo. That's not a lot." Not much to be killed for anyway. Yeadings considered asking precisely what instructions Webb had been given; how far he was expected to risk his neck alone without police back-up. But that aspect was beyond his own remit, certainly being the subject for a future disciplinary hearing that would have Merton carpeted by his own bosses.

"What do you want us to do?" the Customs man asked.

"Talk to the dead man's sister. How well do you know her? Enough to take her into your confidence, or will you hand her the suicide story?"

"She's a sensible woman, but for her own safety it will be better for the present if she's given the official version."

Good. Yeadings hoped that after this sharp lesson the man would be doing everything strictly by the book. "If you send someone to work with us undercover make sure he's unknown hereabouts and totally trustworthy. I'll inform you instantly when we pick up a trace of these people. Until then we'll go with the flow, publicly satisfied with the theory of suicide, but keeping our eyes open and an ear to the ground."

Even as he said it, an imp in his mind remarked that prostrate at ground level was no vantage point for an obbo. He hid the resulting grin in a cough as he stood to grasp Merton's hand and send him on his way. Poor devil, who would be in his shoes, carrying the worst of news to the dead man's sister?

At the door Merton turned. "About the formal identification. Is it necessary for Miss Webb to do it?"

"She should really, but under the circumstances, maybe not. We could log it in your name. Unless, of course, she insists on seeing him."

"I don't think that's very likely. I'll try to put her off anyway. Thanks, Superintendent."

What next? Yeadings asked himself, left alone and moving across to the window. He inserted a stubby finger between slats of the flexible blinds and squinted out at a summer sky dotted with little ovine puffs of cloud. The sort of day to spend in the garden, spraying rosebuds, clipping grass round the flower-beds. Despite the exhilarating challenge of a new murder case, he acknowledged a special kind of distaste for this new job. Not because of the killer, but the victim – the way the poor devil had been left out on a limb.

There were disturbing factors about the dead man, and it seemed possible that as the case proceeded unsavoury details could emerge. Webb's run of misfortunes could well have left him open to temptation. He'd been keen to take on the job when his boss was reluctant and if that in itself wasn't suspicious, what about the fact that his quarry had picked him up so easily.

Leaving the body as an apparent suicide suggested the killers might have known there was a history of distressing events which could justify Webb's taking his own life. Was this because they had worked on him to force those wretched admissions out?

But why did the body have no means of identification left on it? If the counterfeiters wanted a rapid conclusion to any inquiry, shouldn't the body have been left clearly identifiable as Webb's, with a handwritten goodbye note in one of its pockets?

So perhaps there hadn't been time to force him to write one. Was he already dead and anonymous before they thought of that refinement? If so, they weren't all that cool-headed and forward-looking. In which case there was a chance they'd panicked and left some kind of trail behind them.

Down in the forecourt a uniformed man was hassling another over parking his patrol car. *Cars*, yes. That was the next move: find Webb's Nissan Bluebird which hadn't yet turned up. Get the team circulating among secondhand dealers; alert patrol men to check deep ponds and flooded quarries for signs of tyre tracks.

He let the blind slats snap back, wiped a light dust off the ends of his fingers and set off to get things moving.

Two evenings later, on Saturday the twelfth, a report of a submerged vehicle was phoned in by the Safety Officer on a practice dive with the local branch of British Sub Aqua. And that was luck, Yeadings conceded, because the entry to Cragg Park pond was barred off from picnickers' cars by a palisade of solid tree trunks, and so the site hadn't been listed as a priority for checking. Whoever disposed of the car must have driven it a long way through the pine woods, over heavy undergrowth and after dark. Which certainly meant it hadn't been a joyride pick-up: kids'd never have had such patience, psyched up for the ritual torching of it.

Minimal fuss was made of the Bluebird's discovery. It was winched out in the early hours of Sunday and transported for forensic examination swathed in dark covers. If the local Press had learned of the event they hadn't considered it important enough to put in print.

"Let chummy think it's still underwater," DI Mott said, "and that we've assumed it's been stolen and already shipped out. Meanwhile let's hope we get a lead from something they've overlooked inside."

But luck wasn't straining itself on their behalf. It appeared that Thames Valley police had received its ration of good fortune for the present. There remained only the alternative of hard slog.

The Superintendent's select team met in his office to consider the forensic scientists' preliminary report on the car. Despite its being submerged they had managed to bring up a few distinguishable fingerprints, but all of them Webb's. Smudges elsewhere, notably on steering wheel, brake and gear lever, were most probably caused by someone wearing thick gloves. There were no traces of blood, no DNA-rich cigarette butts, giveaway scraps of paper or marks from shoe soles.

"Total negative," Mott said gloomily.

A description of the Bluebird as a stolen car, and requests for sightings of it were still being made in the Press. Thames Valley Traffic Division dutifully examined three burnt-out cars, the victims of joyrides, implying that they expected the suicide's abandoned car had been stolen from above the railway line. Nearly a week went by without any progress at all. And still no flood of new counterfeit notes flowed into local shops or banks.

Reduced to trawling through reported minutiae in back copies of the Bucks Advertiser for the period of Webb's death – *Timothy's Pet Tortoise Goes AWOL; Jail for Absconding PO Manager; Grocers' Society Honours Retiring Chairman* – a frustrated Superintendent Yeadings suddenly had second thoughts and turned back to the front page item of a domestic fire in Little Chalfont.

He remembered hearing of it from Amersham nick as a bit of a puzzle still left as an open file. At two a.m. a passing motorist had reported by mobile phone that smoke was issuing from a second-floor flat. Prompt action by Amersham Fire Service had prevented widespread damage to neighbouring apartments but the blaze had almost completely gutted the original rooms.

And although it had no connection with his own inquiries at the time Yeadings remembered that it had been an arson case: the place doused in accelerant, but no insurance claim ever made, and the tenant had mysteriously disappeared overnight.

With rising hopes quite out of proportion to the likelihood of any relevance, he sent for the Incident log and a copy of the fire chief's preliminary report. These confirmed what he recalled of the case. And hadn't he agreed at the time with the investigating DI's theory that someone needing to cover his tracks had made a pretty thorough job of it?

Anti-terrorist branch had shown interest, suspecting the flat could once have been used as an arms dump or IRA bomb factory, but no evidence was found and the inquiry quickly went cold. Now the only reason he had for looking again was the coincidence of dates. The fire had broken out during the night on which Oliver Webb met his death. The flat could have been torched to cover up any number of existing crimes, but there was a chance, just a slim one, of a connection with the murder inquiry.

Yeadings reached into his desk for an Ordnance Survey map and traced the distance by road between Little Chalfont and the railway line at Great Missenden. It looked little more than ten miles. Then go west and south another dozen, and guess what? Cragg Park pond. Could the figures look so promising and still not add up? He picked up the phone and barked out an order for Mott and his two sergeants to be called in.

"First," DI Mott decided, when they had assembled and been put in the picture, "we need to know if Oliver Webb was ever seen in the vicinity of the arson flat. I believe there's a row of shops almost opposite. Beaumont, take one of the photos Merton gave us and show it around. If I remember aright there's a patisserie and tea shop which he could have used for obbo. Try those first but keep it low key: he's your long lost brother or whatever."

Yeadings turned to the woman DS. "Zyczynski, I want you to

find out everything about the missing tenant. Blast the neighbours with Social-Security speak. You can't understand why
they've gone off and not drawn money they were due, and so
on."

He scowled. "And if you both prove I'm on the wrong trail
here, don't ever dare remind me."

Mott was looking happier than he had for days. "The railway
runs close to the flats, but it makes sense they should take the
body some miles farther down the line. I think we can trust your
nose, boss. Meanwhile I'll check on any scraps retrieved from the
fire scene. Hopefully it was done in an almighty hurry, and
they've slipped up somewhere."

Beaumont was the first to report back. Oliver Webb's photograph had been recognised in three of the shops almost opposite
the burnt-out flat. At the patisserie he was remembered for
coming in three days running and once causing quite a scene
over claiming an occupied table as his regular one.

Even that wouldn't have been a perfect lookout since the shop
was narrow with a single line of tables parallel to the long service
counter, and the disputed one was the first in line from the door.
Webb had spent some considerable time in the shop over those
three days. He'd confided to his waitress that he was a software
rep dealing with home computers, and she'd felt sorry for him
the way he had to hang about until his clients were able to see
him.

"Did he mention any of those clients?" Beaumont had inquired. But no, he'd asked a few questions about people in the
flats opposite: whether they might be interested in video games
and calculators. She hadn't been able to help much, but she told
him where the kids hung out who were probably into that sort of
thing. Not that there were many. Most of the residents were
middle-aged or retired people.

When Beaumont remarked that it looked as if there'd been fire
damage over there at some time, that was when she'd come up
with the goods. Actually, she'd said, the man in the top flat – who
didn't seem to be employed because he never went out much,

except to get supplies – he'd been a client of the man Beaumont was asking about.

"Your brother," she said significantly. "Only he wasn't, was he? And you're a copper, aren't you?"

At that Beaumont had felt obliged to pay her over the top for his Danish and milkshake.

DS Rosemary Zyczynski wasn't far behind him. Her clear-lens heavy-rimmed spectacles and drab outfit hadn't saved her from clumsy compliments from certain of the retired male flat-dwellers. "What's a pretty girl like you doing in DSS?" was about par for the course.

The women she approached were more voluble but not necessarily more helpful. Nearly all aired personal complaints against Social Services about inadequate payments or unanswered letters. One single mother on income support was angry at being falsely charged with cohabiting. But another, apparently contented with her life, invited Z in for home-made lemonade.

From her the DS learned that the late Olly Webb had actually made contact with the now missing tenant from Flat Twelve, directly above this woman's apartment. There'd been just the one man – a Mr Collins, rather rough-looking with a beard. But he'd had a friend to stay three or four days before he disappeared.

She'd glimpsed the gentleman whom Z showed her the photograph of, just the once, going upstairs with Mr Collins. She was sure it was the same gentleman because she'd stopped them in the hall at lunchtime and asked if she could help, the gentleman not seeming at all well and needing Mr Collins to help him get up the stairs.

Asked if she could remember what day this had been she wasn't sure at first, thought it was a Thursday, then suddenly beamed as she recalled, yes, it was July the third, the day she'd bought a birthday present for her young nephew, William. A model ambulance complete with paramedics and stretchers inside. She'd packed it the same afternoon and sent it off by first-class post so he'd get it by the weekend for sure. There was no doubt about the date.

Zyczynski almost hugged herself with satisfaction. So now

there was a sighting of the Customs officer at midday on the day before Yeadings encountered his body on the railway line.

"This other 'friend' who'd visited Collins," Yeadings pressed when the DS reported back, "did you get a description?"

"Yes. It tallied with the photo of Nederhuis that Customs gave us. Droopy moustache, but otherwise rather ordinary, although, there was one interesting thing. She said he spoke with an American accent, but she thought he was some other nationality and he'd simply learned to speak English that way."

"So we've a witness for the last sighting of Webb alive. Get her to come in and look at some mugshots," Mott ordered her. "We need to get a fix on that Collins."

"That would blow Z's cover," Yeadings reminded him, "and she might need it again. See her yourself, Angus. You've got a way with the ladies. She may open up even more."

Zyczynski hesitated at the door, unsure if she was needed further just then. "Did you get anything from the fire chief's investigation team?"

"Yes and no," said the DI inconclusively.

"You'd better all sit down and we'll pick it over together," Yeadings offered. "Beaumont, get some coffee perking while Angus explains."

The DI waited until they had all found seats. "It seems that among a lot of seemingly useless junk there was an overturned tin waste-bin in the kitchen. In it was found a badly burnt scrap of paper, covered over when the ceiling fell in. Fortunately for us, because arson was suspected, all fragments have been carefully preserved."

Mott unfolded a sheet of paper taken from the breast pocket of his jacket, slung over the back of a chair. It was a photocopy of a handwritten note. A widespread pattern of charring had destroyed the main part of the message, but the two sergeants leaned close to make out the remaining words "close down he—". And, on the line below: "—ater to . . .—ylings".

"The first bit's easy," Beaumont claimed cheerfully. " 'Close down *here*.' That would fit in with the arson. This was a note left by Collins for someone due to arrive while he was disposing of the body. Whoever it was, he was instructed to clear their stuff out and torch the place."

"It seems a reasonable assumption," Yeadings commented. "Or it could come from written instructions left for Collins by a third party. What do you make of the rest?"

" '—ater'," Zyczynski considered. "It could be 'water', or a surname, like Slater."

"Or less the S?" Yeadings suggested. "Some rendezvous arranged for *later* at a place ending in '—ylings'?"

"Or at somebody-*yling*'s house?"

"Yes. We have a choice there: a person or place." Mott quietly groaned, taking the hot mug from Beaumont's hand.

"It's not much to build our hopes on," Yeadings pronounced, "but it's all we've got. We must milk it for what it's worth. Assuming that Webb's death has made some change of plan necessary, they're going to need a new venue. So, putting all our stake on '—ylings', I want local directories and large scale maps scoured for persons or places that end with those letters. So sup up and get to work on it."

It took the best part of the afternoon, and the only acceptable words to come up were Grayling's or Fraylings – as in Fraylings Court, an old manor house which had passed from that family through the female line two generations back.

And the name rang a bell in the back of Yeadings's skull. He swivelled the leather chair and reached for a phone. When he was connected with his wife he asked, "Nan, have you still got that wad of notices about arts and crafts courses? You have? That's great. Could you drop them in for me? Or Z can come out. Right, that's great. Thanks.

"She's just going to pick up Sally from school, so she's bringing them in," he told the others smugly. "There's something which should interest you. The family at Fraylings Court are finding times hard. They'd considered putting it on the Stately Home circuit, then fought shy. Instead it's to open for residential theme holidays.

"Nan had some idea of trying a week there while I took the

25

kids to the seaside, but it didn't work out. Which, if my wild surmisings are anywhere on target, is probably just as well. I could send one of you lot instead—" he eyed the other three sardonically – "if any of you has artistic or intellectual leanings or wants to do *t'ai chi*. We can decide who that'll be when we've taken a look at their brochure."

Mott had his keen-whippet look on. "It sounds promising, a landed family down on its luck, needing new infusions of cash. A sizeable estate: plenty of places to stash the counterfeit stuff. And any extra coming and going can be put down to a renewable flow of mature students. I like it, Boss. Let's go for it."

# Dealer's Choice

*Sunday, 11 May*

T he brochure, the family had all agreed, was inviting, even enticing, while remaining in discreet good taste. The disputed words 'hotel' and 'country club' had been voted out. The boldface heading offered THEME HOLIDAYS AT FRAY-LINGS COURT.

There was an aerial view of the main house, outbuildings and grounds, with a hint of rolling Chiltern countryside beyond. There were fetching colour shots of a bedroom suite, the lounges, studio, ballroom and stables. Catering was referred to in mouth-watering terms, offering special diets on request, a distinguished chef, home-produced vegetables and fruit in season. Treat yourself, it implied: escape to luxury living and indulge your dream hobbies.

The list of courses available included painting, both in oils and watercolours; sculpture; creative writing; voice production and public speaking; aerobics; music appreciation; horticulture; and riding for the disabled. All suitably upmarket interests likely to draw only those with money to scatter to the winds.

"You don't think –" Sir James had anxiously inquired – "that it's offering too much? I mean, all things to all men, what? A bit sharp, eh? Don't want it to sound like a con, do we?"

"We have to spread it wide," his daughter, Constance, countered firmly, "to sound out the market. Once applications start to come in, we'll know more precisely what it is that people want."

"But they'll expect it ready set up, m'dear. You can't produce all that at the drop of a hat."

"We don't have to, Father. Just do a quick job on producing one line that most people go for. One study subject at a time: specialisation. We simply explain to the rest that the current lists are full and offer to consider them for the next round."

He still looked uncomfortable. The programme on offer struck him as distinctly sharp.

"I'm sure Connie has it all thought out," his wife said serenely. "Once the demand is known we can go ahead with the necessary adaptations."

She forbore to mention the proposed first-stage onslaught on the bank, armed with grandiose forward-planning figures prepared by son-in-law Julian. The mere hint of loans, mortgages and repayments – however modest – tended to afflict the old war-hero with hysterical paralysis.

"Liese, I'm afraid you're an incorrigible optimist."

"Only from necessity, darling. Someone has to restore the balance. You're so discouraging, James. You should be grateful for the young folk's initiative. If we want to stay on here we must make money somehow. After all, anything's better than wildly throwing the place open to the public, as you pointed out yourself."

Well, yes. He had done, visualising hordes of spike-booted hikers and sticky-fingered children let loose to destroy his precious, fragile relics from bygone generations.

"At least this way we'll have some control over whom we allow under our roof."

*Guests*, he told himself, trying to find compromise. Yes, not actually an invasion. Perhaps endurable, although large house-parties had always driven James in near panic to some temporary hermit cell.

"You'll see, Father," his daughter assured him briskly. "It will all be controlled and highly civilised. And think of the cultural benefits for Joanna."

At mention of his grandchild the old man brightened visibly. "Where is she? Haven't set eyes on her all morning."

"Oh, somewhere around," said Constance vaguely, fluttering her fingers. "She's decided to write a book."

*     *     *

A handful of straw had removed enough cobwebs and accu-mulated grime from the small oriel window in the stable loft for Joanna to keep tabs on the family discussion. Across the sunlit courtyard, Grandfather's wheelchair was centrally posi-tioned in the morning-room's big bay window, with Granny Liese sitting alongside at a low table as she arranged irises and azaleas in a china ewer. Mother flitted behind them sketching in the air with small impatient hand movements, abruptly abandoning her clipboard to lean a moment on the open window's sill and twitch free an invasive stem of wistaria.

Joanna watched their mouths and reconstructed the unheard dialogue. The women were working on the old soldier, demol-ishing his final defences – and by now no more remained than a small pile of soft sand. He'd no choice but to let it happen: bend the knee before wave on wave of invading Attilas, pillaging and enslaving the natives. Grandfather nagged into raising the white flag, betrayed by the lower ranks. It was outright treachery, it was pitiable. It was damnably *unfair*.

Prone on the scratchy straw, Joanna paused, scowled, chewed at the end of her pencil and resumed the fierce scribbling in her journal. It was no airy 'Dear Diary' effort, but in dramatic form, TV-scripted.

*Lt-Col Sir James Siddons* (Close-up), she wrote, and under-scored the name. Then a colon and the speech: If needs must, then t'were well t'were done quickly. (Raises head nobly. Strikes fist on knee.)

She doubted the speech was original. She frequently found exciting turns of phrase while sniffing through the leathery books in the old man's library. Too many to memorise the snippets' sources, but they had a way of lingering in her mind, to pop out at suitable moments.

Joanna peered again through her window. Mother was speak-ing now, turning away. Must have won her point. No. She'd merely gone for some newspaper to clear up Granny's broken stems and leaves.

Joanna continued the imagined dialogue.

29

*Mrs Julian Tinsley*: It is all for the best. In time you will come to bless our names for saving the House of Siddons.

Really that was rather good. A fine place to end, even if a rhyming couplet would have had more punch. But you couldn't start off as a Shakespeare. It took time to work up to.

Joanna finished with a practised arabesque of her initials and added the date: May eleventh at eleven seventeen of the forenoon. And may the Lord have mercy on your souls.

Even before the first outside reactions to her advertisement could suggest the shape of final arrangements, Constance Tinsley found herself torn between priorities. Thank God they had continued to live in a civilised manner up to the limits of available income. (Almost beyond it, Julian had warned.) But still so much needed doing if the Court was to be made acceptable to paying guests.

Cosmetic improvement to the outdoor pool vied with renovation of the clay tennis court. An English summer gave no guarantee of prolonged warmth, but if the project was to take off in late July, people would expect to swim, whereas the tennis frenzy over Wimbledon would have peaked and (she hoped) fallen away.

"School holidays," her mother unhelpfully countered. "So you must be prepared for couples with youngish offspring. Tennis would help burn up their excess energy."

"M'm. Not keen." Connie frowned over the prospect, an accidental and out-of-depth mother herself. "Anyway, those sorts of children will have bullied their parents into jetting to more exotic climes. No, the pool wins. It's simply an all-ages *must*. I suppose we might get by with a few dozen replacement tiles and some new sun loungers. Pray God the filter system hangs on a little longer."

She swept off to survey the tennis court's pitted surface and rusted wire surrounds. It was even more of an eyesore than she remembered: thistles and dock leaves lushly bursting through like some prize vegetable crop in an oversized roofless fruit-cage.

"Get rid of it," she ordered Jolly, the odd-job gardener. "Hire a mechanical digger and turn the ground over. I'll see if I can contact someone selling turf. If it's mostly crumblies who answer our ad, they may fancy a putting green."

Jolly scribbled on his pad and made the usual harsh bullfrog sound in the back of his throat. Connie fielded her reading glasses from the ornate gilt-chain hanging from her neck and peered to read his comment.

Crokay? the pad inquired. Voiceless and poor speller though he was, Jolly remained an inveterate snob.

Well, why not? Miniature golf course or croquet lawn, what difference? Both needed grass. "Right," said Connie, "so that's settled."

Jolly plucked at her cardigan sleeve. She sighed, turned and repeated her last sentence facing him, mouthing exaggeratedly. Jolly responded with a display of portcullis denture.

If Napoleon had had lieutenants of like mettle, Connie considered, he would have gone back to digging the family plot in Corsica and the French would never have become so boringly uppish in the EU. Wondering fleetingly what heights of glory her own shackling assistants deprived her of, she waved the man off.

Provided the sun shines when they arrive, she told herself, slowly walking back towards the house, the old pile could really make an impression. Its warm golden stones, transported from the Cotswolds by an inspired Jacobean Frayling, had stood the centuries well, sand-blasted and steam-cleaned some quarter-century back in a wild burst of patriotic fervour at the Queen's Silver Jubilee.

Money hadn't been so tight then, and had stretched to soft furnishings and interior upkeep. Ever since, the Court had been allowed to slide – well, to *mellow*. One did expect a historic house to look dignified; even a trifle dowdy – like fine lace yellowed by time. *Smartness* – she comforted herself – would be frowned on as distinctly parvenu by the right kind of people.

Elsewhere, Sir James was pulling his weight; also a four-by-two strip of flannel on a cord through the barrels of a treasured Purdey. Seated in his wheelchair, he contemplated the walls of the gun-room – rendered and whitewashed brickaged to a cosy parchment colour. Over them, arranged in serried ranks or radiating fanwise, were displays of pikes, blades and firearms used by his family in skirmishes from the Civil War through to World War II.

These weapons, unlike his cherished hunting guns, evoked in him ambivalent feelings. Convinced that warfare was most often the outcome of governments' political ineptitude, he deplored that innocents must become involved and die for such failings. As a career soldier – by his father's choice and in submission to family tradition – he had led his men through bloody horror in North Africa and Italy, determined that they should honourably survive, and only secondarily concerned with putting down an enemy. A Yeomanry officer, he saw himself under a personal obligation – a shires baronet protecting his own. Alongside the fallen of his regimental family, he honoured and regretted the more distant dead of his own blood who had borne the clumsy cuirasses and other body armour stacked now between flagstones and wall. Over centuries they too had discharged duties as heavily heaped on them. But he found he could not glory in their bloodier exploits.

A modest man – retiring crippled as half-colonel – he remained in awe of the ancient pair of regimental flags which, grown threadbare with age, dipped ghostly grey from opposite sides of the vast stone-flagged outer entrance hall. To him they appeared substantial, his own military effort skeletal.

Hopeful that life might impose no further unwanted role upon him, he was wryly content to watch his only daughter take present command, a fitter campaigner than ever he could be, but inheriting like him the stringy frame, sheep features and strawlike hair of rugged Frayling forebears.

His only grandchild, who for him embodied the promise of a fairer future, seemed to have skipped a generation, taking after his plump and pretty Viennese wife, with her creamy skin, dark eyes and near-black hair. But Joanna was something more, something special: farouche, he decided – an untamed creature, possibly with hidden fangs, wildly unpredictable, imaginative, insatiably curious; at the same time shy and fearless as only the untried dare be.

He considered her now, questioning the effect on her of whatever changes her mother was about to inflict on their secure and unpenetrated family life.

Squinting down the first gleaming barrel of his side-by-side, he grunted approval, laid the heavy gun across his lap and prepared to thread the pull-through into the second chamber.

Early May, he considered; and their little world at peace. It was a very serious move the family was taking on so light-heartedly. How unalterably would things have changed in two or three months' time?

*Mid-July*

Constance Tinsley surveyed the final programme. Four projects were now listed as definite. Oil-painting was out for lack of teachers; but determined scouting among ancient school friends, the extended family and listed evening classes locally, had produced two candidates to present a course of sketching and watercolour. Which was, apparently, the desire most commonly held by applicants for the advertised holidays.

She had interviewed the tutor-applicants separately in a hotel in Henley, with her father present to add gravitas. The first – an emaciated and wild-bearded young man reeking stalely of some herb she had disdained to enquire into – would be fitter, it struck her, as Scarecrow-in-Field than Artist-in-Residence. So the position fell by default to the sweetly vague-seeming, plump little lady of a certain (but undisclosed) age whose surprisingly strong pen-and-wash landscapes had been exhibited in a number of London galleries and the present Summer Exhibition of the Royal Academy.

Her paintings were all signed D Crumm, and when pressed she admitted shamefully to having been christened Désirée. Since she appeared to be temporarily in straitened circumstances and was enchanted with the opportunity to keep her easel set up after the two fortnightly sessions for which students had signed up, a loose arrangement was made for her to stay on afterwards as a paying guest on special terms.

Simultaneous with the residential art course there were to be twice weekly afternoons of Riding for the Disabled, supervised by Connie herself and a nurse friend from the village; also – during the school holidays and with an option to continue indefinitely – a Saturday series of junior dancing classes (classical ballet, mornings; tap, ballroom and modern, afternoons); and – twice weekly – synchronised-swimming tuition, (Connie's last-minute inspiration to help cover expenses on the outdoor pool).

The instructor for this floodlit evening course was to be a plain-clothes policeman by the name of Mott, himself a water polo enthusiast. An aquatic ballet corps for Thames Valley force and their friends had been reluctantly disbanded as female officers were often required on duty at short notice or posted away. Two or three surviving members wished to continue, and applications from the general public now guaranteed a full team with two reserves.

Within Fraylings Court's walls, modifications were being pursued with varying degrees of vigour. A new set of five guest bedrooms and two bathrooms was being developed off the upper east corridor – unused since resident staff had been pruned during World War I. As ever, the right kind of workman was scarce when needed, and a band of semi-skilled amateurs from the village had set to with a will, jostling each other to remove existing walls, construct partitions, plumb, tile, wire for lighting and radio, apply paint and fit carpets almost simultaneously, while two of their wives provided refreshments from the distant kitchens, along with a flow of matronly advice.

The kitchens themselves had been inspected by a firm of industrial caterers whose damning report had been stonily received by the ladies of the house. ("They've a nice way of saying 'primitive'," Sir James had commented mildly.)

Alternative tenders for renovation had been scorned, pared, and ultimately adopted in a modified form. Modern industrial catering equipment was being installed, also a goods lift to deliver from the basement kitchen to the dining-room and newly created buttery.

Mrs Dalton, partially sighted cook-housekeeper aged seventy-eight, gave notice. Thankfully the family presented her with a pretty Worcester tea service – superfluous to requirements – as her retiring present, and Connie promptly contacted the three nearest polytechnics with a view to re-staffing from their final-year catering students.

O-Day (for Opening, Overture or Oribull Fiasko according to Connie, Liese or the man Jolly) was to be Friday, July twenty-fifth. Even with the bank's co-operation, that date promised a close-run race between hungry creditors and the required "settlement of the basic fee on arrival" quoted in the prospectus.

Julian Tinsley had notified his City partnership of an intended two-week holiday from the Monday following the opening, "Just in case of complications", and Connie, in a rare eve-of-battle failure of confidence, had accepted her husband's offer as a supportive move rather than additional hassle.

Sir James, having installed in the library a microwave oven (with handbook) and a small refrigerator – both included on Connie's catering equipment account – was preparing to dig in and sit out the invasion.

Liese had removed plastic covers and swathes of tissue paper from her collection of Ascot gowns for the past fifteen years, and was making a selection for her Ladyship role. Connie had bought two sets of jodhpurs and five new shirts.

Only Joanna, released the previous week from her prep day-school, had no plans, moping in seclusion as she mourned friends absent on family expeditions or summer camps. The TV script dried up from lack of inspiration as she wretchedly promised herself a long, miserable summer of alien interference.

Friday, July the twenty-fifth began sticky and overcast, the successor to three days of glorious sunshine and steadily rising temperatures. Even at seven a.m. fingers were easing collars loose. By noon distant rumbles augured badly for the intended Welcome on the Terrace with a Strawberry Tea.

By seven p.m. the (mainly) assembled would-be artists were peering out through windows sheeted with rain at the roll call of the Aquatic Ballet corps barely visible under the vast colonnaded porch. Their instructor, a well-built blond young man, had grinned cheerfully at Connie's confident assertion that, "We never get lightning strikes here. The storms always head for the ridge at St Peter."

"Just the same," he declared, "I'm not letting anyone into the pool." Since his last words were lost in a deafening clap of thunder directly overhead, Connie could only admit his wisdom and lead the party up the grand staircase for 'dry run' instruction in the ballroom.

After checking out the dining-room, she returned to take stock of her guests socialising over their aperitifs, and was shocked to realise that although the roll call of attending students was complete, no one had yet set eyes on their instructor. Ms Désirée Crumm had simply failed to arrive.

Nothing could equal the horror of the discovery. It was like being mobbed by a flock of unruly sheep when the collie had run off. No, it was far, far worse, since the guests were showing some enthusiasm for the coming course and none of the family could even make small talk about art.

With Crumm's defection and Father like some staunchly uncooperative Colditz inmate determined to tunnel out of his social obligations, Connie was immediately faced with being two short for the dinner table which was already formally laid. Unless, of course, she made an exception for the evening, inviting Jennifer Yorke's little girl Clarissa (a much resented stowaway whose existence had never been hinted at until she was being unloaded with baggage from the blue BMW) to join the adults. Which also meant summoning Joanna from whatever grubby pursuits she was involved in, overseeing rapid sanitisation, and trusting she would cope with keeping the other child out of everyone's hair.

Connie nodded meaningly to Julian to repeat the round of aperitifs while she went on the necessary quest.

\*     \*     \*

36

"Stuffy. Shit-stuffy," Joanna mumbled into the olive-green taffeta which was being forced over her head. Under the fiercely hissed threat – "You eat, don't you? Well, tonight you eat this way or never again" – she had submitted. But, as a measure of independence after her mother left, she had travelled downstairs via Granny Liese's dressing-room, presenting herself to the company with inexpertly applied scarlet lip gloss and black eyeliner.

The kid, she saw at a glance, was no challenge, blancmange soft, with drippy long blonde curls and big blue eyes. China doll stuff. Fleshy big; maybe her own age or even ten. She lifted a superior eyebrow at her and gazed emptily through the storm warnings on her mother's face.

As the meal progressed, the company's initial stiffness began to ease. The older ladies, having rapidly given each other a challenging top-to-toe survey on meeting, were now able to check their first impressions against a more protracted examination of the respective male partners.

Connie, offered an abundance of applicants, had selected her first fourteen aspiring art students on the dinner-party principle of balancing the sexes. Of the three married couples, one was elderly, one middle-aged, the other – surprisingly – in their middle twenties. Another couple (of separate surnames, but Constance chose to overlook this and referred to them as Mr and Ms Dunne) struck her as a pair of ill-matched Lawrence inversions – Lord Chatterley and the Land Girl.

The remaining six would-be artists were single, unless you bracketed Miss Finnegan and Mrs Fellowes, unmistakably teachers from the same girls' private school, who had booked a twin room. Which left Dennis Hampton, retired journalist; Douglas Jeffries, fiftyish, an aeronautical draughtsman; Jennifer Yorke, the blonde widow of thirty rising fifty, and finally NL Smith, accepted as a supposed male but proving on arrival to be a wraith of a woman who appeared as characterless as her name – until you encountered her huge watchful eyes, green as ripe gooseberries.

Jonna found one compensation in the bargain her mother had

struck: the food was fantastic. She was keeping her side of it. She was there, she was eating, so OK. But nothing more.

There was a lot of stilted waffle around her: references to opera, long-dead film stars, disapproval of media treatment of famous noddle-heads. Relinquishing her carmine-streaked fork, she looked up with momentary satisfaction and met the bright, humorous eyes of the elderly man opposite.

He was amused at her. The cooling embers of resentment flared into open fury. She would have stretched over and accidentally knocked his wine glass into his lap except that something in his expression warned her he might well expect it of her. Joanna searched her mind for the word to describe him. Was it maverick? Anyway he was right out of place here, uniquely alive in the company of the drivelling dead.

Fortunately, she was spared further discomfort under that disconcerting gaze by the arrival of coffee.

"Darling, take Clarissa upstairs and show her your room." Connie instructed, her voice honey-soaked like baklava.

They trooped obediently out. In the hall Joanna whooped and cartwheeled, finally rolling like a puppy on the tiles and cycling with her legs in the air. "Clarissa," she howled. "*Clarissa, Clarissa, the boys queued to kiss her!* How could they give you a name like that?"

The other stood abashed like the pudding that she was. "Everyone calls me Clary," she defended herself.

"Clary. That's better." Joanna sat up cross-legged. "So, what shall we do, Clary? I know, I'll show you the stables. I bet you're scared of horses."

The girl looked down at her satin pumps. "But it's raining."

Joanna stared long at her. Clary quailed.

"All right, then."

They moved towards the great archway that gave on to the flagged entrance hall. Some economical body had turned out the lights there and its bleak enormity was full of unaccountable shadows. As they neared the outer doors a sudden black figure appeared momentarily, flattened against an upper glass panel.

38

Silhouetted by a vivid flash of lilac lightning, it flapped monstrous bat-wings and uttered a banshee wail.

". . . Can't find the bell," came the distant lament, then the spectre disappeared.

Joanna drew a bolt and looked out. Driving rain blew in between the columns and, staggering again up the steps, came a little bundle of a woman lugging various bags and boxes under each arm.

"I'm rather later than expected, I'm afraid," panted Miss Crumm. "What a lot of wriggly little lanes there are round here, with signposts all offering the same destinations."

"Are there? Didn't you have the map Mother sent you?"

"Goodness child, I can't read a map when I'm driving."

"No wonder you got lost."

The little lady planted her bundles on the flagstones. "Not lost. Gracious me, no. You can't get *lost* on an *island*. It just means taking a little longer sometimes, going another way round. And being sure to start out with a full tank of petrol." She seemed in no way put out.

Joanna, a practical cartophile from her earliest years, regarded her with wonderment. "I'll say it could, if you went by Edinburgh or Southampton."

"Well, anyway, I'm here. The name's Crumm." She was beaming. So nice of you to help with the luggage. I've got some more things in the car."

She bustled off again, clutching a shawl over her raincoat's shoulders. The two girls looked at each other. Joanna nodded towards the larger suitcase which Clary began to drag in, and then marched behind with a collapsible easel and stool.

Still panting slightly from her exertions, and dripping rain, Miss Crumm was welcomed by Connie and Julian while Liese sailed off to the kitchen to order a supper tray for the newcomer's bedroom.

"We won't trouble you with introductions this evening," Connie offered, viewing the woman's happy disarray with some unease. "I'm sure you'd prefer to relax in peace and meet your students tomorrow. Let's leave your – er, equipment here for the moment, shall we, and just have your personal requirements taken upstairs?"

"Good idea. Clothes and such. Let's see. That'll be that one." Miss Crumm indicated a small tapestry bag, its handles mended with green gardening twine, and contentedly followed Julian upstairs.

At the division of the grand staircase they were met by the first of the synchronised-swimming class, dismissed, excitedly chattering, from instruction in the ballroom. Miss Crumm's bright eyes lit on them with interest.

"Not your students, I'm afraid," Julian admitted, and explained. She crowed with laughter and stomped on.

Connie, below, steered the dry-swim stampede towards the rear of the house. "Perhaps it'd be more convenient if you all went out by the kitchen garden," she suggested. "It's closer to where you left your cars."

They trooped down the back corridor, past the one-time butler's pantry, Angus Mott bringing up the rear with two girls from the original police team. A padded door swung suddenly open and a surge of small white dogs exploded on them, excitedly yapping and challenging the strangers.

"West Highland Terriers," Connie introduced them proudly. "Marvellous guard dogs, very lively and independent. I'll let them out for their airing, but see they don't follow you all through that door in the wall."

As the crowd filed through they could hear her shrieking to call the dogs in. "Rory, here! Good boy! *Angus, don't piddle on the chervil!*"

"I don't think she means you, sir," whispered Sergeant Barbara Wayne.

Detective-Inspector Angus Mott hunched his shoulders against the rain. "Good. That leaves me free to suit myself."

"Well, m'dear, how did it all go?" inquired Sir James anxiously, emerging from cover when he judged the company had finally dispersed.

Connie was perched on the arm of a leather chesterfield in the staircase recess. Seldom accepting hard liquor, she was clutching a brandy balloon. "Well, at least they all turned up. In the end," she said carefully.

Liese appeared from the kitchen corridor wearing the smile of a satisfied tiger. "I am going to bed now, where I shall say a little prayer to St Hobart."

"St Hubert, surely, m'dear. Though why this sudden taste for huntin'?"

"St *Hobart*," she insisted, taking her husband's arm and planting a kiss on his weathered brow. "He is the patron saint of dishwashers. His name is all over that wonderful machinery in the kitchen."

Connie leaned back and drained the last of her brandy. "I think it's going to be all right," she ventured on a final sigh. "Nothing too dire so far. Though tomorrow will be the real test."

The (dry) swimmers having left the ballroom in good order, Connie's inspection on Saturday morning was quite brief. The new practice barres fitted across the full-length mirrors still looked odd to her, but the carpenter who had installed them swore they could eventually be removed without damage to the walls.

Madame Clovis's first ballet class was scheduled for nine a.m. but she was the fussy kind who would arrive early and start picking holes in arrangements. Fortunately Liese was deputed to deal with the lady and Connie had total faith in her mother's upstaging ability.

Hopelessly clumsy at infants' ballet classes herself, Connie had nevertheless discovered in adolescence a passion for Highland reels, and during her father's military career had become a notorious feature of the more cavorting regimental occasions. Liese, loyal Viennese, had despaired of her galumphing, certainly inherited from Sir James who, before his injury, could convert the swooniest Strauss waltz into smart marching order.

Despite her admitted failings, Connie paused now before a wall mirror to watch herself perform a carthorse curtsy before darting a guilty glance at her wristwatch and plunging off to check on preparations for the art class.

Across the cobbled courtyard from the stables was the coach house, its ground floor converted with a minimum of expense into a studio. Connie endeavoured to avoid the puddles, blessing the fact that yesterday's clouds were fast dispersing. There was no one present as she peered in, but clearly Miss Crumm had risen early and set things up before breakfast. The big room was divided into four areas each with a central subject for study and a half-ring of chairs. One model was a set of coloured wooden cubes, spheres and cylinders. In another corner was arranged a still life consisting of a green wine bottle, a partly peeled orange, an open magazine and a pair of reading glasses. The third exhibit was a twisting branch of stephanotis (surely wrested without a by-your-leave from the Fraylings conservatory) arranged in a plain glass jar against a drape of blue brocade which Connie recognised as the window curtain from the downstairs staff lavatory. The fourth corner held a dais topped with an empty chair. The white double sheet draped across it gave pause for thought. A *nude* Life Class? Wasn't that a bit – well, you know?

A caw of delight from the doorway announced Miss Crumm's return. "Are you joining us? Oh do, it'll be such fun!"

Connie hurriedly assured her that she was there merely to make certain the class had all it needed.

The little lady whirled, arms outflung. "You see, I have just helped myself. Everything's perfect, perfect." She beamed, bird-bright eyes under bird's-nest white hair, round as a robin in some all-enveloping dark stretch garment, topped by last night's tatty shawl and stopping short at a pair of neat ankles and tiny moccasined feet.

"Water jars." Miss Crumm waved towards the stone sink which was crammed with kilo jam jars. "I found about a hundred in a cupboard in the pantry. Didn't think you'd miss a few."

"Er, no. Quite. What about paints, pencils, paper, all that sort of thing?"

"Sent 'em all a list of what to bring, after you gave me their names and addresses. Brought along some supplies anyway, in case they forgot. People do, I find."

Slightly dazed by an unexpected organising talent that rivalled her own, Connie went back to report that on the art front all appeared to be ready to roll.

The breakfast room was emptying, one of the two catering students on duty at the long chiffonier checking what was left under the covers. It was the lanky boy, Andrew something: red crewcut and bobbling Adam's apple. "Got the portion control about right," he murmured. "A bit short on the kedgeree and long on the kippers."

"If ordinary house guests are anything to go by," Connie assured him, "it could be the reverse order tomorrow."

"Did you arrange with a pig farm about the leftovers?"

"No need," Connie quelled him. "It'll all be composted." But not, she conceded silently, until the family had relished their delayed — and of necessity reheated — breakfasts.

"You do the crocks," she ordered. "I'll see to this little lot."

She transferred the remaining food into the small goods lift and went up to the buttery where she found Julian and her father unloading it.

"Where's Joanna?" she demanded, apprehensive.

"She's had hers, m'dear," Sir James apologised. "Went in with the little Yorke girl. They seem to be hitting it off. They'll keep each other out of mischief, I expect."

Privately Connie suspected that the reverse might be the case, but for the moment her daughter was a problem shelved.

As they settled to tuck in, Liese arrived in a dashing Cossack-style linen suit from the seventies. "Really that Clovis woman is extrao-o-o-ordinary," she told them. "Thin as her wand, magenta rouge from eyebrows to chin, and — would you believe it? — black silk Directoire knickers!"

"How on earth do you know that?" asked her son-in-law, intrigued.

"Because she throws her legs in the air. She must be eighty if she's a day, and she's showing off like a young ballerina."

"She's seventy-two," Connie corrected. "And she's still a name among the Covent Garden crowd. We're lucky she lives locally and responds well to flattery."

"Let's hope she doesn't overdo things," her father said anxiously. "The very last thing we want here is a fatality."

# Ace High

I t is in the nature of human endeavour that sooner or later some disaster must occur, but the first three days of the Fraylings project passed with only recoverable lapses. Gayle, the other half of the catering pair, scalded her left arm with an upset pan of boiling water. After an obligatory visit to Casualty at the local hospital she took twenty-four hours off. Her place was taken more than adequately by Liese whose apfelstrudel was out of this world, and her secret ingredient in the coffee won glowing comment from several of the company.

On the second evening Sir James's library was invaded during his absence by the elderly couple seeking a dictionary for their compulsive nightly games of Scrabble, but even that had a happy outcome. From a framed group photograph on his desk they discovered an acquaintance in common; the Gilchrists' nephew had briefly been Sir James's adjutant in Germany. On his reappearance the colonel was hailed as near-family, their incursion was explained and forgiven. Taken unawares, Sir James was temporarily overwhelmed, submitting to joining their next game of Scrabble. And subsequently found himself a convert.

Connie was perplexed over lack of progress on the putting green/croquet lawn. Jolly seemed to have disappeared off the face of the earth. The new turf had been duly laid during early June and required frequent attention. It had rapidly soaked up Friday's rain and was now drying out again without benefit of being further rolled. Nor was the wretched man attending to duties elsewhere; the midden was rising to a steaming and odorous offensiveness behind the stables; the kitchen garden had not been hoed, and the supplies of produce brought in for house use had been only perfunctory.

The mystery was explained by the first exhibition of the art class's output. There, hideously grinning in collarless striped shirt and straggling water-smarmed hair, was Jolly, enthroned on the white-draped chair.

Life Class indeed, Connie thought; decidedly *Low* Life. But at least they had been spared his nudity.

Miss Crumm declared herself delighted with the promise of her students. The retired journalist, Dennis Hampton – he of the lively eyes which had so discountenanced young Joanna – showed strong leanings towards caricature.

Mrs Fellowes and Miss Finnegan, forever inseparable, had found the flower study's challenge too subtle, and switched to portraying Jolly (head only) in line-and-wash with left profile and full-face respectively. The results were a childish study of a cheese-coloured gibbous moon and a ruddier much-knobbled potato.

Jennifer Yorke's appreciation was a lopsided splosh which by happy accident perfectly suggested the ungainly man's louche leering. Only Dunne's painting displayed any technical skill, but the overall effect was of a strangely sad person with Jolly's features superimposed. Dunne's female partner had omitted neck as well as body, submitting a charcoal sketch which suggested a skull shrink-wrapped in clingfilm.

The remaining exhibits were incompetent flower studies or wildly inaccurate Still Lifes. Only one meticulously shaded pencil sketch reproduced the mundane collection of wooden cubes, spheres and cylinders.

"Yes," said Miss Crumm, sighing as she eyed it, "we shall have to liberate this one. It looks as though he uses a ruler. Poor Mr Jeffries, he draws what he knows is there, instead of what he sees."

On Tuesday, Julian Tinsley, having assured himself that matters at home were in safe hands, decided to check with his city firm that no clients were upset by his absence. Connie dropped him off at High Wycombe station when she went shopping at eleven a.m. By his return over seven hours later the scene had somewhat changed.

"It really is too bad!" Connie stormed at him the moment he reappeared. "I was quite prepared for people to drop out, so I'd organised a pretty tight operation. Now, to have an *extra* coolly dropped on us – as if we were subject to a billeting order – well!"

"But if people haven't booked they just can't come," Julian said reasonably.

"You try telling *him*!"

"Who? I hope he doesn't imagine he can steamroller his way in. Where is this person? Would you like me to go and have a word?"

"You can't. He's asleep. Up in Mrs Smith's room."

Julian ran a nervous hand through his thinning hair. "I'll get us both a drink, Connie. It sounds like a long story."

He poured two dry sherries from their private supply in the locked cabinet. "Now. Who is 'he'? And what's he doing up in Mrs Smith's room?"

"I knew that woman was going to be trouble the minute she turned up," Connie complained vehemently. "Signing herself 'NL!' Naturally I thought she'd be a man. And she's no more 'Smith' than Santa Claus. Goodness knows what her real name is. When I queried it, quite humorously, she calmly said it didn't matter: we wouldn't pronounce it right anyway, so Smith was easier all round. She sounds English herself, but goodness only knows what *he* is. I never imagined we'd need to ask people for passports or identity cards."

"You're telling me that Mrs Smith's husband has turned up?"

"That's what they claim he is. But how would I know?"

"Well, you did accept the Dunnes, and they don't pretend to be married."

"With the Dunnes I'd already *catered* for a couple, Julian. Don't you see? Mrs Smith's in a single room, naturally. Somehow I've got to produce another double or we shall lose both Smiths. And a double fee."

"Isn't another available?"

"Mrs Yorke and her little girl have the twin-bedded room opposite. I could move her to a single and suggest putting Clary up in the old nursery with Joanna. But this man who isn't really Smith insists on a double bed, king-size if possible. It would mean moving other people around as well."

"He sounds more trouble than he's worth, Con. Why's he asleep at this hour anyway? Has he been drinking?"

"Jet lag," she said shortly. "He's just back from Honolulu. Julian, this is our first real challenge. We've got to manage something. Besides –" She looked at him imploringly – "he simply drips money, and you know how expenses keep going up and up."

Connie had obviously surrendered her disgust at the man's arrival to the overriding need to balance the books. It seemed inevitable that they must go through the lists again and see who would perhaps agree to exchange rooms. Just the same, Julian had every intention of pointing out to the man how inconvenient his unannounced arrival was – and exacting a sizeable surcharge.

Mrs NL Smith came down alone for pre-dinner drinks. For once she appeared quite congenial, inviting the company to call her Nadia. "My husband," she explained, suddenly informative, "has returned unexpectedly from a business trip abroad. He will not require dinner, but you will all be able to meet him later tonight, or at breakfast tomorrow."

"And what aspect of art interests him most?" Miss Crumm enquired briskly.

"Oh, he hasn't come to paint. Just to relax."

"I'm still not entirely sure," Connie said, bridling at the woman's calm presumption, "that I can meet his requirements."

"I'm sure you will, Mrs Tinsley. You are such an admirable manager." Nadia's wide green gaze slid over her hostess and away serenely into the distance. She was very slightly smiling.

And I had thought her unremarkable, Connie raged inwardly. *Patronising* me, in my own home!

Julian had no need to wait for next morning to encounter the newcomer. As he approached the grand staircase just before dinner, from the family's private sitting-room, he was aware first of the rich aroma of a Havana cigar and then of a tall, slightly stooping figure standing halfway up. A lean face framed with black hair and trimmed beard topped powerful shoulders in pearl-grey mohair suiting. Long white teeth showed in a scimitar slash against swarthy skin as his sardonic features curved in parody of a smile.

The man came slowly down to tower over Julian's adequate five feet ten. Deeply set in the vulpine face, his dark eyes dominated.

"Tinsley?" the man asked softly. Perhaps there had been just a hint of 'Mr' first.

"Er, yes. And you—"

"Mr Smith, shall we say. But you may call me Boulos. There is no call to be formal." His voice was sibilant, the accent impeccably upper class. Perhaps suspiciously so, like a foreign language perfectly imitated.

With horror Julian added the forename to the appearance. They had never met in the flesh but, although notoriously evasive of cameras, the man had been adequately described in the financial press. There could surely be no mistake.

"Mr – er, Smith, I—"

"Boulos, please. Or even 'B'. Yes, I think we would find that more convenient."

"I understand from my wife that you require—"

"A suite, yes."

God, now the man had further upgraded his requirements! "I'm afraid we don't have one. This isn't a hotel, you see. We are a private family."

"You have a delightful home, Mr Tinsley. I know you will do your best to accommodate me."

"Of course, but—"

"I think you will find I am not too difficult to please. And certainly – appreciative." Then, with a gracious inclination of the head, the man passed on, through the open doors of the drawing-room, heading for the terrace.

Julian made for the domestic offices where he found Connie checking tradesmen's bills.

"I've just seen – the Smith man."

"Ah. Did you have a word?" she asked, barely looking up.

"I just about got one in, yes."

"So how did you find him?"

"Impossible. A menace. Connie, we've bitten off more than we can chew here!" Julian sank back on to a chair and set about explaining the depth of their present embarrassment.

"So the decision's up to you, Con," he ended, "whether we turf the pair of them out or somehow make room. I know it's hard on you either way, because you've already packed everyone in like sardines. But, then again, we *are* counting on the money."

"But a *suite*, Julian! The only thing we've got that approaches that—"

"Is either our suite or your parents'. I know. And I'll not have you inconvenienced while you're slaving away as at present. We could ask James and Liese if they'd give up theirs."

"M'm. Just beautifully redecorated, of course."

"For their Ruby Wedding present. Yes, it's an awful lot to ask—"

"But why not? Father would be the first to admit we're doing a good job and that he hasn't contributed so far. We could simply explain that this is a very prominent man in the international markets. The connection could even do you some good career-wise. It's not, after all, as though he's a fugitive from justice or a terrorist."

So far as has yet been proved, Julian added silently. There had been rumours of late among some who kept their ears firmly to the ground. The term financial buccaneer had been voiced.

He sucked at his lower lip. "Yes, I'm certain James would help out. Not so sure about Liese."

"She won't like it at all. But then . . ."

"What?"

"Well, you saw her at dinner last night. She's impressively into her grande dame act. Provided we stress to this Boulos-whatever how terribly his request has inconvenienced her personally, he may have the wit to butter her up. Then she'll be total graciousness."

"I doubt it, Con. From all accounts he's anything but the sort to kowtow."

"Not perhaps to other men, but Mother is something else. I don't know how she does it at her age, but she can be a pretty high-powered woman."

"In which case, it'll cost him."

"Provided he gets the best, Julian, we can see that he pays through the nose. Oh heavens, there's the gong for dinner."

With his back to the house, and with the taped orchestral Lehár covering any sound of an approach across the grass, Angus Mott was unaware of the man's presence behind him. Only as the *tableau vivant* dissolved on the final chord did the sound of handclapping make him turn.

"Beautiful, beautiful," the newcomer pronounced silkily. His dark eyes slid across the floating nymphs and swung to encounter their instructor. "An aquatic corps de ballet. How charming."

"Don't let them hear your compliments," Mott warned. "That last figure was ragged. But they're mostly beginners, so I'm not displeased."

He turned back towards the pool. "Anybody finding it too chilly? No? Right then, we'll try the chain again from corner A, then centre-circle. By bar five you should be linked up. Joan, you'll have to hold back or you'll overshoot. Check you've squared up with that marker in the grass. OK, group up. Counting, and music on three."

He reset the tape and gave instructions over the top. "Wheel with spokes, two, three, four, five, six. Starfish, two, three, four, five, six. Spokes, two, three, back five, six. Lift, two, three, four – get those legs up! – six. And down. Are you drowning, Nancy? Well, don't squawk. What a shower! Break, and everyone back to the start."

The spectator stayed on through another repetition, then Mott ordered the girls to pack it in. They climbed out of the pool, tossing their hair, running hands down streaming limbs, laughing and wisecracking as they made for the dressing-pavilion.

Mott wound a towel round his waist, dropped his trunks and

51

moved across to where his clothes were folded on a lounger. He was aware of the other man considering his athletic build. He stared coolly back. "Do *you* swim?"

"From before I could walk. But never in such delightful company. I must compliment you on your team. It must be – rewarding."

His suggestive meaning was unmistakable, and Mott chose to ignore it. "We'll be putting some shows on later, when they've had more practice. They've a long way to go yet."

"And this is their only – *activity* you organise?"

Mott strolled across to the pavilion, took a bunch of keys from his pocket and unlocked a metal box fixed near the door. At a flick of a switch the underwater lighting was extinguished. He re-locked and moved away, drawing the other man with him. "These girls are all amateurs. This is a hobby they follow after their day's work."

"And they do this every evening?"

"Just twice a week, while the weather's good. From October we have to rely on the public swimming-baths, competing for booking with other events."

"Yes, I imagine it is more pleasant here in the open. So there is no move to build an indoor pool at Fraylings?"

"It would require too much upkeep, I imagine." Mott had tired of being on the receiving end of questions. "We haven't come across each other before. Are you one of the house guests?"

The man looked amused. "I shall be staying here for a while, yes. I arrived only an hour or two ago."

They had almost reached the terrace, where several of the company were now settling to enjoy after-dinner coffee and conversation. Mott pulled up short. "I have to go back now and round up the team. Nice meeting you, Mr – er . . ."

"Smith."

"Mr Smith," repeated Mott thoughtfully. "Good-night."

The man accepted his dismissal, amused at the stratagem. Smiling to display strong white teeth, he watched the younger man striding away across the grass to rejoin his charges.

# Cold Hands

He stroked his bearded cheeks. No matter. There would be other evenings, other opportunities.

Tonight the mermaids had parked their transport in a part of the driveway beyond the protective shrubbery of the pool. When Mott arrived back they were stowing their possessions, slamming car doors and belting themselves in, several to each car. His own passengers – a woman sergeant from Uniform Branch and her sister, a nurse – were still checking the pavilion for straying garments. Mott pocketed the keys when they had locked up.

"Who was the audience?" Sergeant Barbara Wayne asked him.

"One of the guests, apparently. I've not seen him before, but back at the house no one queried him when we strolled up. He claimed he's a late arrival."

"Another would-be artist?" The girl sounded doubtful.

"There may be some other course running at the same time. It's all a bit of a hotch-potch. The family are throwing themselves in with more enthusiasm than discretion. They've just added a dog-handling class on Thursdays."

"You didn't care for him." It was a statement.

"Fortunately I don't need to. But we must see the girls take no chances, with stray men about. I wouldn't say he was quite drooling, but . . ."

"I got warning vibes too." Her tone was abrupt. Well, she should know; Barbara Wayne's speciality was sex cases.

"Lovely evening," said his other passenger luxuriously, folding herself into the car's rear. "Wouldn't mind being swooped on and carried off into the sunset myself. Looked as though he knew how to entertain a girl. Purely wining and dining I'd go for, of course." She rolled her eyes with comic exaggeration and the slight tension eased. "You can't really blame the man for watching. Some of our youngsters do take the eye."

The other cars had left a few minutes before, but four miles out, as they took the steep road winding down towards the river, they were suddenly on to a tailback.

"Looks like an accident," Mott said, grimacing at the line of rear lights.

53

A contraflow started streaming past as they remained stationary. "Didn't know they got so much traffic on this route," remarked Barbara Wayne. "It must have been building for ages."

She had her window open and was craning out. "Wouldn't you know? It's the fluffin' police holding things up! Blue lights up front!"

They waited and eventually the oncoming traffic was stemmed. Mott put the car in gear and followed the line ahead. After a hundred yards of crawling they were waved out into the opposite lane by a patrolman. Tyre burn marks on the road surface to their nearside led to tracks through torn-up grass at the verge. Police in Day-Glo vests were taping off the area as firemen with an emergency tender deployed hoses.

"There's a burnt-out car down below on its roof," Barbara announced. "It's still smouldering. Do you want to go down, sir?"

"Leave it to Traffic," Mott said philosophically. "They wouldn't thank us for nosing in."

Barbara sat back and whizzed the window up. "No ambulance," she pointed out.

Her sister snorted. "It's gone on ahead. Some doped-up adolescent will be in Casualty screaming at doctors half-dead from a sixteen-hour shift to put him back together."

"Can't be one of our girls," Barbara said thankfully. "It must have happened a while back. Betty was the first to leave, and she was barely ten minutes ahead of us. I'll give her a buzz when we get back though. She may have got a better view of what happened."

Mott stole a glance at the dashboard clock. "OK if I drop you both by the bus stop near the Feathers?"

"Fine," the sisters chorused.

That way he would be almost on time for the boss's rendezvous with Beaumont and Zyczynski. The call had reached him just as he left for Fraylings Court.

\*   \*   \*

54

Perhaps as a concession to the woman in the quartet, they had moved away from the bar to a table in a corner of the lounge. The eldest of them, a big man with dark hair and mobile eyebrows above a comfortably creased face, had been given the vantage point of one wall-seat with the woman on his left at right angles. The two younger men presented a rear view to the watchers from the hatch of the public bar, but a corner mirror caught their faces as they leaned forward to speak.

"The blond feller, hefty shoulders, is DI Mott," said 'Carver' Ward, nodding towards the latest to arrive. "Fancies himself at water polo. Not the easiest to push under. The other one's his sergeant, name of Beaumont."

"Ventriloquist's doll," said the trainee, scornfully eyeing the latter.

"Don't mistake him for a wally. There's them inside as knows different. Got a *torchewous* mind, that one."

Still, he could see what the kid meant. Beaumont had the round-eyed face of a wooden puppet. That Pinocchio character in the Disney film.

"Who's the girl belong to?"

"She's another jack, a DS. Seen her in court. She's a looker, got what it takes, but she don't give on who's getting it. Got a long Polish name starting with Z, so Z's what they call her."

"And the one against the wall's the boss, eh?"

"Superin-bloody-tendent Yeadings. He's the brains orright. Got mental radar. If he looks yer way, you'd best scarper, and bloody fast."

"I don't reckon on hanging around anyway," said the other. He was younger, shorter, dressed anonymously like Ward, in leather jacket and jeans, but instead of trainers his feet were encased in calf-length boots. Beside them on the floor he'd set his skid-lid, which he'd worn until he sat down. His blotched skin looked tender and inflamed, as if overexposed to sun on top of pitting like ancient smallpox scars. He'd had plastic surgery after his last spill at Brands Hatch, and the scars had become infected.

"All yer gotta reckon on is doing what yer bloody told," Ward said coldly. "If yer wanna stay healthy."

The youngster muttered into the dregs of his tankard, wiped the back of his hand over his mouth and belched elaborately to indicate he wasn't impressed.

He'll learn, Carver thought drily. The hard way. Or else he won't last. Nobody wants a Jonah around.

"Get their faces in yer head, then on yer bike," he ordered. "There's no call to make yerself remembered."

The lad derisively skewed one end of his mouth, but he also reached for his skid-lid and gauntlets. "See you, then," he said jauntily and swaggered off through the crowd milling at the bar.

Carver sat on, from time to time leaning slightly sideways to get a view of the four jacks in the lounge. Conniving bastards, planning some poor bloody oaf's downfall so they could sit crowing like sodding cockerels on top of their midden. Well, it wouldn't be his own toss. There was nothing to connect him with this recent thing, and it wasn't in their line of business anyway. Not yet, if ever. And it didn't worry him that his own face was known to at least two of them. If they recalled seeing him here, it'd do very nicely as an alibi, back up the landlord who'd noticed him come in coupla hours back.

Superintendent Mike Yeadings finished his pint, reflecting that he'd tasted better. "So I've passed you the opinion from on high," he said conclusively. "Any comments?" He looked towards Mott as next in command.

"If proactive policing's to be anything more than a buzzword in the brass's annual reports," said Angus doggedly, "we've got to have some guarantee that intelligence operations won't be interrupted by reactive duties."

"You'll not get that. It's a question of available resources and costs."

"Housekeeping," Zyczynski said sadly. "Everything comes down to budget restrictions nowadays."

"Forget the finance side for the moment," Yeadings suggested. "How could any guarantee work in practice? It's as questionable as performance-related pay for individual effort, and in teamwork that can't properly be assessed: it's like a post-war puzzle of who gets the medals. No, we have to accept that intelligence-gathering, however vital, is the background picture, and in the early days of an operation we must be prepared to drop anything we're on and switch instantly to whatever emergency arises. All I can promise you is that when the search is hotting up – when we've got some villain in our sights with his fingers crooked for the kill – it'll be over my dead body that you get called away to any lesser current crime."

He looked round at the others. "However, we've been given three days' grace to pick up some lead at Fraylings. Let's hope chummy shows himself before the time's up."

Mott nodded: the boss had his headaches too. They arose mainly from needs to bat off the instant demands of certain senior ranks. It was because he was good at it that their little team had survived intact for so long.

"You could see it as a compliment, that your peculiar gifts are so widely sought after," Yeadings said drily. "Sergeant Beaumont, we haven't heard anything from you yet."

The Pinocchio features barely moved as he uttered the one word, "Ward."

"*Ward?*"

"Carver Ward. Sitting behind the hatch to the public bar. Thinks I haven't spotted him. We thought he'd gone back to Brum when he came out. Anyone know of a knife job on the books?"

Nobody made an obvious move to take a look. "Should I phone in for a rundown on recent attacks?" Zyczynski asked.

"Whatever he's got on his mind, he's quite easy about," Beaumont told them, scanning the mirror. "He's seen us. Keeps sticking his head out to see what we're at. On past record, once he's struck he never hangs around."

"Going straight in his old age?" Mott asked sarcastically.

"Or passing on the torch?" This was Yeadings's contribution. "Might be an idea to check on his chums. Beaumont, you had a line on his ex-landlady at one time."

The sergeant winced. "Spare me that. I know a bloke who lives opposite. He'll open up on anything he's noticed, if I stand him a jar."

"Good enough. We'll hang in here while Z checks with base."

The woman detective rose, swinging her shoulder bag, ran her fingers through her cap of brown curls and made ostensibly for the door marked Ladies. Cued to make their gathering seem casually social, Beaumont filled in with one of his shaggy-dog stories. Zyczynski returned to a more convivial party and a general groan of appreciation as the sergeant wound up.

"He's still there," she reported.

"Waiting for someone?"

"Past tense. There was a second glass, empty, and he's nearly finished his own. I rang the nick. No recent knifings reported in this area. One mugging with a cosh in Henley tonight, but they've picked up a lad for that. Oh, and I asked about the RTA Angus passed on the way here – one body recovered, badly burnt, no ID, sex unknown. Front licence plate's barely legible and back one's missing, but it could be a Volvo."

"Nothing for us, then?" Yeadings grunted. He relaxed visibly. "So, Angus, how's the sync swimming coming on?"

"Shaping up, you might say. The girls aren't bad at all."

"Some even more shapely than others?" Beaumont suggested. "They could get in trouble as *agents provocateurs* with our local perverts."

"Drew an audience of one tonight," Mott answered. The memory of the man Smith persisted in the back of his mind, alien and slightly disturbing.

"Are they running many courses at Fraylings?" Yeadings enquired. "Rather an off-beat enterprise for that family, I'd have thought." He'd briefly met Sir James Siddons during a series of country house burglaries. Following a tip-off, they'd staked out the house and grounds, but the actual haul had been five miles away at a film producer's weekend cottage.

"They've a heavy schedule, from all accounts. As well as the residential art course, there's our twice weekly syncswim, Riding for the Disabled, full-day dancing classes on Saturdays and now Sir James's daughter has started a dog-training course. Not that their own pack are much to recommend her!"

"I've met 'em," Yeadings agreed. "West Highland Terriers.

58

Small, rough-haired whites. Companionable little beggars, but independent. If you can train them, you can train anything. What about the human element? Has anyone surfaced that we need to check on?" He angled the question at Zyczynski.

Z assumed Miss Finnegan's best schoolmistress pose, perfected now after practice among the Fraylings' crowd. "Nothing yet to link with the Webb case. They're a motley lot. The artist woman's a bit dotty, but seems harmless: takes her half of the road in the middle, driving an old wooden-frame Morris Minor van. It must be nearly as ancient as she is. *Désirée* Crumm by name – the class call her 'Dizzy', and she regards it as a compliment. Otherwise everyone's giving very little away, taking time opening up."

"There's this new man who turned up late. He may change things a bit," Mott offered.

"A catalyst?"

"Flamboyant. Expects to get his own way. Assumes you'll oblige him. Most people don't take easily to being patronised. There could be interesting reactions. And he's a bit of a mystery, arriving out of the blue. I'd understood from Connie Tinsley that this first art group was already complete."

Yeadings grunted. "A robust ego? Well, with an extra ace slipped into the pack, that may help the play along. But is there any way he could be connected with the business we're interested in?"

The question was directed at Mott. While he hesitated, Z offered her own opinion. "I think we're talking kingpin here. Really big money, probably legit. He wouldn't court attention as he does if he'd anything criminal to hide. Anyway we'll know soon enough what his line is. He's too self-important to resist showing off how good he is at it."

Yeadings eyed her reflectively, noted the touch of waspishness and asked himself whether Z was pushing beyond her experience. "Well, get as much on him as you can, Z, but don't risk blowing your cover. You're all we can spare in there full-time." He looked round at them all and nodded dismissively.

"Need a lift back?" Mott asked her.

"That's taken care of," Beaumont put in. "Her gear's in my car. She's supposed to be taking an after-dinner stroll, so I'm going to drop her just short of the gates."

B Smith and Nadia had spread themselves over Sir James's refurbished apartment as to the manner born. After her public graciousness in surrender, Liese Siddons remained tight-lipped, pouring suppressed spleen into physical activity, rapidly re-disposing the armfuls of dresses, hats, underwear and shoes snatched from one of her walk-in wardrobes, and turning the locks on all other property abandoned for the duration.

Between them the Smiths had only the two suitcases with which the woman had arrived. Her husband had turned up without luggage, implying it would follow on. They should find ample room in the space vacated.

Smith had magnanimously produced five hundred in cash as an advance supplement on the suite.

Jennifer Yorke had previously declined the offer of a smaller room at a reduced charge, insisting that Clary should stay with her in the second twin bed. This had left Liese and Sir James with no alternative to a straight swap with Nadia Smith's single room. This had required the relocation of an old brass double bedstead from a junk-room, provided with a lumpy flock mattress which would have to suffice until a replacement could be delivered from a Wycombe store in the next day or two.

With this cramped rearrangement hurriedly effected, those involved were reacting diversely. Liese had stormed to the kitchen, commandeered all equipment and threatened an all-night baking session in preference to submitting her generous curves to the lumpy embraces of the bed on offer. Sir James had covered the library settee with down cushions and stacked a selection of biographies alongside with which to withstand the wakeful hours of darkness. As soon as day dawned he intended to be out in his motor-powered chair shooting crows and bagging the odd rabbit for the pot.

Connie and Julian, expressing profuse regret for any necessary inconvenience to the older couple, retired for the night comfortably congratulating themselves on achieving the nigh-impossible and even ending up in pocket over the exchanges.

From the windows of the newly achieved apartment, Nadia Smith observed her husband's departure to wander the moonlit grounds, smiled sardonically, closed the curtains, tried out and approved the king-size mattress, then ran herself a deep and fragrant bath.

Emerging from a spinney path alongside a breach in the outer estate wall, B Smith clambered through and found himself on the village road, empty except for a lone pedestrian making for the main gates which lay behind him. As she neared he recognised the younger of the two schoolmistresses, apparently unalarmed by dark country lanes and the night noises of wild animals. A naturalist perhaps; therefore to some extent a romantic. The idea amused him.

Zyczynski – back in disguise, and forewarned by a hint of Havana on the still night air – gave a convincing cry of alarm as he detached himself from the shadow of the high wall, allowed herself to be reassured, and flutteringly accepted the man's company back indoors, as far as the stairway that led to their respective quarters. Along the way she burbled of her fascination with the stars and her total inability to navigate by them, so getting hopelessly lost in the winding lanes. Faintly bored, he endured her frothy inconsequence, bowed as she breathlessly thanked him for his company, and wished her good-night.

He watched her climb to the upper level, observing trim ankles in the clumsy walking shoes, a dipping hem on the overlong grey skirt, the untrimmed bush of mousey hair; and he marvelled what perverse genius the English spinster had for making the worst of herself. Then, gazing about the panelled stairway and relishing the aura of ancient lineage and privilege, he permitted himself some satisfaction at where he had arrived.

Learn to recognise the best; demand the best; achieve the best: none but such principles of Caesarean conciseness could properly be his own. Tomorrow he would start to build on present success.

# One Pair

J oanna filled her bowl with cereal and doused the sugar-coated crispies with orange juice. Then she considered where to seat herself among the interlopers.

Clary was already there, dormouse-demure between her mother and Philip Pomeroy, the middle-aged Pickwickian husband of the tie 'n' dye woman seriously into art. He was working hard at being jolly, Joanna thought, but he should save himself the effort. Anyone could see that Mrs Yorke wasn't a morning person. And anyway she would never respond to "Rather a lark, eh? Heh, heh!"

From first arrival she had been showing distinct interest in the dark and brooding Mr Dunne. Perhaps she thought she could outshine the Cockney-voiced girl everyone pretended was his wife. But at lunch yesterday Gerald Dunne had responded to Mrs Yorke's playfulness with a whip-crack remark which Joanna hadn't understood; and Clary's mother had flushed, then gone pale and trembly. Hal Carrick, of the young couple, had jumped up and offered to take her to her room. But he'd done it in a funny sort of way, exaggerating his body movements like a ballet dancer. It was Harlequin he'd reminded Joanna of; long-limbed, toe-pointing, lean and teasing.

Mrs Yorke had pulled away, rushing out of the room with her face hidden. That evening after dinner she'd been rather quiet, arranging herself artistically under the standard lamp. She was ignoring both men, but was all cow-eyes whenever the bearded newcomer, Smith, looked her way.

Disdainful, Joanna looked for a place farther away. Dennis Hampton nodded to an empty chair beside him at the breakfast table. "Good of you to join the aliens," he greeted her.

Aliens, she considered, ought to be small and green with froggy eyes and antennae. But he was right: these people, now that their first good manners were wearing off, were all quite odd in their way. In their different ways. Even Mr Hampton himself. Sort of red squirrely.

"Did you like writing for a newspaper?" she demanded critically.

"Loved it, hated it. Got bored by it, can't stand not doing it any more. That surprise you?"

"You could have been a real writer instead."

"M'm. Who says I wasn't? Amn't?" He gave her a mock wounded glance. "You don't think much of the daily press."

Joanna scraped her bowl clean before answering. "All that stuff about politics and wars and football results. Nobody reads all the way through. I've watched."

"Different pages suit different people. Isn't there anything you like?"

"When I'm older I might do the crosswords," she claimed loftily. "And the ads aren't bad. The ones for compost bins and rubber knickers and clippers for your nose hairs. They make me laugh."

"Joanna, there you are," said Dizzy Crumm, popping up behind her chair. "We need a new model for our Life Class. Would you like to help us out?"

"I – can't. I have to go somewhere for Granny Liese," she invented desperately.

"Oh, what a pity. Such a nice chin and cheekbones. Ears too. Well, perhaps another time? I suppose, then, it will have to be the other little girl."

Who hadn't any bones so far as you could see; was all candy floss and dimples. You could tell Dizzy was disappointed, but Clary would jump at the chance, and try to score off it somehow.

"Sorry," Joanna said tightly, moving in on the idea. "She's arranged to come with me."

Miss Crumm tutted and went off, tugging at her shawl as its fringe threatened to tangle with a carved chair-back.

Now Joanna would have to draw Clary off and make sure she lay low until after Dizzy's next approach. Joanna could see the girl hanging about with her mother by the door, and made faces to get her back.

"Like to go somewhere special?"

"Where?"

Oh Lord, where? Somewhere out of bounds it'd need to be. But Clary wouldn't like the sound of Hangman's Wood. "Picking raspberries."

"All right. I'll just tell Mummy."

Not as if her mother would know where she was in any case, once the art class started. Wouldn't care much either. "Tell her quietly. Or everyone will want to come."

She waited for Clary at the door to the kitchen garden and observed that she brought with her an empty shoebox.

"Haven't you got a basket or something?" Clary asked.

"We shan't need one. Raspberries are for *eating*. Got this, though," and she picked up a plastic carrier holding some leftovers from the breakfast buffet. Waving off a trio of yapping Westies, she made for the door in the garden's flint wall.

"But they're over the other side!"

"Not those raspberries, idiot. *Wild* ones. They're much better."

The two girls went through and kept to the path under the wall as far as the shed housing the old waterwheel – still with its ancient bar for a donkey to drive it by – then struck off into the shrubbery, hidden from any watchers at the upper windows. Scratched by unyielding branches of rhododendron, they left the landscaped grounds by a broken fence, pelted down the open hillside and were soon safe from view in the dappled gloom of Hangman's Wood.

"Ever seen a crocodile?" Joanna asked. "Real close, I mean?"

Clary shuddered. "No. There aren't any wild in England."

"There wouldn't be if we let people know. They'd come and shoot them. You'll have to be quiet. *Dead* quiet, or you'll wake them. This time of day they're asleep."

Clumsily Clary tried to keep up with her, sliding down the spongy bank, turning her ankle on hidden rocks or roots, her hair-ribbon snatched by a low-hanging hazel branch.

"Can't you wait for me?" she wailed.

"You should have worn trainers. And don't you have any jeans?"

"Mummy doesn't like me to wear trousers. She says – *Ow!*"

This time she had taken a header and landed awkwardly on her shoulder against a tree trunk. She sat up, clasping one arm bared by a shredded sleeve. It was bleeding slightly and there were brown specks of loose bark in her hair and on her cheeks. As Joanna watched, fat tears gushed from her eyes and made tracks down her cheeks.

"God, you're hopeless!"

At that Clary began to howl out loud.

There was nothing for it then but to do as promised and take her on to the part of the wood with the raspberries, which meant crossing the swampy end of Crocodile Lake on the bouncy single-plank footbridge.

Joanna had some experience of sick ponies and incontinent puppies. She tried now to summon the same understanding for this – this wimp. She cleaned her face off with the hem of the voile dress, put her arm round the quivering shoulders and said, "There, there." Eventually the girl stopped sniffing, and whimpered she was sorry.

"OK, then. Let's get on, shall we?"

It was still and dark here just above the water. Blackish grey with islets of green scum, it lay sullenly unreflecting. Like slabs of lichen-spotted slate, Joanna thought, watching a fine silver line lengthen where some underwater twig broke what little flow there was.

She squeezed the other girl's hand and whispered, "Shush! There's one!"

She felt Clary recoil at sight of the half-submerged log, grey-green, scaly and smeared with slime. For half a minute, more, they waited for some sign of life, a movement of the long spine, a tail twitch, the sudden opening of a watchful, malicious eye.

A *whole* minute; then, pulling free her sweating palm, the girl cried, "It isn't alive. It's an old tree trunk."

Joanna looked at her in disgust. "But it's more fun as a crocodile!"

Anger at the deception took Clary halfway across the plank

bridge, then suddenly she saw it for the impossibility it was, gave a hopeless little cry, wobbled, tilted on one edge and toppled off.

The pond's swampy end wasn't deep, but Joanna had to get in to pull her upright. Even she was surprised by how quickly the girl had become coated in the black and stinking grime. Clary's face was entirely covered, with only the gritted teeth and eyes shining out white. Too terrified now even to scream, she huddled in abject misery and squalor, knee-high in filth.

"Look. You'll have to get everything off," Joanna ordered. "Can you swim?"

It was one thing the girl could do, but only in heated pools. Joanna dragged her into deeper water. Under duress she floundered and moaned, renewing the filth each time she tried to pull herself up the bank again. At last, heaved out by Joanna, she stood numbly naked and watched her clothes swished in the pond on the twiggy end of a branch to clean them.

The girls had arrived on the far side of the pond. Because it lay in an old gravel pit most of the sides were steep and there was only this one shallow bank to climb out on. And return must be by the way they had come, over the plank bridge.

Joanna rubbed down her jeans with a handful of sycamore leaves and lay down to rinse her shirt in the water.

"What shall we do-o-o-o?" wailed Clary.

"Go on. What else?"

Like old Dizzy Crumm, Joanna thought: reach Fraylings by a roundabout route. She remembered there was a hut of some kind in a clearing farther on. Grandfather had taken her there once; said they used to raise pheasant chicks in it. At least it would be shelter, and maybe they could find something to start a fire to dry out their clothes.

Clary would never venture on the plank bridge again. She was stiff with fear. So they'd no choice. They had to go on, farther into forbidden territory. Wasn't it lucky she'd thought to bring some food along?

Immersed in paperwork, Superintendent Mike Yeadings reached blindly for his coffee mug, felt its disappointing lightness, deduced that he must already have consumed almost a litre of the stuff since lunch, sighed, and decided that another little drink wouldn't do him any harm. He pushed back his chair, stretched stiffened limbs and set about refilling the filter machine. As the first comforting burbles began there was a knock at his door. A woman PC looked in, holding some papers.

"Sir, a report just passed on by Traffic about an RTA on Tuesday night. These were addressed by error to DI Mott, sir, and he's—"

"He's off on a three-day course. Do I need to know about it?"

"Funny sort of accident, sir. If it was one."

"In that case, I'll take a look. Is there anything else on the DI's desk?"

"Nothing important, sir. Just a note for Sergeant Wayne about taking over the sync-swim class while he's away. I've passed that on, sir."

"Right. I'll check on the traffic accident."

He took the printout across to the open window and stuck his head through, snatching deep breaths of late afternoon air. Above the thinly toxic fumes from the station's car park he seemed to detect the familiar faint country scent, the almond-nut hint of sun-drenched gorse, against the suburban sweetness of privet in full flower.

This RTA. He remembered now: it was out towards Fraylings Court. Mott had mentioned the road being taped off. There was a tailback when the swimmers were leaving. So what was 'funny' about it?

Two things, apparently. One sheet reported Traffic's finding of secondary tracks on the grass verge where the car had gone over. A motorcycle had been driven off the road there, stood up on its bracket, and then ridden rapidly away. The tyre marks crossed over grass freshly ploughed up by the car as it hurtled into space. So, after the accident but before the emergency services' arrival, a biker had stopped to watch the car burn, then driven off. Without reporting it. And the car's driver had still been inside.

The only 999 call had come from a baker's delivery man who passed in his van while the flames were at their fiercest. He'd stopped too, but the heat was too great for him to get anywhere near. There had been no mention of any other traffic on the road at that time.

Interesting, Yeadings thought. But not necessarily significant. There were bikers who didn't care for contact with officialdom, even granted the anonymity of a public phone-box.

But linked with the second report, which originated from the Fire Department, the incident took on a fresh and sinister possibility.

It appeared that a small explosion had occurred *prior* to the petrol tank going up. Remains found suggested a small incendiary device. And with the presence of an incinerated corpse, the incident now passed from a Traffic case to one of Serious Crime.

Such a development justified a personal trip out to survey the scene. Yeadings shovelled papers wholesale from desktop to drawer, locking them away with some gusto. So heigh-ho for the open road, and other such Toad-like utterances!

In a little over twenty minutes he was there. He had no difficulty finding the point at which the car had left the road. The plastic marker tapes were guarded by a single constable. Nothing had been done to restore the grass verge, but the ground showed ample evidence of the fire crew's heavy-booted activities. The scientific experts would have had their work cut out to identify earlier traces.

Yeadings drove his Rover into a field entrance fifty yards on, crossed over and walked back.

It was unbelievably peaceful, standing there on the ridge with the breeze riffling his hair and the wide valley opening out below. No sound but a distant tractor in an invisible field, and the trilling of a lark somewhere overhead. Again the scent of gorse reached him and he located its source down the fatal hillside, a ballooning of brilliant yellow where the trees were thinner. And then, as he trudged down, there were blackened, twisted branches, as skeletal as the remains of the burnt-out car.

So what must he suppose had happened here? At its simplest, someone had intended arson. Not necessarily the way it had turned out. So where, and to what? The car's movement under

69

sudden braking could have set the device off prematurely. In which case, had the driver, now in the morgue, contemplated fire-raising elsewhere? Or been the unwitting victim? Had the bomb been planted on him with the intent it had actually achieved?

Yet again, had the skid itself been contrived? Had the anonymous biker been involved? Swerved past, perhaps, and driven a nervous driver off the road just at the most dangerous point? And had he come back fearful of the consequences, or to make sure he'd succeeded in his intentions? Could he have had knowledge of the device and intended it to complete destruction if the wrecked car failed to ignite of itself?

Diabolical, if that was so. But then the idea of any bomb was. And even if no second party had been involved – striking murder off the list – it had to rank as a suspicious death.

He'd have to set up a Serious Crime investigation, check anyone recently in the neighbourhood who was worthy of another's murderous intentions, or else urgently needing compensation for insured property.

Vehicle examiners would be required to pick over the wreckage and identify the car. If the licence plate was genuine the Police Central Computer could give its registered owner. Which, in turn, should lead to a possible killer. Of known bombers who would be the most likely – IRA, Animal Rights, or some vicious individual working on a private agenda?

But if the car had been stolen there'd still be no clue to who the dead man was. Dead *person*. Because even the corpse's sex wasn't clear yet.

Meanwhile there was the biker to be found and questioned.

Most of the tailback that delayed Mott was due to the outflow of cars from Fraylings Court after the sync-swim practice. Normally there would be little traffic on this country road, but the surface had suffered from activity by the emergency services outside the section originally taped off. Photographs would have been taken of the car's tyre-burns on braking, but he doubted whether lesser marks from a motorcycle would still show up on the metalled surface. It remained to get a lead on the make of tyre from indentations on the grass verge.

Beaumont had given Zyczynski a lift and arrived at the Feathers well before Mott. He hadn't mentioned any crash. Maybe they'd be able to put a precise time on it. But then, there were alternative routes and certainly Z would have stayed on at Fraylings for dinner and been picked up in some minor country lane. He doubted they could help after all.

Yeadings walked back to his car, and radioed to base. He got through to Beaumont who sounded suspiciously alert.

"What's new?" Yeadings demanded, ever quick to pick up vibes.

"It may be nothing. Coincidence perhaps." Beaumont's warning voice had toned down from red to amber.

"But . . . ?"

"There's been a panic call from Fraylings Court. Two kids have gone missing. Girls, aged nine and ten. One of them is granddaughter to Sir James. The other came with her mother who's attending the art course. They've not been seen since breakfast this morning."

"Who's dealing with it?"

"Sergeant Morris has taken some uniform men to organise a search. It's only nine hours they've been gone, but in the case of children . . . shall I go out and help, sir?"

"No, keep away. We may need you in there undercover sometime, if Z pulls out a plum. I'll go myself. In the meantime there's a development about Tuesday evening's RTA which Angus mentioned." And he gave Beaumont a précis of the Fire and Traffic reports.

"I'm on the spot now, taking a quick shufti. Warn Uniform I want a fingertip search carried out there before dark. I know they're thin on the ground if Morris has a priority on the missing children, but this is a possible murder case. I'll speak to Allocations personally, and be in early tomorrow."

He drove back on to the road and continued in the direction of Fraylings Court. No need now to invent an excuse for speaking with Z. He'd be a senior CID officer alerted to the serious possibilities of two young girls as Mispers. Everyone present at Fraylings Court would need to be questioned.

*     *     *

71

Jennifer Yorke, viperish in her frenzy, was blaming everyone except herself. How could she possibly have known where the children would go? Clarissa had definitely said they'd be in the kitchen-garden picking raspberries. Clary didn't lie. And she wouldn't have gone anywhere else on her own – or with another child – without asking permission. She knew all about not talking to strangers: she'd been warned time and time again. She was a sensible child; you could rely on her. The trouble was she wouldn't see the other people at Fraylings as strangers. Because she'd had meals with them. She knew her mummy talked to them. You couldn't feel safe anywhere nowadays. People were so *awful*!

And so on and so forth, DS Rosemary Zyczynski thought to herself. She had some difficulty mastering an ingrained habit of diving in and sorting out the facts. However, her schoolmistress role did seem to authorise some interference in matters concerning the young, so she hung about, hopeful of picking up dribs of information from those sympathising with the distressed mother.

Connie Tinsley, she noted, was distinctly less hysterical over her daughter's disappearance, even suspiciously thoughtful.

"Has this happened before with Joanna?" Z managed to enquire quietly while Jennifer was otherwise distracted.

Mrs Tinsley screwed her mouth into what the French called a *derrière de poule*. "She's quite an independent spirit, but she knows the rules."

"And would she break them?"

Connie drew a deep breath. "It has been known, but there's always a reason."

"You mean she can always find some excuse," said her grandmother, livid because she felt that this time Joanna had deliberately and personally abused her in planning this deception.

"She's an imaginative child," Sir James pleaded. "With a strong sense of romance and adventure."

"She's led my baby astray!" wailed Jennifer Yorke.

Dizzy Crumm plonked herself down on a nearby seat and rested her hands on splayed knees. "She told me she couldn't pose for the Life Class because she had an errand to run for her grandmother," she said sadly, staring into the carpet. "And when I suggested asking the other little girl, she said no; Clary was going with her too."

"I sent her nowhere! *Himmel*, I know nothing, nothing at all about all this." Liese was almost in tears, shredding her handkerchief between agonised fingers. "I was myself the model. All day I have sat there, except for lunch and tea. It was not until the children had to dress for dinner that we found we had two different stories about where they had gone."

"I was there all day, too," Jennifer claimed. "Well, most of us were. Naturally I supposed the children were on the putting green or out with the horses as usual. Where was Joanna's mother, I want to know? She's supposed to be in charge here. Why didn't she keep an eye on the girl if she's so out of hand?"

"I had the household to run," Connie said indignantly. "And this afternoon I had my dog-training class."

"Dogs!" The anguished mother's voice rose to a peak. "How can you be any good with them when you allow your own child to be a wild thing?"

There was a confused hubbub of dissent, then mercifully Sergeant Morris arrived at the front door, ready to keep the factions apart. He quickly summed up the combatants, dispatched Connie to order dinner to go ahead and drew Mrs Yorke with him into the small salon to pour out her fears and complaints.

"Right," he said, after three or four almost incoherent sentences, "I've got the rough picture. What's been done about a search party?"

"Some of the men have gone. Mr Hampton, Mr Pomeroy and Joanna's father, I think."

"Good. That's a start. I've sent out four of my men on foot and there are three patrol cars circling the area. I don't suppose any of your vehicles are missing? Could either of the little girls drive?"

The very thought finally struck Jennifer speechless. She let him march her to the door where he looked out for the next person to question and discovered that the Superintendent was now of their number. "Sir," he said, "shall I carry on?"

73

"I'll join you," Yeadings offered. "Let's have another of the ladies in. You, m'dear. What's your name?"

"Finnegan," said Z. "Maeve Finnegan. That's M-A-E-V-E."

Sergeant Morris barely blinked, falling back as the other two followed him into the room and Yeadings shut the door firmly.

"Good man. We don't want her cover blown. DS Zyczynski's here on a quite separate job for me." Yeadings paused, looked hard at them both and added less briskly, "At least I think it's separate. I sincerely hope so."

As soon as Zyczynski had given a résumé of all opinions on the girls' disappearance they asked for Connie Tinsley to follow on. Z avoided the sparse group in the dining-room and, as instructed, made for where Joanna had been temporarily lodged in the old nursery. There she made a rapid search, though without any clear idea of what she might be expected to find. After drawing a blank, she knocked on the Yorkes' bedroom door, found it locked, and fought shy of being caught using her skeleton keys.

Confronted by two policemen, Connie Tinsley was less confident. "Do you truly believe there's cause for . . . ? I mean, one does hear of such awful things, but here we've never had any trouble. Even the village boys – a bit of horseplay, no more . . ."

"What would that be then, ma'am?" Morris inquired.

"Oh, Young Farmers' Union sort of thing. High-spirited, a little too much to drink perhaps. Some damage in the public bar, a hayrick that caught fire – purely by accident, Sergeant. And the young vet's moustache, of course."

"The vet's moustache?" Morris echoed faintly.

"They ambushed him and cut it off with sheep shears. Most of it, that is. He took it in good part – eventually."

"I see. As you say, just a bit of fun." He sounded unpersuaded.

"Did Joanna have any favourite hiding-places that you know of?" Yeadings pursued.

"Not hiding-places exactly. Places she liked to be private in. We've looked in them all."

"So where do you think she would have gone, if she'd been free to choose?"

"Walking," Connie said after a short pause. "I don't know where, but she took quite a lot of food with her. At least I suppose that's how it disappeared. I went to clear up after the guests' breakfasts, and there wasn't anything left. Only kedgeree, which she doesn't care for."

"Which is why you aren't too anxious about what may have happened?" Yeadings asked sympathetically.

"I wasn't. Only, *now* – you see, it's not like her to stay away so late. She'd know we would worry once we realised." She shook her head. "You mustn't think we're careless of her. It's just that for a nine-year-old she seems so – capable. And then we're used to thinking things are safe round here. Perhaps we shouldn't; times are changing. Things don't get better, do they?"

There wasn't any answer to that. "Have there been any new faces around here just recently?" Morris asked, and she almost exploded at him.

"They're *all* new! What do we know about any of them, except what they chose to tell us in their letters!"

They let her go, to carry on worrying but warned not to let on too much to others. She fled to the kitchen, where the two caterers were glumly surveying an almost untouched dish of chicken korma sent back from the dining-room.

"There's only three of them in there," said Gayle. "We're holding the rest of the meal back until the search party returns. If you'd like us to stay on late, we will. I mean, it's the least we can do."

"Would you? Just for the moment I don't think I can . . ."

"You go and lie down, Mrs Tinsley," Andrew comforted her, "and I'll bring you up a nice big brandy."

She explained she didn't want to sleep, but she had to get away on her own. It had been a disastrous day all round, she reflected, stomping out into the courtyard. She found herself heading for Joanna's lair in the barn loft, climbed the rear stairway and seated herself on a bale of straw.

First there'd been that worry about the mare. For the second day off her food, in obvious discomfort, with difficulty in swallowing. Connie had looked it up in her cure-all book and it sounded like Grass Sickness. Which meant damaged nerve supply to the gut. She'd checked for muscle tremor and patchy sweating, came up with a positive; didn't think there was weight-loss yet, but there would be if the beast couldn't soon be made to eat.

Grass Sickness could be serious. It had been around for decades but nobody seemed to know for sure what caused it. Maybe a toxin in grass produced from a fungus. But it was normally a cold weather, cold-climate disease, not usually diagnosed so far south, as far as she knew.

She wanted to call the vet, but she was ashamed of worrying over a horse when Joanna might – just might – be in danger.

She raised her head from her hands and became aware in the half-dark of something strange about the loft. It wasn't as Joanna normally used it, but rearranged with bales of straw pulled into a circle about a table taken from the east-wing landing. And in a dogfood carton beside the bale she sat on was a selection of items Joanna would hardly have any use for.

Connie scrabbled through the contents, counted the ash trays, burrowed further and came on the sealed decks of cards.

So this was where the men went of an evening; why she'd seen one or two of them, baggy-eyed, slinking back in the dawn's early light through the conservatory door which was secured only by inside bolts. They'd started a poker school, up here above the barn.

What was it Father had once called the game? 'The supreme competitive male-bonding ritual'. More than a game, in that case.

Men. She would never understand them, but at least if they poured all their energies into stag-fights of this kind, they would surely be of no danger to the children? It appalled her that in seeking to redress the family's financial embarrassment she could have laid them open to the risk of vicious strangers in their midst.

Maybe not, but *smoking* up here – and certainly accompanied by boozing, otherwise why that opened box of plastic beakers? – was a distinct fire hazard with all this loose straw around. She'd no objection to their gambling, but it would have to be contained indoors, under regulated conditions. Spoilsport or not, she felt obliged to confiscate the carton and its contents, marching back across the courtyard with it in her arms like some self-conscious school prefect.

Arrived via the domestic offices, she was immediately aware of a hubbub in the inner hall, an outburst of voices abruptly hushed, a silence, a single low male voice, and again a torrent of anxious questions. She rushed in, crying, "What is it?"

Her father swung his wheelchair to face her. "They're found!"

The big superintendent was still there. He came in from the drawing-room's open french doors, sliding a cordless phone into his pocket.

"Mrs Tinsley, Mrs Yorke, it's all right. Our men caught up with the search party. They've found the little girls. They are scared, but they'll be fine in no time."

"But where, what—?"

"Let's wait until they're ready to tell us, shall we? They're bringing them back by the road, so we shall soon know. Say ten minutes? How about having some hot soup ready? And may I suggest that everyone outside the immediate families should disappear for the present?"

His voice was kindly, masking his horror that it was the children's clothes the searchers had first stumbled on before shouts and thumpings drew them to the hut where they'd been shut in. There was no obvious sign of who might have been holding them prisoner. He went out again on to the terrace to contact base and order a Scenes of Crime team to be sent out immediately.

"This first, Connie," Sir James said severely, producing his private supply of brandy while the crowd gradually dispersed, excitedly chattering. "Now, give me that box, sit down and take a few slow breaths. Andy will scc to the soup business, won't you, young man?"

Connie dropped on to a nearby armchair, recognising Jennifer Yorke prostrate on a chaise longue opposite. "No, she's had enough already," Sir James said, heading off the offer he saw coming.

"Warm dressing-gowns," Yeadings was quietly advising Liese. "And, as soon as the doctor's had a chance to examine them – but not before – hot baths. Then get them straight up to bed before they're questioned."

He returned to sit with Connie and the somnolent Jennifer Yorke until a commotion in the outer hall indicated a car's arrival. "No, stay here," he ordered, standing in the doorway while he checked that Liese was wrapping the children in their own things and discarding the men's jackets. He noted that one of the policemen carried a bulging plastic sack destined for the forensic scientists.

A woman doctor was with them. Liese and the younger schoolmistress were herding the girls upstairs. "They'll see to them," Yeadings warned, holding Connie back from streaking after. "Let them get to bed first. A doctor's going to check up on them. Purely precautionary."

At least she could make a preliminary examination, take any necessary swabs, and determine whether the children should be sent on to hospital. The dark one had looked more angry than frightened, but the fair one was in shock, having to be carried in and supported on the stairs. Yeadings glanced again at the two mothers and guessed which child belonged to which.

"No," Connie said with sudden determination. "My place is with Joanna," and she pushed past Yeadings' restraining arm.

He let her go. Nan would have been the same if anything had happened to Sally. The very thought made him feel sick to his stomach.

Sergeant Morris came striding over. "Not as bad as it might have been," he said grimly. "We're looking for two men. The girls were chased through Hangman's Wood and fell in the mire end of the pond there. Tried to wash the mess off their clothes, took shelter in a hut out near the main road, leaving some outer clothes to dry in the clearing. That must have been before midday. Seems the men came back and dropped the bar on the door so they couldn't get out. No physical assault, though. Never actually laid hands on either of them."

\* \* \*

Fierce little hellcat, Zyczynski thought, supporting the child's arm as she stepped over into the foamy bath. Joanna's brows almost met in a single line above stormy eyes. She had positively spat out the answers the doctor had demanded. Was this outrage at losing face, or defensive guilt? Thank God anyway it wasn't trauma from a sexual attack.

"I can bath myself," the girl snarled between gritted teeth.

"Good. I'll leave you to it, then. Nightie's on the hot rail."

Z found the child's mother sitting on a bed in the old nursery. She seemed to have regained some of her organising zest.

"I've seen Clary Yorke," Connie said. "She's more or less speechless. Just keeps crying for Joanna. So I'm putting them together in here. I'm afraid her mother's out cold."

Both children together? Not ideal for questioning, Z regretted, but with children's cases you had to play it mostly by ear; comfort them first; sort things out as soon as possible later; above all be sure a responsible adult sat in on the questioning.

Joanna was ready first, glowering at the superintendent who was feeling foolishly oversized in the scaled-down nursery.

"Two men," he said. "We'd like to catch them quickly before they go frightening anyone else. So anything you can tell us about them will help us do that."

Joanna swivelled to watch a shuddering Clary deposited on the bed alongside. She gave her a hard stare before turning back to her questioner, and Clary covered her face with her hands.

"One was black." Joanna spoke loudly, very sure of herself.

"Black?"

"Well, very dark brown, then. And large."

"As tall as I am?"

She considered him. "A bit bigger. With a fat face and bulgy arms."

"What was he wearing?"

"A string vest, dirty jeans and trainers."

"Good. You're very observant. How about the other man?"

"He wasn't so tall. But thin. Not so old. I can't remember what he wore." Her voice was trailing. She had every right to be tired.

Behind him the door opened and Yeadings was aware of

someone coming in. Unsteadily Jennifer Yorke made her way to her daughter's bed and drooped over it. "Poor baby," she crooned. The child curled up small, turning her face away.

"She's still very upset," Connie warned.

"Maybe she noticed what the second man was wearing," Yeadings said hopefully.

Jennifer leaned over the bed. "Baby, tell us what the horrible man was like. You really must tell us. The horrible, horrible man! He frightened my baby, didn't he?"

Clary opened her eyes and stared back, her pupils distended. "His face," she said stiffly.

"What about his face?"

"All lumpy and pink, like . . ."

"Like someone you know?" Z pressed her.

"Lumpy like rhubarb crumble. All pink and juicy." And her own face screwed in a spasm of horror. She whipped her arms round her knees and began to rock, forward and backward, moaning in rhythm.

Z caught a quick glimpse of the other child's reaction. She had sat suddenly bolt upright in amazement, her jaw sagging.

Connie Tinsley left the light dimmed and only half-closed the door, then she joined the others on the landing.

"Did you get what you needed?" she asked the superintendent.

"For the moment. Thank you, ladies, for your help. We'll keep a close eye on the woods and surrounding areas tonight, and one of my men will be back in the morning. Meanwhile we'll leave you in peace."

She saw him to the door and into his car. Everyone else seemed to have gone to the dining-room for a belated supper. The children were safe, would soon be asleep after the mild sedative with their soup.

Which left Connie to resume her previous worries. She looked at her watch. Too late now to expect the vet to come out tonight, but she could phone and put her request on his answering machine. She'd do that, then go out to the stables and check again on the mare.

# Two Pairs

"**P**ull yourself together, woman," Smith said coldly. "It is one thing to play the brainless bimbo. Quite another to reveal that you are one."

Jennifer Yorke flinched. God, the man was a shit. He couldn't understand that terrifying abyss she'd teetered on just hours back when she thought something had happened to Clary, something unspeakable and meant as a warning to herself.

He waved a dismissive hand. "What happened to those kids has nothing to do with you or me. I have no connection with this place. Officially I am not even in the country. It was purely some local low-life, poachers or suchlike. It is unfortunate that the police have shown up, but it is simply because they panic over anything involving children. Now that both little brats are back safely they will ask a few questions, round up any known child-molesters, pick on someone to blame and then decide there is nothing that will stand up in court. Within a few days it will be totally forgotten."

"You can't be sure there's no connection! Someone could have talked out of turn. They *could* know you're here and that I am. Someone from the past. This thing with the children could be intended as a warning."

"The only one talking is you. Babbling hysterical nonsense. There is nothing for anyone to worry about. I tell you nobody outside knows I'm back in this country, no one at all. If they did, then they would have followed up my decoy and I should have heard of it by now."

He smiled, his teeth fiercely white in their fringe of black beard. The sight of them chilled her. She knew he could be savage when opposed.

Her fear amused him, having nothing contagious in it. At Manchester airport he'd taken no chances on recognition, having sent the bearded actor on a meaningless tour in the Rolls ordered in the name he'd travelled under. Double indemnity, with himself a muffled invalid helped by wheelchair from the men's room into an unremarkable car. *Triple* indemnity, considering the final stroke of luck with that car which had delivered him without luggage half a mile from the gates of Fraylings Court.

Tuesday night's crash and the charred corpse, which the police had been gossiping about while served tea after the kids' return, had to refer to the Volvo. He'd noticed the back licence plate was missing, and cursed the driver because it might have drawn unwelcome attention. Now even that was part of his natural good luck because it proved to him that yet more of his tracks had been eliminated.

"Your presence here isn't really secret. You could be got at through Nadia." Jennifer was still in cringing mode.

His lip curled. "Nadia knows, even better than you, how *foolish* any indiscretion would be. It is common knowledge that she and I had long gone our separate ways. There is no love lost, as one says. She would not be worth anyone's following. She is colourless, transparent; has never excited public interest – just your present jealousy, which I find quite amusing under the circumstances."

Jennifer turned away from the boldly mocking eyes.

He reached for her hand, and his own was cold as a corpse's as he squeezed, increasing the pressure while he spoke. "I don't need to emphasise, I hope, that since no one else, no one at all, has knowledge of my whereabouts, if anything should get out, the blame must fall on you."

He smiled at the prospect. "An impossibility, which I have nonetheless taken precautions against in advance. You must appreciate by now that I am always careful over details."

She shuddered, not only from the pain of his grip, and he relinquished her hand in sudden contempt. "So you will be very discreet, Jennifer. As you have already indicated, it would be devastating to have any misfortune befall your little pink and white cherub.''

They had reached the end of the terrace walk and now turned slowly, their shoes crunching on gravel. In the distance they could see others of their company seated at little tables, some leaning on the stone balustrade talking, with drinks in their hands. Even Sir James had come out to socialise on this airless evening. His wheelchair was drawn up to the table where old Gilchrist was shaking the bag of Scrabble tiles ready to play.

Rosemary Zyczynski, in her persona of schoolmistress, broke off from fascination with her colleague's deft hands working on a crochet shawl. Seeming relaxed and inattentive, she had observed Jennifer's overtly sexual attempt to attract Smith's attention, and found it somehow phoney.

The body language of the pair as they walked together into the distance, and out of others' hearing, contradicted the claim that they'd met only a day or two before. They were old enough acquaintances, she decided, to be arguing with some barely suppressed tension, at least on Jennifer's part.

Smith, although he had stopped to take the woman's hand in his own and lean intimately towards her, was neither impressed by her nor soliciting anything. Rather he was exacting compliance. There was more than his normal hint of arrogance about the movement, and something like contempt when he rapidly relinquished her fingers. As they approached the company again Jennifer seemed unable to cover her disquiet, while the man exuded purring confidence.

Where was his wife in all this? She hadn't come out on to the terrace with the others. Z shifted her chair slightly, fanning the air as if to chase a dancing gnat. And then she saw the still figure at the open upstairs window, binoculars trained on the same pair she had been watching.

Even more interesting. Yet from the woman's stance there was no way of knowing what her emotions were, if any. Nadia Smith was uncannily self-controlled. Whatever she made of this unlikely pairing, she would not be displaying any public reaction.

On the ground floor, Connie Tinsley leaned from the nearer

drawing-room window to address the company as Smith and his companion came within earshot. "I must tell you that I've moved the card-playing things to the little salon. Much safer for everyone there, I think. Too great a fire hazard, smoking among straw in the barn."

There was no rejoinder, but several sets of eyes met in half-guilty admission.

"Probably thinks poker's immoral," grumbled Dunne under his breath.

"Poker," said Miss Finnegan with unexpected interest. "What fun. I haven't played since I was a student."

"You never did!" exclaimed the motherly Mrs Fellowes.

"Ah, I was young once," the schoolmistress regretted.

"You still are," Dennis Hampton assured her, grinning like a garden gnome. "I'm sure you won't have forgotten how to play. It's like swimming or riding a bike. Why don't you join us?"

"Yes, indeed," Smith purred, seating himself alongside. "We should certainly open the school to the ladies. At least until midnight."

Serious play presumably began *after* the witching hour, Z thought, smiling gauchely. "I didn't mean to push in," she said.

It appeared she was to be the token female, on sufferance. No other lady admitted to an interest in the game.

Towards ten thirty p.m., Smith carefully extinguished his cigar and looked round at the others. "Well, to more serious considerations," he invited, rising. He swung his discarded jacket from the chair behind him, slung it over his shoulder and turned towards the house. Falling in behind came Dunne and young Hal Carrick. Dennis Hampton leaned over Z's chair. "How about it, Miss Finnegan? Are you on?"

"Why not?" she demanded with an air of girlish daring.

"Maeve, really!" chided her colleague, but benignly smiling like a seashore mum watching her children build sandcastles.

"Andy's night off. So we're just five, unless anyone's told Jolly we've been moved on," Hal said briskly when they reached the little salon. "I'll fetch the booze."

Dennis Hampton was sorting through the contents of the

carton. "Mrs Tinsley appears to have provided us with a set of tumblers. Enforced gentility."

They were disposing themselves round the card table. "I'm afraid you'll have to remind me a bit," Zyczynski said diffidently.

There came a tapping on the uncurtained window and a face pressed against the glass, gawping like an aquarium exhibit. Jolly had found them. Dunne flung the sash up and he was helped over the sill.

This could be a challenge, Z told herself, anticipating the deaf-dumb handyman's coming play, but he proved equal to the occasion, lip-reading easily and sticking up the required number of fingers from a bunched fist for draw cards.

She had no difficulty establishing her play personality. As a schoolmarm she must be cautious, holding her cards close, puckering her brows over future action, barely masking her relief as others' moves seemed to follow rules learned way back.

It was, in fact, a more recently practised skill than she let the others suppose. After-hours her relief in uniformed branch had set up a hard-playing school, though the pot was usually safety matches, and on one memorable occasion – after the custody sergeant's annual leave in Italy – a shared two-litre can of black olives.

Tonight Smith, as first dealer, had opted for plain five-card draw and they were modestly betting with pound coins, the ante being a fiver each. The rounds built up smoothly and she stayed in, matching the previous bid, until eventually a hand she held was too tempting and, to keep within the chosen role, she felt obliged to drop, discarding her hand blind.

The next deal, from Hampton, brought her three of a kind, and when in that round nobody had staked, she checked. Then Smith opened for two – not such a skilled player as he made out, because his weakness was setting out to win on each hand. She could feel him watching her covertly. The others stayed for two and she followed. In the draw she took a useless seven of hearts but raised two and the other three players folded. Smith doubled. She grimaced and threw in her hand. She hadn't bought a sight of his cards but he couldn't resist showing that he held a flush in spades.

As the poker continued, the five men's play tended to confirm the opinions Z had already formed of them. Dunne was unpredictable, his sagging face from time to time betraying only impatience, as though he moodily questioned why he wasted time in this way. Hampton was controlled, making steady but unspectacular gains. Jolly was unruly and optimistic. Young Hal Carrick's play was flashy, annoying Smith with a run of luck until he seemed to get the measure of the young man's reactions. As he reached for the pot he glanced showily at his wrist.

"Twelve twenty-five!" Z exclaimed, checking with her own watch. "Past my bedtime. And I'm enough out of pocket for one session. So I'll say good-night, gentlemen. And thank you."

"Come again," said Smith, leaning back but not rising. "Anyone who loses as sweetly as you is welcome any time."

Toad, she thought, but treated him to a bemused smile. They waited until she had left the room, then Dunne, ready to deal, lifted an eyebrow. "Seven-card stud." he announced firmly.

"Will you walk into my parlour?" Smith was all expansive bonhomie.

Zyczynski smiled to herself, listening with her head against the panels. Dunne was waking up, behaving true to type. There was a streak of ruthlessness there, perhaps desperation. Well, stud should pander to his tastes. You could seriously win or seriously lose at that game.

She went out through the drawing-room's french windows to the terrace and came back to watch the spotlit game from the darkness of the flagged path. One good way to learn about people was to be driven by them in their own car. An even better way was to watch them in concentration when they'd no idea you were there.

She left twenty minutes later, feeling a little surer of what lay behind each poker face. But still she was no nearer guessing which of them might be the reason for her watching brief.

The undercover operation might well be a wild-goose chase, based as it was on only a scrap of charred paper. Forensic scientists had done a good job to pick up those few letters from the brittle ashes, but still '—ylings' could refer to another place or person. Suppose the original word had an apostrophe. It would have been simpler to decipher if typewritten; then a clear space would show between g and s, indicating a house where a named person lived. As it was, the team had been groping in the dark. And assuming an awful lot.

On a hunch the boss had decided that the villains had decamped, so this scrap must be part of instructions left behind for a gang member.

So he/she – whoever – was the only one the team had a chance to follow up. And doing so meant that a lot of taxpayers' money was going to be spent on a proactive cobweb.

When Z was instructed to infiltrate the gathering at Sir James Siddons' home, she had invited her one-time history teacher as back-up to her new identity, and the semi-retired woman had been delighted, agreeing to cover her own expenses. Together they made a convincing pair of holidaying schoolmistresses with a taste for amateur watercolours. It had allowed her to mix freely with family, staff and guests. But after five days of observation she still had no suspect to connect with the murder of Webb.

Not that they were a totally innocent-seeming bunch, because when you're looking for dodgy characters don't they turn up on all sides? She thought she could discount the Siddons-Tinsley family itself – at least for the present – and the two children. But who else? Maybe Andy and Gayle, the catering pair, too busy to have time for other interests – but then, wouldn't that be the ideal cover? She had used such a one herself in her second murder case with the Yeadings team.

Beyond those provisionally eliminated, her possible suspects comprised all the would-be artists plus the late-arriving and slightly sinister husband of Nadia Smith. There were, besides, numerous unnamed comers and goers because of the other classes on offer.

She agreed with the Superintendent's opinion: Fraylings Court would be ideal for stashing a large counterfeit stock and taking the next delivery. It offered the camouflage of numbers, like Charing Cross at rush hour, with clear routes for rapid departure. And there were a hundred suitable places on the estate for hiding the counterfeit consignments before distribution.

But still no news came through of anything big being circulated on the street since Webb's death. As always there were false notes being handed in but only with the normal fluctuations. If it had been drugs the gang was dealing in, no break in operations could have been considered, because users got dangerous without their regular fixes, and there were always competitors eager to take over dealing. But with counterfeit notes the gang could risk temporarily disbanding, to wait while new supplies built up with fresh shipments from Holland. They needed only one person here to take delivery. But he/she must be a principal who could be trusted not to cut the others out. So who? As yet no one appeared to fit the role more than any other.

She rose from her cramped position beside a stone urn, brushed grit from the drab floral frock and turned gratefully to thoughts of bed.

Bed alone, unhappily, with Cynthia gently snoring on her identical narrow mattress across the room. On the job, Z must forgo the personable Max Harris's company. She wondered how he would be faring, alone in his London bachelor pad.

She had seen no evidence there of earlier female occupancy. Yet for Max – popular columnist for a national newspaper – there must be plenty of opportunities on offer. It seemed that at heart he could be a serious man under the droll humour. She had even begun to wonder if something lasting might come of their relationship.

It pleased her that, while keeping her location secret, she could now contact him with a legitimate Press query. Max could verify or refute Dennis Hampton's claim to have been a journalist with the *Independent*. It wouldn't necessarily eliminate Hampton from her list of possibles, but any background Max dug up could suggest whether he'd criminal connections, an expensive habit or an overriding passion for money.

She would ring Max early tomorrow. No, she realised, glancing again at her watch; today, of course. And it wouldn't be all that early, unless she got instantly to bed.

Despite this, she hesitated on the landing to her east-corridor room. The little girls' adventure in the woods still disturbed her, although in fact they'd escaped a close encounter with the men who'd chased them. She decided she must look in on the old nursery before getting finally to sleep.

On the upper corridor a wedge of dim yellow from a night-light shone from one of the far doorways. As she approached it she heard the two children's voices, one low and accusing, the other little more than a sniffing grizzle: Joanna grumbling at a crumpled and defensive Clary.

"I told you to leave it to me. A face like rhubarb crumble – whoever's going to believe that? Why did you make up anything so crazy?"

"But he *was*!" Clary wailed. "He was horrible. You didn't see him. His face was all lumpy and pink!"

Zyczynski barely caught Joanna's scathing rejoinder because at that moment a door on the floor below opened and shut, letting out a short burst of canned music. For a moment she doubted what she had heard the child say.

She would have walked in on the two little girls to demand an immediate explanation, but she caught herself in time. Nothing would be lost by waiting for daylight. It would give her a chance to decide how best to tackle them, and, Lordy, after the poker and accompanying Scotch she was dropping in her tracks.

Silently she made her way back down the top flight and reached her own room, passing a closed door from behind which came more low voices. She stood a moment, head tilted, listening, but she couldn't identify the man's nor make out any words. Enough, anyway, that Mrs Jennifer Yorke was profiting from her daughter's absence by entertaining overnight. Since all other rooms on the corridor were silent, it must have been her door opening that allowed music to escape as she let her visitor in.

Now who, Z asked herself, would that be? She had to eliminate the poker players set for an all-night session, and Sir James who had no chairlift for this end of the house, so that would leave only old Gilchrist the Scrabbler, Pickwick Pomeroy, and the diffident widower Douglas Jeffries on leave from aeronautical engineering. Unless, of course, one included mine host Julian Tinsley, who appeared so very correct and should now be properly asleep in company with the indefatigable Connie.

But Jennifer Yorke's amours were her own business, so perhaps no matter. From the start she had given the impression of being on the loose. Perhaps her opinion was that all cats were grey in the dark.

Tired as she was, Z found it hard to switch her mind off. In the next bed Cynthia Fellowes snored delicately on the in-breath and hissed as she expelled. The faint, mixed noises of the night came through the open window: a distant train, the call of hunting owls. Z slid gently towards sleep.

In mid-dream she came suddenly awake, alerted to an intrusive sound.

Surely not rain: the sky had been cloudless and there wasn't a breath of wind. It struck her that she'd been hearing similar sounds on and off all day as a background: the steady crunch of gravel on walkways beyond the stone terrace. But this time it was gentle, and unbroken. Not footsteps.

She stole to the window. Her room overlooked a corner of the kitchen garden. As she watched motionless, a lumpy shadow crossed moonlight reflected in glass cold-frames. A bulky animal? Not tall enough to be human.

Then it stood erect a moment, light glinting on the oversized spherical head. No astronaut, but a biker in his helmet, *pushing* his machine towards the drive, for fear its engine should rouse the sleeping residents.

Perhaps Andy leaving late, after a marathon baking session? No, he drove an old Ford van, and someone had mentioned it was his night off. So – one of the guests? Or an intruder? Either way, why so furtive?

By the time Z had flung on her bathrobe and reached the kitchen garden (unbolting the side conservatory door which she had learned was independent of the alarm system to allow for family comings-and-goings after hours) she was teased by the sound of a distant engine revving and slowly fading into silence.

Even with her torch she could find no tyre tracks. It was

unnerving to realise that someone from inside the house had probably re-bolted the door after the biker left, and they couldn't be far away. She didn't fancy resorting to the excuse of a lost brooch to justify her creeping about the garden in the early hours if someone was alerted by her light.

Any real search must wait for the morning when Sergeant Morris would come to question the little girls about the men who'd chased them.

*Supposedly* chased them because, thanks to her eavesdropping, it appeared now that their escapade wasn't at all how they'd described it.

Grimacing at the need, Z set the alarm on her watch for seven twenty a.m. Barely four hours on. Whatever had happened to set hours of duty?

As soon as the two village cleaners were let in by the conservatory door, she left the house in jogging gear and ran a circuit, ending outside the main drive gateway. There she hunkered beside a clump of brambles to await the police presence.

It was eight fifteen a.m. before an official car came over the humpbacked bridge with Sergeant Morris at the wheel and a woman constable beside him. Zyczynski stood up and moved out into the road.

"Swap," she crisply told the WPC when they'd stopped. "Sergeant, would you loose the bonnet catch and let her inspect the engine?"

"At risk to her life if she lays a finger on it," he growled. "What's up?"

Z got in beside him, ready to dive below dashboard level if any stranger hove into view. "First, the job you've come on. Seems it's a hoax, but I'd be happier if you just accept everything you're told and fade quietly away. The two little girls went off on some scheme of their own, and the story about being chased was a total fiction."

"Hang on now. No men in the wood? In that case who shut the kids in the hut?"

"I don't know. You saw it. Was there any way they could have done it themselves from inside?"

"But I never did see it. I ran into the search party after they'd got them out. I'm going there this morning to have a look at it."

"*Before* you have a word with Joanna and Clary."

"If you insist. But how come you've got this different version? Did they cough up?"

"I overheard them talking, and guessed the rest. Joanna's the imaginative one. It was her invention. She was livid with Clary for adding her bit on. But the odd thing is . . ."

"What?"

"Clary – if I'm not mistaken – is just as her mother said at the beginning: a truthful child. She's too damped down to dare be anything else. And I don't think she has a gram of imagination in her."

"But she gave that weird description of the second man."

"That's the odd part. The boss was sitting there taking in Joanna's bit about the big black man. Convincing enough, because she stopped short of a scarred face or a limp or a parrot on his shoulder. And she decided she couldn't properly remember the other man. I guess she'd invented as much as she thought safe. At the time, Clary was rolled up tight on her bed, scared out of her wits, dead silent."

"What started her off, then?"

Zyczynski thought a moment. "Her mother had just come in, still woozy with drink, and started fussing about her precious angel. 'Clary, tell Mummy what the horrible man was like,' and so on."

"So you got it wrong about her having no imagination. To dream up a man who looked like a fruit pudding! It's pure Hammer Horror."

"*Rhubarb crumble*. Visualise it. The fruit's underneath with baked pastry crumbs on top. When it's cooked right through, the juice wells up round the sides and bubbles through the spaces, bright pink."

"A bit like apple crumble, then. But not like any *man* I've ever seen. The kid's been scared by some monster on TV, or in a book."

"Maybe." Z sounded doubtful.

"And *maybe* you'd like me to put out a wanted notice on him." His voice was heavy with sarcasm. "Plus an artist's impression."

"God forbid! Nothing dramatic while I'm here undercover. I'll catch Joanna at breakfast and try to get her to admit to her parents that it was all a bit of nonsense. It shouldn't be too difficult. She's decidedly off Clary at present. If she's on her own I'll make a buddy of her. She could even be useful: she's an observant child, with definite ideas about people. She sits back watching everything they do. Intends to become a writer, so she told me."

"All of that just concerns the kids. How about your obbo job here?"

"That's why I wanted to catch you. There was someone in the grounds last night with a motorcycle. I saw it from my window."

"Doing wheelies, that sort of thing?"

"No! Leaving the house. Dead quiet, really furtive. He – or she – left by the gate in the kitchen garden about three-o-eight a.m., pushing the bike, engine off. While I tackle Joanna, would you take a look for its tracks?"

"Can do. My WPC's a camera buff. She brought her Nikon along for a sneak go at the house. Jacobean, isn't it? Quite a picture anyway. If we find any tracks she can shoot them."

He tapped thoughtfully on the steering wheel with the heel of his hand. "This biker. An intruder? Or perhaps one of the inmates sneaking off somewhere?"

"It could have been either. Or even some Romeo visiting on the quiet. I heard a male voice in one of the women's rooms a while before and couldn't identify it."

"There'd be a lot of bed-swapping shenanigans on a do like this," Morris warned, darting her a sideways look. Everyone in the Area knew Z wasn't game for anything of that sort. Pity she was frigid; you needed to be human to make a good cop.

"No doubt. What concerns me is whether an outsider was contacting this woman for some *non*-amorous reason. It might make her one of the lot we're after."

"You want me to put your boss in the picture on what you've just told me?"

"No, I'll contact him when I've more to work on. Which reminds me, would you run me down to the village, so I can ring someone else? I might just catch him before he goes off to work. My mobile has gone screwy, and I need a replacement fast. Report that, would you? You needn't wait for me there. I'll jog back."

But Max wasn't available. Z fed her query about Dennis Hampton into Max's home answerphone. "Can't give you my number, I'm sorry," she ended. "Hang on to the information for me, please, until I can next get in touch. And thanks, Max. Take care."

Joanna was frankly uneasy. She had to stay close and keep an eye on Clary for fear she opened her prim little mouth to blab when people – especially the returning police – asked more questions. Clary wasn't made of heroic stuff and would squish under pressure. There was bound to be a lot of curiosity shown, since the little stinker had made up that ridiculous description. She should have left details to the expert.

Joanna was so fed up with the kid that she could barely trust herself not to strangle her with her own golden curls. Perhaps that temptation showed, because, passing in the hall, Mrs Yorke had steered Clary away as though Joanna were covered in plague sores. Everyone, in fact, was giving her a wide berth. Guilt prevented her seeing this as tact.

It was a relief when the younger schoolteacher brought her cereal across and sat opposite at the breakfast table. She just nodded and got on with eating, which was Joanna's preferred attitude to mealtimes.

When both finished together she slid off her chair and held out a hand for Z's bowl. "Want seconds?"

"Oh, what a good idea! Are you going to . . . ?"

Joanna nodded. "Silly little dishes." She stalked across to the chiffonier and ladled out two generous helpings. Again they enjoyed the cereal in silence.

"I was wondering," Z said at the end, wiping her mouth with her napkin, "if I could see your mother's horses."

"Do you ride?" Joanna countered suspiciously.

"I haven't for a year or two. But I used to go hacking with the girls at a school where I taught previously."

Joanna nodded slowly. She knew better than to let absolute ignoramuses into a stable. They'd get themselves kicked or something equally flabby.

"I'll take you. Now, if you like?"

Zyczynski did like. They collected some carrots from the kitchen and she followed in Joanna's wake across the cobbled courtyard, having great faith in the ability of animals, outside the human kind, to melt the stoniest child's defences.

After a few appreciative remarks about the roan gelding, Zyczynski observed Joanna's gloom lifting in the ammoniac and sweet hay scent of the stables.

"That police sergeant's somewhere around," she said casually. "He may want a word with you, but they don't seem very bothered. Too much real crime on elsewhere, I expect."

"*Real?*" Joanna repeated, aghast. She wondered if Miss Finnegan had a schoolmistress's second sight.

"*Serious* crime," Z corrected herself calmly. "Yes, Clary's effort wasn't very convincing, was it? Not in that context, anyway."

"You didn't believe her?"

"Joanna, I've been a girl myself, and schoolmistresses live among girls for the best part of every day. I didn't believe either of you."

She went on stroking the soft muzzle of the gelding, then turned to smile at the child. "And I don't think that big detective who was here last night took it all that seriously either. How about your mother?"

This was obviously a sore point. Joanna was left standing on one leg.

"I think she may have her doubts," Z went on serenely. "If I were you, I think I'd just settle it for her. She's got a lot of responsibility on hand at the moment. It would be one thing less to worry about."

"She'll be furious."

"Not in front of a stranger. Should I come along, help take some of the heat off?"

Joanna considered the alternative – Clary blabbing her version first, and to the police. There was no knowing where it could end. The police got stroppy, she'd once heard, if you wasted their time.

"I expect," Z suggested, "that your mother could just pass on what you tell her, and the sergeant will leave it at that. He may not need to bother you again."

"Would you? Say a bit for me, I mean."

Z nodded, offering up the last carrot on the flat of her hand. "Shall we do it now?"

Connie was taking a rare break from organising in the scullery. She put down her coffee cup with an air of foreboding as they approached.

"You tell," Joanna insisted.

"I expect you guessed," Z began, "that Joanna's imagination ran rather wild yesterday. They were in the woods and, drying off after a fall in the pond, took refuge in the hut out there. The bar fell across after the door slammed, and they panicked, knowing they were shut in; imagined they'd heard someone outside. They realise now that there weren't any men chasing them."

There was a brief silence, then, " 'Big and black'," Connie said damningly. "That's more than just imagination. It's lying, Joanna. And almost racist. I don't know what your grandfather will say."

"Need he know?" the child mumbled, looking away.

"Everybody will know. They're going to think you're a very silly little person."

Joanna squirmed.

"But she's putting it right now," Z pointed out. "Which is quite brave really."

"I don't know how we can explain to the police when they come."

"Don't you think they're probably used to things like this? Maybe you should tell them how it was. I thought Joanna and I

Cold Hands

might go for a little nature walk this morning – to give her imagination a rest. If you approve, that is."

Clearly Connie was glad to leave the child in the company of a responsible adult until the matter was sorted. She agreed, sighed and returned to still-room matters until Sergeant Morris should make his presence felt.

Joanna was subdued as they walked along the terrace in the direction of the open summer fields. We make an odd couple, Z thought to herself.

The notion recalled her observation last evening of another mismatched pair opting for each other's company. Jennifer Yorke's sudden enticement of Smith was unconvincing in the circumstances, because she hadn't fully recovered from her genuine panic at the supposed attempt to molest her child. Smith was hardly the person to turn to for advice and comfort on such a matter. And at best his attitude had looked like one of scorn.

They couldn't be strangers to each other. She would give a lot to know how well acquainted they were and in what circumstances. Then again, how soon had the poker school actually broken up after she left it? Could it have been Smith she'd overheard in Jennifer's room, availing himself of what she'd earlier seemed to be offering?

The biker seemed a much more likely alternative, because Smith would hardly throw in at poker so soon after they'd switched to serious stud. Yet there was certainly a link between him and Clary's mother. A link she must give some serious thought to.

# Three of a Kind

The elderly trio had set up their early-morning game in the library. This was by Sir James's invitation. Mona Gilchrist – who, her husband had confessed, was 'tiresomely shrewd' – suspected that it was for greater privacy because Sir James suffered a slight puritanical pang over self-indulgence before lunchtime and he hoped his new weakness would not be re-marked on by the family.

"It's not any worse," Mrs Gilchrist assured him, "than doing the *Telegraph* crosswords over one's breakfast." (She had already excused her own abandonment of the more literary puzzles of *The Times* on the score of that newspaper's having 'gone colonial'.)

Sir James considered her. She was curiously like his daughter, but while Connie channelled her energies into active organisa-tion, this large and indomitable old lady directed hers into opinions. Each, in her way, was formidable. He bore with her mainly for the pleasure of her husband's company. And she would be away shortly to her morning watercolour class.

George Gilchrist was, frankly, an old dear. Not a fanatic over art, he had declared his eighty-year-old bones too barely fleshed for the collapsible metal-framed chairs the class took on their sketching session to the nearby farmyard. Mona too had almost defected, without similar excuse but because she held it her wifely duty to accord him little time to himself. Between them the two men had persuaded her not to disappoint Dizzy Crumm, and this eight a.m. session was her idea of compromise.

So here they were, indulging the new *aficionado* – however untimely Sir James might secretly consider it – choosing a tile each to decide who should open play.

"I'm told," said the old soldier, exhibiting a G, "that we have a poker school on the premises. How enterprising. Does either of you play?"

"*Play?*" Mona Gilchrist snorted. "As I understand it, it's more like war."

"M'm. Unarmed combat. You could be right," said her husband. "Couldn't afford it, myself. Sort of thing where you must dive in the deep end. I'm rather more a paddler in the shallows. Suit that new feller, I should think. Likes to put everyone down. Terminal one-upmanship."

"Smith," his wife supplied. "Mine's a W."

Sir James was familiar by now with Gilchrist's inability to remember names. He more than made up for this lack with his trenchant descriptions. There was never any doubt about who it was he referred to.

"E," Gilchrist announced. "So I start." He helped himself to his tiles and almost instantly produced the word "caverns".

The other two groaned. "Plus fifty for using all seven," he gloated gently.

Despite that excellent start, he lost out to Mona who managed to collar four out of the desirable red squares on the board, using high-score letters. As Sir James shook the tiles for their next round, she commented, "So the police aren't doing anything more about yesterday's little drama?"

Sir James sighed. "My daughter tells me it was all a deplorable fiction of Joanna's, hoping to avoid blame over taking the other child out of bounds."

"You can't blame her entirely," Gilchrist suggested. "The way I heard it, the little candyfloss one was equally inventive. If not more so."

"Yes." Sir James paused. "Which implies collusion. Rather worse than one of Joanna's normal overflows of imagination. I must have a word with her. Can't let her lead our young guest astray."

"Wishy-washy little girl, that Clarissa," Mona offered. "She wouldn't need much leading, to my mind. You often get that: considerate parents with selfish children; loose ones with goody-goodies. Jennifer Yorke has her little girl tied down with petty rules and regulations so that she daren't say boo to a goose. That child would do anything anyone told her. Disciplined spiritless, so that her mother's left free to do as she likes. And we've all gathered what it is she likes to do best."

"But not spectacularly successful in that line to date," her husband remarked absently. "Showed some interest at first in that sarcastic feller who brought the nurse along. But he wasn't having any. A bit out of her class anyway."

"Dunne," Mona supplied the name.

"Nurse? Are you sure?" Sir James queried.

"Well, *attendant*. Couldn't say how well qualified the girl is. But she gives him his injections. Carries the stuff in her handbag. I was at my window. They thought they couldn't be seen on that seat in the shrubbery."

"You don't suppose . . ." Sir James began, fearful they might have a drug addict among them.

"Then she turned her attentions to young Hal Carrick, but his wife warned her off," Mona steamrollered on regardless.

Sir James with difficulty grasped that she was still on the subject of Jennifer Yorke.

"Mind you, that Fay Carrick has a wandering eye herself. I don't know why a flashy young couple like that would want to come here. After the first two days they haven't attended any of Dizzy's classes."

"Er, shall we continue with the game?" This was getting serious: Sir James didn't relish scandal. Even less did he care to think that Connie's scheme had let in a horde of alien deviants.

"I'm playing truant myself this morning," George reminded his wife. "And that green-eyed willy isn't a very regular attender."

"*Willy?*" Mona repeated, offended. "Really, George!"

"Don't be stupid. I mean willy as in that ballet thing where they all go around flapping their arms and the girl dies. Grave on the stage, and all."

"Giselle."

"If you say so. I need two more tiles. What, they've all gone?"

"I'm out," said Sir James thankfully. "What's your score?"

He resolved to change the subject. "M'daughter's had a bit of worry over one of the horses," he confessed. "Thought it was quite a serious complaint, but the vet was here early and put her mind at rest."

"What sort of complaint?" Mrs Gilchrist demanded, ever a fan of TV hospital serials and willing to expand her interest to cover domestic animals.

"A disease called Grass Sickness."

"Just fancy! The things they discover these days. Of course, I've heard of Metal Fatigue, and then there's Concrete Sickness . . ."

"I think it means sickness caused by grass carrying a certain fungus. In its fatal form the nerve tissue in the gut is destroyed. But its early symptoms are the same as for both colic and laminitis: heavy sweating, trembling from pain, inability to eat. It seems in this case it's just laminitis – inflammation of the horse's foot. But it has curious side effects. Anyway it should be cured soon, given careful treatment. And I understand the horse is starting to eat again."

"How very odd," Mrs Gilchrist decided. "You'd think even a horse could distinguish between its – er, intestines and its feet."

Lying relaxed in the long grass, Zyczynski too was scrolling through her mind the cast of characters at Fraylings. But without paper she found it hard to be systematic.

One person she had failed to consider before was Jolly, having assumed that his disability put him out of the running as a suspect. But last night's poker game had proved he could communicate as well as anyone, given sight of others' lips. And what sharp eyes he had: he missed nothing.

A bumble-bee, staggering to the tip of a long grass-stalk, wobbled off, drunkenly took to its wings and alighted on the flushed cheek of the little girl asleep beside her. Z waved a hand and the insect took off again. Joanna murmured, shifted position and then was suddenly awake. She sat up. "I fell asleep. Gosh, I never do that."

"You're tired. *Were* tired. Ready for some action? I thought we might go and see how the sketching is coming along. It's only a couple of fields away."

They walked along by the hedgerow, and in the farm lane came on Dizzy Crumm scrabbling for something in her ancient car. Her face brightened at sight of them. "Come to join us? Splendid! Run out of chairs, I'm afraid. But young backsides never did suffer from hard ground."

"Here!" She handed out two sketching-blocks and followed them with a handful of soft-lead pencils.

Joanna looked on the point of rebellion, but Z nudged her and at once she saw the humour of the takeover. "What are we supposed to draw?" she asked submissively.

Dizzy darted her an incredulous stare. "Well, there's plenty of rural interest, but in your case . . ."

Joanna wriggled under her sharp inspection.

". . . something more imaginative, I think. An illustration. Want me to suggest a title?"

The child nodded, grinning.

"The Bogeyman!" And Dizzy marched back towards the farmyard where the class was widely spread. "The light's a bit dazzling," she called back to Z, "but it throws some exciting shadows."

The two new recruits separated, Joanna sitting cross-legged with her back to the others, Z on a low wall of what had once been piggeries, from where she had a good view of everyone and faced a dilapidated outhouse. As Dizzy had promised, deep shadow at its gaping doorway offered a dramatic contrast to the bleached wood and sun-drenched brick of its outer walls. Rapidly Zyczynski drew in the outline and began to cross-hatch it with shading. When she realised that Dizzy was herself settling to sketch, she felt safe enough to turn the page and concentrate on her real work.

She made a new list of the persons under observation and, before considering them singly, ran through the Boss's précis in her mind. The suspect must be a trusted member of the distribution gang, a reliable guard for existing stocks and have authority to deal with whoever delivered the next consignment of counterfeit notes.

When could they expect delivery? Impossible to predict, but Customs, already watching the channels previously employed, should get a warning through in time.

And where would the handover take place? Not wherever the existing stock was stashed if the British end was an independent client. As distributors they would go for neutral ground; so she must look for someone with transport who was free to leave Fraylings over a short period without causing undue comment.

Which meant any of the art class and all those attending the non-resident courses; the Siddons-Tinsley family and possibly Andy and Gayle, the caterers. Having already met the two cleaning women who came in daily by bus, Z was satisfied they didn't qualify. So who was left unlisted?

Her gaze roamed round the farmyard and came to rest on the little art teacher. Dizzy Crumm? Was that likely?

But what better cover? She had an established function here and must have set up the dates for her two consecutive fortnightly courses well in advance of her students. And Connie Tinsley had mentioned that at their conclusion Miss Crumm would be staying on for a while as paying guest. All of which set her ideally in the right place over an extended period. And she had transport which everyone was accustomed to seeing in strange places.

But *Dizzy*? Wasn't she sufficiently occupied without any secondary vices? She was an eccentric little body, showing little interest outside her own obsessive profession. Was there room in her life for criminal ventures?

Maybe, if she had the art side well organised, leaving her free to cope with other demands. And one remarkable thing about the elderly little woman was that, while seeming bumbling and vague, she was really on the ball, could even rival Connie Tinsley in management enthusiasm where her own interests were involved. What was more, she was politically shrewd with it, viz her treatment of Joanna a few minutes back. She handled people just as capably as art-room equipment.

And she appeared to be hard up. Which could be a smoke screen covering wealth illegally acquired. Or, alternatively, she could be genuinely poor enough to need whatever sidelines could supplement her feeble funds. Poor Dizzy, condemned either way in a heads-I-win, tails-you-lose situation!

Whichever, she must certainly go on the list. Zyczynski added a tick alongside her name. She ran her pencil down to the next one.

Dunne: Gerald Dunne, with no known profession, but apparently well-lined pockets; partnered by a sharp little female, not wife or family. Secretary? PA?

There was a deal of tension in the man. He attended the classes regularly, alternating in attitude between near desperation and utter indifference. Two or three times he had exploded with impatience, but the girl seemed unaffected by his rapid changes of mood. Which implied little feeling. So just a tom he had brought along for the ride? Possibly.

But wasn't Dunne too obvious a candidate? Professional villains normally took some trouble to sink into their background. He was offering himself up on a plate as an erratic man of independent means, open to outside distractions. And yet under pressure of some kind, driven by furies. A closet depressive? With a drink or drugs problem? She decided that either he had something badly on his mind or . . .

Or what? Z shook her head. Keep him on the list. Again she ticked the name.

Dennis Hampton: with any luck, Max would soon come up with confirmation of Hampton's journalistic background. He was supposedly retired, but what ex-reporter could resist the temptations of a crime story about to break? If not in fact criminally involved, had he sniffed something out, and – like herself – come here expecting something to erupt?

She hesitated before following his name with a question mark.

Douglas Jeffries: dubbed 'Judge' Jeffries by the others because of his self-contained gloom; a draughtsman in aeronautical engineering; claimed to be a widower and at present on annual leave. (DS Beaumont was following up that claim with the firm which supposedly employed him.) A loner, certainly his artwork confirmed a skill rigid enough to be the despair of free-style Dizzy. She had complained that Jeffries' precision was the opposite extreme from crinoline ladies and rose-wreathed cottages.

Art-wise he was trying to throw off his long-acquired disciplines, but without notable success. Even now he persisted in wearing a tie and long-sleeved striped shirt when out sketching, while the other men sported jeans and T-shirt. Again this one qualified for a question mark, through lack of information.

Jennifer Yorke: this one too was a puzzle. Feebly following the art classes, she could have signed on in a genuine wish to share a country holiday with her daughter. It could be pure coincidence that she had chanced on Smith here, first encountered elsewhere. Their relationship was complex; close enough for them to be at odds with each other, suspect enough for them to need to dissemble in public.

Could the man be an ex-husband, grasping at an opportunity to see a daughter left in the mother's custody? Unlikely: he treated the child with something approaching disdain. And while Jennifer Yorke didn't appear without funds she didn't exhibit lavish alimony. Perhaps they had once been lovers, or involved together on some business project. Find out what work she ever did, Z scribbled in brackets.

Were she and Smith even now uneasy accomplices in some illegal activity? The one which Yeadings' team was currently interested in? Whether they were involved with the counterfeit gang or something more personal, for now Jennifer Yorke had to be one of the possible suspects.

Now Z had arrived at the couples. First she could almost certainly eliminate the Gilchrists, on the score of their age, and being so totally involved with art classes and Scrabble marathons with Sir James. They each earned a cross.

Then Philip and Jane Pomeroy, the middle-aged couple. She hadn't seen a lot of them, avoiding his invasive bonhomie. Jane by contrast was art-dominated. She was the most devoted of Dizzy's disciples, seriously into Bohemian dressing, in tent-like tie-dye hessian and sandals.

Z supposed this might simply be her chosen holiday gear, with a contrasting style for the home-role of wife to a bank's branch-manager: Pomeroy's post which inquiry to NatWest had already confirmed.

Z put a cross after the Pomeroys' names, then added a query after the man's. It seemed laughable, but weren't bank personnel, however Pickwickian, in a wonderful position to distribute false money?

Hal and Fay Carrick, the young twentyish couple in Dizzy's class, made no pretence of belonging in any group. A self-sufficient, puckish pair, they gave the impression of being sardonically amused by all that went on around them. Physically fascinated by each other, but in too blatant and familiar a manner to be honeymooners, they were increasingly reckless exhibitionists. Each had made open advances to others of the opposite sex, but mockingly as if joking at their expense. Z thought they must be on something more than speed. And that suggested a connection with Rotterdam.

The counterfeit money was printed in the Netherlands, which was also Europe's main channel for illegal drugs, both cocaine-based from South America and morphine-based from Turkey and the Indian subcontinent. But she had to discount the Carricks being involved with phoney money. They invited too much attention; risked exasperating Connie almost to the point of asking them to leave. Unless more positive indications came along, she must write them off as young decadents on a self-destructive jag.

Which just left the Smiths, or whatever they were really called. The woman was shadowy, seeming to be here for a rest, following the art course fitfully with only mildly expressed interest. The man was totally different, a rank poseur, intent on exciting interest with his mock bid for anonymity. From the start he'd suggested he should simply be known as 'B', with the result that nobody called him anything to his face, and referred to him as 'Smith' or 'that new fellow'. At the same time it wasn't a put-down. They were reluctantly impressed by his arrogance and moneyed air.

For herself, Zyczynski reserved judgement. She had met more conmen than real millionaires. For the present his name earned a tick.

She expected some useful lead on most of these characters to come shortly from Superintendent Yeadings. One positive outcome from Joanna's escapade had been that DS Morris asked for, and obtained, the permanent addresses of all residents at Fraylings Court. Beaumont would be checking on them now. What she most hoped for was that one deliberate deception – apart from her own – would reveal a criminal past under wraps.

DI Angus Mott could have done without a re-training course on Team Management interrupting his heavy schedule, but at least it ended early, permitting a detour to London and the chance of an hour or two with Paula. He rang her Chambers in Middle Temple and learned that his fiancée was defending a client at the Bailey for her boss Grant Wheatman.

So probably no opportunity to talk, but at least he could see her in action. He identified the court, slipping in at the back as a woman witness was called. She was small, middle-aged and distinctly nervous, stumbling over the words of the oath. She agreed that she was Adelaide Field, head of the typing pool at Melody Matchmakers of which the defendant, Oscar Ryman, was Managing Director.

The man in the dock was a flashy fellow with a broad, sloping forehead and a pugnacious jaw. Overweight, he sat leaning forward, his puffy fingers, covered in rings, dangling like bananas over the rail that confined him. A prefabricated bouncer if ever there was one, Mott decided. Paula would have an uphill grind getting this one off if the jury went by appearances.

He gathered it was a complicated case, a charge of fraud and conspiracy to commit blackmail. The woman was a prosecution witness, stumbling over her evidence that Ryman had used the firm to provide immigrants with British nationality through marriage to native-born partners. There was also the possibility that more than one case of bigamy had been recorded and Ryman had been extorting money regularly from the wretched dupes he had drawn into his web.

When the prosecuting counsel sat down it looked an open and shut case. But then it was Paula's turn. She looked ridiculously

young and stern in her wig and black robe. Beginning gently, she
gave the nervous woman the impression that she was sympathetic to her intentions.

"Would you describe Melody Matchmakers as a dating
agency, Miss Field?"

"I like to think of it as a Lonely Hearts Club."

"And you have been working there for a considerable time, I
believe, helping these lonely people to find a suitable partner to
share their lives with?"

"Eight years, yes."

"So you are in a position of some trust?"

"Yes. I have always tried to give satisfaction."

"And do you enjoy your work, Miss Field?"

"Well, yes, I must say I do."

"And what do you enjoy most?"

Miss Field almost smiled back. "I like to think I have helped
make some unloved people happy."

"Which is the intention of the bureau, and of its staff?"

"Yes."

"And besides holding a post of some trust, am I right in
thinking you also need to exercise a great deal of discretion about
your clients?"

"Oh yes. Their files are completely confidential."

"To outsiders, that is?"

"Yes, that's right."

"But you are conversant with their contents yourself?"

"Of course."

"And have been so for the eight years of your employment
with Melody Matchmakers?"

"Yes." She sounded doubtful now, perhaps half-sensing where
she was being led.

"Miss Field, I will ask you to look at the document listed as
Chancellor One and dated fifteenth April 1993. Are you familiar
with this extract?"

"I think so."

"I think so too. Are those not your initials in the margin
against the date of the final settlement fee?"

"Yes."

"And the amount of the fee is that required on conclusion of a satisfactory matching? Following a marriage, in fact?"

"It is, yes."

"I shall ask you now to look at this copy of a document listed as Chancellor Two."

Miss Field accepted the second paper from the usher with trembling hands.

"Can you tell the court whether the sum paid and initialled by yourself is the same as on the earlier receipt?"

"It is." Her voice was little more than a whisper.

"And will you also say what date is given on this second document?"

There was no answer. The woman's shoulders were shaking.

"Miss Field, did you hear the question? Shall I repeat myself?"

"It's the twenty-third of April 1994. But you know that! That's what I told the police. She was marrying this second foreign man, and just a year after the first!"

"And this transaction – if I may call it that – was your responsibility throughout. You were, in fact, even as long ago as that, knowingly aiding the commission of bigamy."

"Not knowingly. No! I was just doing what I was told. initialling the receipt."

"Told by whom, Miss Field?"

"By Mr Ryman. He was my boss."

"But in this particular case, Miss Field, he could have given you no instructions, because Mr Ryman was at that time on holiday in Lanzarote. And I can give you other dates on which your signature on specimen papers germane to this case were dated at a time when Mr Ryman's authority would have been unobtainable."

"It was general practice. I had overall instructions."

"Mr Ryman had no personal contact with these clients, Miss Field. Where his signature was required on withdrawal or paying-in slips for the bank there was no reference back to specific cases. It was you who prepared and produced the forms which he signed in all good faith."

"Yes. That is the way we work. It's normal office practice. Mr Ryman has a second account into which—"

"Did you have access to this second account, Miss Field?"

"No. It was for his private money."

"Then if you had no responsibility for it, that account is outside your sphere of interest. It is, as you say, private, and therefore irrelevant to the present charges."

Paula drew herself up to deliver the final blow. "You were entrusted with a high degree of freedom. I am suggesting to you, Miss Field, that you went far beyond the remit of an agent, taking it upon yourself to encourage, condone and connive at these illegal practices and, now that this has come to light, you are willing to pass the blame to one who could have been in no way involved."

There was an immediate protest from the prosecuting counsel which was overruled. Mr Justice Longthorne consulted his watch, beat the bench with his gavel and declared the day's proceedings over.

Mott sat on, observing the principals' reactions. The unfortunate Miss Field, lost in a cluster of wigs and obvious police support, was devastated. Ryman stood up, a big man in every way, and looked across at her with open contempt. Paula, coolly composed, gave him a distant nod, inclined her head to take in some remark he made, then turned away to speak to the clerk of the court. Mott reserved judgment for the moment and went outside to catch her up as she left.

"Angus!" she cried in delight, when she saw him. "How long have you been here?"

Long enough, he thought. But he shrugged. "I'm just passing through. Thought you might be able to snatch a meal with me."

"Tea's possible," she offered, dragging off her wig and shaking the thick, dark hair loose on her shoulders. "But I'm dining with Old Wheatears later. I promised to let him know how the case was going."

"Justice being served, and all that," Mott said with heavy irony.

"Oh come on, Angus. You know the way it is. I have to use anything that's to hand to protect my client."

"I know too well how it is. Having an almost watertight case thrown out through the twisted casuistry of a clever barrister. How do you think that poor woman feels now after what you did to her?"

"Chewed to bits," Paula admitted. "But my client hasn't a chance unless I rubbish everything that's thrown at him. Miss Field should have been more aware of what she was handling. I'm paid to win, Angus, not play bleeding hearts."

He looked hard at her and felt the storm rising inside him.

"Darling," she said persuasively, but he was thinking she'd call anyone that nowadays if she couldn't remember their name, "we've argued over this ever since student days. It's the British system of trial by champions. Whatever kind of shit I may suspect my client of being, I have to do my darndest for him."

Just as I'd do my darndest to get him sent down, Mott acknowledged silently, galled that it left him and Paula on opposite sides. "I thought you'd had your fill of keeping the corrupt in circulation."

"It's part of my job," she said simply. "And I'll stand up for it just as you have to for yours. There's hardly anything worth doing nowadays that hasn't its seamy side. Come on, I know a place where they've umpteen kinds of tea to choose from and gorgeous cream pastries. We can talk more when we get there."

He wasn't sure he wanted her winning him over by persuasion. And certainly not with cream cakes. He should have known better than to meet her on her professional ground.

"Whatever happened to old Wheatman's intention to retire?" he demanded when she had poured his Darjeeling and her own Earl Grey.

"It's on hold."

"What became of his charming wealthy widow in the West Country?"

"Oh, didn't I tell you? She died. It was quite sudden, and he was terribly cut up. So it's just as well he hadn't given up entirely. His work is all he seems to care about now."

"Not enough to see his own cases through, apparently."

"Well, he started this one actually, then decided I could handle it. The client was willing, Mr Justice Longthorne has a leaning towards a feminine line of argument . . ."

"Has a lecherous eye, the old goat."

"We need to use everything we've got on this one, Angus. It's going to get sticky later when we get to the blackmail charges."

"So you do know this man Ryman's guilty?"

Paula gave him a reproving look. "I may suspect as much, but he's never admitted anything. Quite the contrary. I can barely get him to acknowledge his name. If he was ever moved to confess I'd expect him to plead guilty and I'd try to prove mitigating circumstances. But anyway why are we discussing my clients? Is that what you came for?"

No, it wasn't. But the sun was hidden for the moment; all the joy gone out of meeting up with Paula again. He didn't even have the heart to remind her she'd intended moving to Thames Valley, eventually taking a job with Crown Prosecution. She was so concerned with Wheatman keeping her on as his junior, that she'd no thought for Mott himself as husband-in-waiting.

"Just passing through," he said heavily. "Can't stay long. We've a logjam of cases at present and as ever we're thin on the ground."

"Poor old Angus," she said, laying a hand on his arm and stroking it gently. "We must try and get a few days off together soon."

But it wasn't a holiday he wanted. A honeymoon was more like it.

He returned on duty that evening to be confronted with an impasse on the burnt-out car inquiry. From Traffic Division it was being transferred to him as a murder case, with Yeadings as Senior Investigating Officer. His first task, after scanning the daily media précis, left on his desk by the assistant press officer, was to examine the pathologist's report on the incinerated body.

Little joy there for identification. The fingers of the right hand had been charred right down to the bone. The ringless left hand, contracted tightly, retained some skin tissue, but it would be a long and doubtful specialist job to look for any recognisable prints, even if the man's samples were on record for comparison.

His blood group, however, had been taken from dry samples and was the rare AB rhesus negative. It would be a matter of weeks before they had access to full DNA details.

These facts persuaded Mott that his best chance lay with the long shot of recognition by medical record – in tracing a long-healed double fracture of left tibia and fibula. It seemed more hopeful than the matching of dental details, which must wait for comparison with a known missing person.

Vehicle examiners reported that the car's front (and only) licence plate had been false, but painstaking picking off of buckled and flaking metal had now revealed the engine number. The murder team rapidly assembled by Superintendent Yeadings was intent on tracking down the car's earlier movements, and a Volvo of similar type was being shown on television's *News at Ten*.

It had not yet been released to the Press that tyre tracks of a motorcycle were found on the grass verge above the burnout. They'd now been identified as Dunlop 204s, new and in good condition; fast riders, indicating one of the more porky road machines, and at a price that implied the biker wasn't strapped for cash.

"Any sighting yet of that biker?" Mott demanded at morning conference. "No? Who's covering this?" House-to-house inquiries, he was told; and, due to sparse population, it was already completed, but without any positive result.

He consulted the Ordnance Survey map on the wall. Although houses were few near the incident, there was a church marked some mile and a half farther on, with a school alongside.

"When were inquiries made?"

"Wednesday evening, sir. When the families would be home."

"Send someone out to the village school. I know it's closed for the holidays, but someone must have a list of pupils with their addresses. See them all. There could have been a scout meeting or organised activity that evening so that some children got missed out at home. If anyone's going to take note of a great beast of a motorbike it'll be kids who would give their eyes to own one. And get me a line to Path Lab. I want a date as near as dammit for those leg fractures."

While he was waiting for the connection he looked round for Beaumont. "What are you on at present?"

"Doing some checking for Zyczynski."

"Has anything come to light out there? Or any alert from Customs on the next delivery?"

"Everything's dead as a dodo, Guv. They're sitting this one out. Whatever scare made them move the last load was serious enough for them to keep their heads down."

"Killing Webb wouldn't have been on the cards to begin with. Let's hope that's all that pressed their panic button. I'd hate to think they know we're on to them," Mott said curtly. "If we've got a blabbermouth, or Customs has, it will be pointless leaving Z on that job. Her cover could be blown by now."

Beaumont looked owlishly at him, questioning what had put the normally sunny Mott in such a tetchy mood. "You want her back here for this car murder?"

Mott didn't answer, phoning a query through to Pathology on the dead man's bone surgery. Which didn't please him much; the medical specialists were being typically cautious.

"Twelve to fifteen years back," he said, ringing off.

He swung round on Beaumont. "That's something you can get on to right away. Pick up photographs of the charred left-leg and get all hospitals in the area to examine them. If that doesn't produce results, spread the net. E-mail them to the moon if necessary. I want a recognition on this one and I want it now."

"And Z, Guv?" Beaumont persisted.

Mott hesitated, remembering the Boss's pledge to resist taking the team off proactive work to fill in emergency blanks. He didn't want to be the first to breach the guarantee.

"We'll hold her there in reserve. If you've chased up any information she asked for, phone it through and warn her she's on her own now."

"Right, Guv." And pass the bone inquiries to someone down the line, he told himself. With patients' waiting lists the length they were it stood to reason nobody on hospital staffs would waste time on such a hopeless quest.

*   *   *

115

Rosemary Zyczynski was familiar with the legend 'For the want of a nail the war was lost'. It was her habit to pick up and employ any usable implement that came her way. In the present case her nail was a wasp sting. She clapped a hand to her right temple and gasped aloud. Joanna looked up from her drawing, got to her feet and came across.

"Something stung me," Z said, wetting her finger in her mouth and rubbing it over the spot.

"Wasp or bee?" Joanna asked, peering close. "It doesn't seem to have left its sting in. Are you allergic to insect bites?"

"Not more than most," Z admitted. She smiled, noticing that the little girl was looking at her with a strange intensity.

"What's the matter, Joanna?"

"Nothing. Well . . ." She looked embarrassed, hesitating whether to be truthful and seem rude. Then abruptly, "Why do you wear a wig, Miss Finnegan? Sorry! Sorry, that's personal, isn't it? Only, I know sometimes . . . Well, if you've had *keemothrappy* . . ."

Zyczynski turned away and swiftly pulled the net edge of the wig's base more firmly into place. She kept her eyes down, avoiding the child's stare. "Do you think anyone else noticed?"

"No, they're too far away." Joanna leaned close and whispered with passionate conviction, "I'll never tell. They can tear my tongue out . . ."

"Thank you, Joanna. There are things, you understand, which one does like to keep private. I think perhaps I'll go back to the house now."

"I'm coming with you. I'll just tell Miss Crumm we're leaving."

Hurriedly she collected her drawing-block and held out a hand for Z's, from which the top two sheets had been removed. "Don't you hand your drawings in?"

"Not today. Just the block."

"All right then." Joanna went across to where Dizzy was sitting, happily splashing away in watercolour. Z watched while they exchanged a few words, then she jumped down from the wall, brushed grit from her cotton skirt and moved off to join the little girl.

This wig accident was unfortunate. How would she escape Joanna's protective custody? She feared the fervently romantic child would seize on the drama of a pathetic victim of invasive cancer.

Joanna was mercifully silent on their way back. On entering the house by the conservatory they ran straight into Connie, bound for the kitchen with instructions for serving lunch. "Oh, Miss Finnegan, your prescription has been delivered. I put it in your room."

Z smiled to hide her mystification. "Thank you, Mrs Tinsley." She turned to Joanna. "And thank you for your company this morning."

"Will you be all right?" Joanna asked with elaborate doubt.

"A wasp sting, that's all," Z assured the child's mother. "It will be fine when I've splashed some cold water on." She felt her smile growing stiff with the effort, turned aside and made for the stairs.

The package was wrapped in white polished paper, folded with meticulously mitred ends and sealed with two blobs of scarlet sealing wax. Just like a chemist's order from Edwardian days. Someone back at HQ had a sense of history. But the outside did bear a label from the leading pharmacy in Wycombe. It was, of course, a box containing her replacement mobile phone.

Unfortunately this delivery must reinforce Joanna's view of her as a very sick woman. The child's sympathy was something she must learn to put up with. And it wasn't certain that Joanna would need her tongue torn out before sharing the sad news.

Perhaps there were compensations. It would excuse Z's necessary absences at times. But if Joanna went so far as to mention the wig, someone might question why Miss Finnegan had chosen such an unbecoming bird's-nest.

Just before lunch, Connie came knocking on her door with the offer of antihistamine tablets. "You should really have taken them earlier," she said, "but I'd forgotten where I'd put them. I've brought you some mineral water as well. Take two, why don't you? And have a quiet lie down until it's a little cooler. I'm having your lunch sent up."

Which would usefully excuse Z's absence from afternoon art class and give her a rest before night-time activity. She had already decided that the farm outbuildings where they'd been sketching that morning deserved a second, more thorough, examination after dark. Anyone with local knowledge might have used them as a cache.

The evening Scrabble game was interrupted by Connie, accompanied by a uniformed policeman. She appeared a little flustered to find her father entertaining company in the library.

"No, no," Sir James insisted, when the Gilchrists rose from their seats and prepared to depart. "I'm sure this is nothing of a private nature. How can I help you, Constable?"

It was a question of recalling traffic on the main road on the previous Tuesday evening. There had been a fatal accident and witnesses were needed. All houses in the immediate vicinity had been visited and now the police were spreading their inquiries wider.

None of the trio was able to help. They recalled that everyone had been present at Fraylings except Julian Tinsley who had spent the day in London, returning sometime before seven p.m., but not from the direction of the car crash. They had assembled for pre-dinner drinks at seven fifteen and could vouch that none of the group had driven outside the grounds before breaking up for bed at a little after eleven.

"At what time did the accident occur?" Sir James asked.

It hadn't been established with accuracy. Flames had first been observed from across the valley at six fifty-five, but not reported. By seven twenty, when a home delivery van passed the point at which the car had left the road, it was burning fiercely. The driver had continued to the crossroads phone box and rung the emergency services. It was much later that an incinerated body was discovered inside the doused remains.

The constable's voice was flatly unemotional, as though he read aloud from a report, but for one of his listeners at least, the effect was traumatic. Sir James closed his eyes, facing again the savage orange fireball of a Chieftain tank as he managed at last to force the blocked turret open. There had been no hope for the men cremated inside. He had been hurled clear in the fireball's blast, to wake up later in a Cairo hospital bed, hair singed off, bandages up his arms and chest, his face unrecognisable.

Fire was a diabolical way to die; small wonder Hell was imagined as a furnace. All his pity was for the poor devil it had happened to in the car.

"So nobody from Fraylings Court could have witnessed either the fire or any road traffic at about that time?" the constable summed up.

"That is correct," Sir James answered for them all. "If you prefer to question our guests individually . . ."

"I think your word will cover for them, sir."

"Good. I'm surprised that you haven't a statement from your own Detective Inspector Mott, who must have used that route after holding his swimming class here that evening. But perhaps you come from a different department?"

"I'm from Traffic, sir. Actually it's DI Mott running the investigation now. Since it's become a suspicious death."

Shock waves told him he'd said too much. Genuine horror showed on the three old people's faces.

"Do you mean murder? Is that why so many questions are being asked?" Connie Tinsley said faintly. "But what a hideous idea! I'm glad none of us saw anything of it."

Small-talk as they met for their final drinks before retiring was overtaken by the startling news the Gilchrists brought of the police interest in Tuesday night's road accident.

"And not a real accident, but murder!" Mona Gilchrist declared dogmatically, almost as a reproof. "Who would expect such a dreadful crime in peaceful surroundings like this?"

"But hardly on our doorstep," Dunne said sardonically. "And in the end they'll probably find it was something more mundane – like our babes-in-the-wood fiasco of yesterday."

Jennifer Yorke barely held back an angry retort. "How could the police tell it was deliberate?" she demanded, to cover up.

Several theories were aired, some frankly ludicrous: the body having been stabbed and left in a passenger seat, or chained to the steering wheel, and other ghoulish inventions.

"What the police most wanted to know concerned other traffic on the road at the time," Gilchrist told them. "Obviously they're hoping for eyewitnesses."

"We explained," Mona said importantly, "that we were all here, and none of us went out again that evening."

Sir James considered the statement afresh. He remembered now that the man who called himself Smith had not been present for dinner on that evening. He had arrived unannounced some time before Julian had returned from the city, presumably brought by hire car from the airport. Then he was supposedly resting in his wife's room until he reappeared while coffee was being served on the terrace.

Yet Smith was not speaking up to point this out. He was delicately sniffing at his fine malt, theatrically turning the glass between long, finicky fingers. Knowledgeable on the subject of grapes and vineyards, he'd had a supply of The Macallan and a couple of cases of fine wines delivered and was patronisingly offering it around. Sir James had declined firmly, while regretfully observing the Montrachet vintage.

He caught old Gilchrist watching the man closely. So he was thinking much the same: that Smith chose his moments to attract attention, and this apparently wasn't one. There was something distinctly unsavoury about the man, yet no one so far had been able to put a finger on what it was.

Sir James had learnt the advantages of being elderly and sitting back to watch others in action. Perhaps, he thought now, although a back-number he was good for more than book-browsing and Scrabble. Next time he and the gossipy Gilchrists met over their shared interest, the trio should pool their opinions on the mystery man and see what they came up with.

With ambivalent feelings – the man was, after all, a guest in his house – Sir James waited until everyone had departed from the lounge before propelling his wheelchair towards the staircase. And carefully folded inside a linen napkin in the chair's rear satchel he tucked the cut crystal tumbler that Smith had recently been using.

Just in case the man had a criminal record – and why else should he want to use an alias? – this might be of use to the young Detective Inspector Mott in identifying him.

# Five in Sequence

Z yczynski waited until all was quiet along the landing then, armed with a powerful torch, she stole from her room in black sweater and trousers, reaching the ground floor by the back stairs. Dimmed lamps in the main hall were scarcely enough to illuminate the unlit kitchen passage. She crept down it towards a bar of light shining under the door. A muffled clink of pans and crockery reached her as she pressed her head against its quilted padding. It seemed that Lady Siddons was at one of her late night baking sessions, so there could be a risk of encountering her on the way back to bed.

In the butler's pantry, Z located a panel governing the house's burglar alarms and switched the system off. That way she'd have options for a return route, if for some reason she couldn't go via the conservatory.

The night was sultry, the almost full moon mainly covered in bars of drifting cloud which offered up spasmodic pools of darkness as she left the shelter of the house and made for the home farm. Twice, as she entered the fringe of woodland, she was startled by the swooping flight of a pair of owls. After the first rush of their passage she was aware of distinct rustlings and murmurs as nocturnal creatures scuttled and foraged. Z stood and listened.

It took longer by dark to reach the stockyard and she skirted around the farmhouse for fear of dogs wakeful for foxes. Upstairs a light still showed at a net-curtained window, but it was feeble; perhaps a night-light for a child's room.

When sketching here, the only person Z had seen was a

121

thirtyish woman in a flowered cotton dress and apron. She'd been pegging out washing on a sagging line and seemed deliberately to avoid any contact with the art class.

The first outbuilding she came on was a hen house. She could make out a peevish, clucking murmur as the inmates gently stirred inside. Did hens actually snore, or were they aware of a prowler close by? (Was it the Romans who had used geese as guard dogs?) Interference with them now would certainly set up a squawking to alarm the farm dogs. So any exploration of the hen house must be left to daylight when the birds were scratching about in the dusty yard.

Next came a byre with eight Friesian cows and two empty stalls stacked with straw. The big black and white beasts did no more than move their weight from side to side and turn to stare at her while still patiently chewing.

A wooden ladder offered access to the loft by a creaking trap door. Z went up and balanced on the top rung, sweeping the beam of her torch to the far corners. All appeared normal: more bales of straw, cobwebs and dust, old brick walls with no sign of recent restructuring.

Then on to a heterogeneous collection of farm vehicles and implements housed in an open Dutch barn. Among the harrows and coulters, drills, trailers and an ancient Fergusson tractor, the emphasis here seemed to be on rust and near-threadbare rubber tyres. Any more valuable materials would certainly be kept in the larger wooden shed which loomed blackly like a hangar against the now lighter sky. And the hasp on the door was, of course, firmly padlocked.

But the more butch the lock the more room it offered to get a picklock in, Z reminded herself, delving in a pocket for the necessary tools. It took her no more than two minutes.

Inside the barn there was a gleaming, barely muddied, giant tractor, a speckless trailer and a wall hung with equally new attachments. Recent money, Z noted. Or, just as likely, recent bank debts.

At the far end, behind the bulkier gear, was the opening to a second compartment. Two overlapping roller doors of heavy timber stood in steel tracks, and this time there was no padlock. Z reached for the right-hand door to grasp the opening bar, directing the torch at the join.

A small, bright projection to the left glinted briefly against the timber and she looked closer. It was a quarter inch of cable exposed from its plastic cladding which disappeared into the thickness of the door. Whoever had channelled it in and filled the space over had been clumsy with the end sheathing and left enough naked wire to catch the torchlight.

Why, she asked herself, when the valuable new equipment was protected only by a padlock, should the barn's inner compartment merit an electrified alarm system? The answer – for the present – had to be guesswork, because no way was she going to risk getting in to find out.

Satisfied that her hunch was apparently on target, Z pocketed the torch, stole out into the farmyard – now drenched in an unwelcome burst of moonlight – slid the padlock back and pressed the tongue home. The return journey was uneventful and she checked her watch as she let herself in by the conservatory door. Barely an hour and a quarter had passed since she'd left.

This time no light had been showing at the kitchen windows, so she felt safe from discovery by Liese, yet at the door to the staff passage she froze. Someone in leather soles was walking stealthily past, towards the butler's pantry. Z opened the door a crack and was in time to see a dark outline vanish round the pantry door.

After a moment she heard a key turn – on the cabinet that housed the alarm system, surely. Then a grunt. Male or female? There was a slight pause, and the cabinet door being shut more loudly. Much as she needed to see who it was, she had to close the door against discovery in a room drenched in moonlight. And then it was too late because the unknown was in a hurry now and had disappeared from the passage into the main part of the house.

So could it be one of the family who, discovering the windows weren't alarmed, had come to switch the system back on? Z went to look. It was exactly as she had left it.

In that case the unseen person had come to turn the alarms *off* and found it already done. Which meant that he/she now meant to go out of the house. Or was expecting someone else to come in.

Z remembered the night-time prowler with the motorbike who would have left by the conservatory door, a convenience known by now to most of the guests. Did this other person not know, then? Or, like herself, was he/she taking precautions against possible emergencies?

She moved silently into the passage and made for the main hall. Here the lights dimmed for night left patches of total darkness where anyone might be standing. She walked round close to the walls. Then suddenly with an appalling clatter her legs were swept from under her. She fell forward on to some hard metallic contraption with bars which rocked and slid away with her sprawled on top.

Damn! Sir James's wheelchair parked in the gloom by the well of the staircase, where he'd have transferred himself to the chairlift for going up to bed. And now the prowler had taken fright. She heard a rush of footsteps receding above her, then pounding on the gallery boards, muffled eventually on the thick carpeting of the upper corridor. Then a second or two later a door quickly opened and closed.

Z extricated herself and limped to the stairs, pulling up with a shock at the chairlift as she recognised Sir James himself seated there waiting to go up. Slumped, rather; because it seemed he'd fallen asleep. Or been taken ill.

But, as she put a hand on his shoulder to wake him, she realised it was a dressing gown she'd touched. And not Sir James at all. Someone distinctly more fleshy, and he was unconscious, perhaps dead.

It was Pomeroy, the bank manager, with a trickle of dark blood running down his neck from his tousled hair and congealing on the crimson silk of his robe.

He was alive. She found the pulse in his neck and he gave a little unconscious groan at her touch. Fetch Cynthia, she thought. Cynthia, the First Aider. Between them they must see to him.

124

She pounded upstairs. In the west-wing passage she came on Cynthia already awake, routing through her travel bag, with light streaming from their doorway and the nearer bathroom.

"Laxative," Cynthia said vaguely. "I'm almost sure I brought some along."

Z gripped her arm, explained there was an injured man downstairs and she immediately reached for her first-aid kit.

When they reached Pomeroy he seemed to be coming round. They set him in the recovery position on the floor and Cynthia fetched a rug from the gun room while Z made a 999 call for an ambulance.

"Twenty minutes," she passed on the message. "Stay with him, Cynthia, will you? I'll have to let the Tinsleys know."

She roused Connie and Julian without disturbing anyone else and they formed an anxious little huddle in the hall, waiting for the paramedics.

Pomeroy had more or less come to, but seemed to have no recollection of what had happened. "Must have . . . slipped and hit . . . my head," he ventured after a while. "What on earth was I . . . doing downstairs . . . in my 'jamas?" Then later, "Haven't sleepwalked . . . since I was at prep school. God, my head hurts!"

"So what else was the outcome of your night walk?" Cynthia demanded of Z when the ambulance had removed Mr Pomeroy, with Julian alongside to keep tabs on him. It had been impossible to get Mrs Pomeroy properly awake after the two sleeping tablets she'd taken on retiring. She had groggily accepted that her husband had gone off somewhere for the present, then curled up comfortably again in bed and began loudly snoring.

"This business," Z told her friend witheringly, "is nothing to do with me. In fact I'd give a lot to know who's behind it." She omitted her find at the farm and explained what had happened on her return to Fraylings.

"Well, I'd agree it was no accident," Cynthia said decidedly. "Pomeroy could hardly have got that knock from falling."

"And then tidily arranged himself in Sir James's chairlift."

"Well, that part's not impossible. Perhaps it was the nearest

125

seat to drop into when he was staggering about? *Then* he passed out."

"But there was definitely someone else in the hall, who made off when I fell over that damn wheelchair. I heard him on the stairs, had glimpsed him in the kitchen passage. He ran back to one of the bedrooms on our floor, either the east or west wing, just a few seconds before I came for you."

"Well, it wasn't the west wing. I'd been hunting everywhere for that laxative, in my own luggage and also in the bathroom. I had both doors wide open, with the lights on. I'd have heard and seen if anyone went past."

"That narrows it to the five rooms in the east wing, then."

"You're forgetting the entrance to the family's private apartments. It could have been either of the Tinsleys, or the so-called Smiths that you saw."

"No. When I went to call the Tinsleys I noticed that one of the double doors is fixed shut. The other has a porcelain knob on a loose shank which rattles. You can't mistake it for the sound of any other door on that level. No, I'm satisfied that whoever was downstairs – and probably bopped poor Pomeroy – disappeared into one of those five rooms in the east wing."

All the guests' bedrooms had brass numberplates on the doors and, to assist communication, Connie had listed them with their occupants' names on a noticeboard outside the dining-room. One of Zyczynski's first precautions on arrival had been to make a copy of this.

At the staircase end of the east corridor, two singles followed the two bathrooms, and these were occupied by Dennis Hampton and Douglas Jeffries. Numbers three, four and five opposite them were twin rooms housing the Carricks, the Pomeroys and the Dunnes respectively.

Zyczynski's own room, number nine which she shared with Cynthia Fellowes, was in the west corridor which was a mirror image of the east. Immediately after the stairs and the bathrooms came single six, originally reserved for the androgynous-sounding NL Smith, but now the cramped quarters of Sir James Siddons and Liese. Dizzy Crumm was farthest at seven. Opposite, at eight, came the elderly Gilchrists. At the stairs end, in number ten, were Jennifer Yorke and Clary (hastily snatched back from the old nursery and any further contamination by Joanna).

That completed the guest list, except for the Smiths – now elevated to unimagined magnificence behind the elegant double doors off the gallery, which kept the family's quarters private. In there too, lay the Tinsleys' room and Joanna's playroom (where she now slept since briefly sharing the attic nursery with Clary).

Z decided that as soon as it was reasonably light she must phone Angus Mott at home and report. It was galling to admit that each time there had been any suspicious movement at Fraylings she had always been a shade too late; too slow to get a good look at the people involved.

She was no nearer identifying the biker of the early hours, but whoever had been downstairs with Pomeroy tonight was certainly narrowed down to one of the east-wingers. It probably wasn't the same unknown both times because the biker had been visiting Jennifer Yorke in the west wing.

Although a verbal report would suffice immediately for Angus, the Boss was another matter. He'd get Angus's précis; then he'd require it fully in writing from her. So she'd better start on that while the details were fresh in her mind. She took the notebook from her locked suitcase and filled three pages with rapid scribble. So much for the past. What really excited her now, so that sleep was impossible, was the prospect of progress.

She turned to a fresh page and wrote room numbers down the margin. Then she added her possible suspects' names.

1. Dennis Hampton
2. Douglas Jeffries
3. The Pomeroys
4. The Carricks
5. The Dunnes

So, subtracting Pomeroy himself, as victim, that gave her a choice of seven individuals. Dennis Hampton was already being

researched, if Max Harris had picked up her request on his answerphone. Douglas Jeffries, remote and uncommunicative, had immediately struck her as worth official interest, so the Incident team were checking his background.

The couples in the double rooms opposite appeared such close pairs that she felt tempted to regard them as single entities. If any one of them was involved in skulduggery then the other partner must surely be in on it too. But they remained enigmas. It was time that the team came up with some background on them.

When the sketching party returned to the farmyard after breakfast and the house resumed its comparative quiet, Zyczynski slipped out into the kitchen garden, with her new mobile phone in a knitting bag, to make two further calls. Angus had been in early for a session with the boss and her opposite number, Beaumont. She caught the DS fresh from the briefing and he had useful news.

Douglas Jeffries *was* the engineering draughtsman at Bristol he had claimed to be; widowed some four months back; childless and overcome by his loss. Dissatisfied with the restrictions of his career, and never one to socialise outside his marriage, he was desperately looking around for a means of occupying the empty hours when he wasn't at his work-desk.

That figured, Z thought. Jeffries wasn't finding it easy to mix with the others. There was an aura of gloom about him which put you off making an approach. She had misread his grief as misanthropy, poor man. The new details made good sense: an unimaginative man at a crossroads in his life, suddenly sensitized to the human condition and wondering what else he'd missed out on. Perhaps, in a state of loss, he'd recognised himself as an industrial robot unable to break out of its programming. He was trying so hard with his painting; could see what was wrong, that a draughtsman's rigid structuring wasn't art.

"Where did you get this personal stuff on him?" Z asked Beaumont.

"From his sister. She'd moved in for a few days, to clear out the dead wife's effects. He hadn't felt equal to tackling it himself and it was getting him down. So much so that she'd advised him to contact the Samaritans. She thought he'd done so, and took me for one of them checking up on how things stood."

That would be a new line for Beaumont. He'd taken on a number of roles in his time. She could picture his Pinocchio solemnity, nodding in round-eyed encouragement as the sad story poured out, putting in a quiet question when the torrent dwindled. A good listener. Negatively supportive, although – like most in the job – usually not slow to criticise the average Social Worker.

"You don't think Jeffries is looking for a substitute career in crime, then?"

"Hasn't the opportunity, nor the time, I'd say. But I've only the sister's say-so to work from. Decide for yourself."

She could almost hear Beaumont shrug as he prepared to wind up. "As it stands, you appear to have a pretty law-abiding lot at Fraylings, whatever your doubts about the Smith man. And you're not alone in that. Some anonymous bod sent Angus a package to the nick. It contained a carefully wrapped tumbler with a set of dabs and the name 'B Smith' in quotes. It's been passed to SOCO for comparison with criminal records. Could be useful, or it could be an act of pure malice. Funny thing though, the name wasn't written in block capitals, didn't appear a disguised hand. Almost as though whoever raised the suspicion was willing to stand by it. I hope this attack on Pomeroy doesn't start up a lot of violence. Not that it seems to be more than a petty spat. Anyway, you're on your own on the Fraylings end now. The guv's got us all tied up with the car murder."

"Sergeant Morris too? I need him to get back to me on the tyre tracks."

"What're they?"

She explained, and received a surprised "*Motorcycle?* When was this? We've found some bike tracks at our incident."

They exchanged details and agreed it was probably a coincidence. There were any number of motorcycles in the area at present, and then, days had elapsed between the occurrences.

"Morris has gone up to Brum to fetch a prisoner," Beaumont told her, "but I'll see how far he's got with it when he returns. Ring me tomorrow."

So the widowed Douglas Jeffries was one less to bother with, Zyczynski thought gratefully. To have even one eliminated was progress. And with any luck her second phone-call would bring confirmation that Dennis Hampton was also genuine. She caught herself smiling as she punched out Max Harris's home number.

Max was there, still cooking himself breakfast. He'd had a late night, missed lunch yesterday to catch a train to Sheffield, been offered no more there than coffee and a rich tea biscuit – whatever twisted sod called them that? – by the octogenarian philosopher he was to interview, then spent the journey back in such earnest confab with an unemployed toolmaker that they'd no thought for food. And at home the cupboard was bare but for cornflakes. So he'd had to start today with a shopping expedition.

The interviews? Dead loss for the first, alpha plus for the second, and it opened the possibility of a series on similar lines. So he'd worked on it overnight, he claimed virtuously: a good week's work compressed into eighteen hours. He sounded tired but on top of the world.

"Glad you're missing me," said Zyczynski drily. "Did you find my message on the machine?"

Max ignored the comment, picking up on the question. "Dennis Hampton, humph. I wish I could find something to put you off him. How come you find yourself in his engaging company?"

"Max, I'm asking the questions. Is he what he says he is?"

"A very competent journalist, even if the *Independent* begrudged him a byline. He turned down a chair in editorial to go and write the Great English Novel. I lost touch at that point. He must have been at it some two, three years. Progress slowed somewhat, I imagine, when he inherited from a rich uncle. Or so Grub Street has it."

"And apart from his competence?"

"Rosebud, I trust you're not demanding references for someone to replace me?"

"Idiot. It's purely work. I need to eliminate him from my list of doubtfuls."

"Doubtful of what? No, ignore that. Mama taught you to be discreet with members of the press. To my knowledge, he's honest, non-violent; all that. Nice bloke. But a bit fond of the ladies, I'm afraid."

"Thanks. Have to cut this short, Max."

"I don't suppose there's any hope of—"

"Not a chance at present. I'm strictly in purdah. Sorry."

"Well, take care. Make it as soon as you can."

As ever, he didn't say goodbye, simply rang off. Z struck the second name off her list for the east-wing corridor.

Slipping the phone into her knitting bag as her keen ear caught the sound of shoes on gravel, she was counting stitches as the man who called himself Smith rounded the bushy screen of runner beans.

"Ah," he said in his over-perfect English, "my companion of the night-walk."

For a split second she thought he was referring to last night's obbo at the farm. But then she remembered her return from Tuesday's meeting of the team at the Feathers. It seemed weeks, not just days ago that Beaumont had dropped her off and she'd met the newly arrived Smith strolling near the gates of Fraylings.

Suitably flustered, Z admitted that she had temporarily defected from the painting group. "Maeve Finnegan," she said, coyly offering her hand and overlooking their common interest in the poker school. "We've never properly introduced ourselves, have we? Please call me Maeve."

He bowed over her fingers. "Boulos – er, Smith, shall we say?"

He couldn't go further to make it obviously false. Again it struck her that no one with something to hide would parade himself so blatantly. Unless, of course, he was very, very sure of himself. Verging on megalomania.

They made small talk until he moved off, doubtless seeking a companion of greater interest, leaving Z to brush off the interruption and return to her list of five room with the first two satisfactorily crossed through.

Which left, as immediate suspects, the Carricks and the Dunnes. There was also Pomeroy's wife because, according to statistics, physical attacks were most often domestic. But Zyczynski had her doubts, because if Mrs P hadn't been truly knocked out by her sleeping pills, then she was a consummate actress.

In the little salon a meeting was being held. Not poker at this hour, but a family council. After assuring himself that Pomeroy was receiving the best attention in hospital, Julian had returned home. Both Connie and Liese had been comforting the shocked Jane Pomeroy before dispatching her, in Mrs Fellowes' sympathetic care, to check on her husband's progress.

Even Joanna had thought fit to attend the meeting, eager not to miss out on any new excitements. But the agenda was to disappoint her, the subject of the actual attack having been exhausted in private.

The question of sleeping quarters was tackled first, brought up again by Liese – the subsequent debate leaving her outnumbered and smouldering. It was agreed by the others that no better room could be found for herself and Sir James than the cramped one they had ceded to under pressure. The attics were discounted, because Sir James's chairlift served only the two lower floors.

Connie rushed in with sweet reason, anxious to avoid all mention of the wretched contraption, which she had censored from the public version of Mr Pomeroy's 'sad accident'.

"Mother, if you exchanged rooms with us," she pointed out, "we'd be less able to keep an eye on Joanna. And at the moment she does need a strong hand."

"As if *I'm* not capable!" Liese protested. "I am her grandmother. And, if you recall, I managed to raise you without creating any great disaster."

"You sleep too soundly nowadays, Mother. And the walls between are too thick for you to hear anything."

"Well, certainly I shall never sleep soundly in that pokey little hole you've put us in at present. And your father—"

"We'll manage, m'dear, when the new mattress arrives. One can sleep anywhere if one's tired enough."

With that it was agreed that Connie must retain her own double since she bore the main burden of management at present.

"Right, so that's settled," she ruled briskly. "What we have to discuss next is staffing. We really do need more help. Andy and Gayle are splendid but they must have reasonable time off. I think all of us are pulling our weight but there are things being overlooked. Just one more person to spread the load would make an enormous difference."

"I have already offered to cook two evenings a week," Liese said grandly. "Do you now want your father to act as butler?"

"Of course not. Don't be ridiculous, Mother. Julian, how are expenses going?"

"We're not expecting to break even for some time, but we are slightly under budget so far. We might advertise for someone part-time. But arranging that will take days, perhaps weeks."

"No, I think the only hope is the village. Not that I can instantly think of anyone suitable. What I'd really like is a *man*, who could serve at table and help Jolly with the grounds, and lend a hand at times with the horses."

"*One* man?" Liese demanded. "Say three at least, especially the way they work these days!"

"Well, I suppose he would have to be full-time."

"Financially out of the question," Julian decided. "Unless, of course, you found someone who'd live in. Not that we really want to use the attics. I suppose we could make an arrangement with the home farm? They'd not charge much for the room and he could eat here. That way we needn't pay him so much. Maybe someone with pub experience whom Andy could knock into shape?"

"Then I'll give them a ring at the local," Connie decided. "They're always taking on new people."

"And sacking them for dishonesty or incompetence," Liese warned.

133

"Well, anyway, it's worth a try." Connie rose briskly and pushed back her chair, turned to the window and momentarily froze. "Who on earth—?" she began.

The others crowded round. It wasn't easy to answer, since both figures, in jeans and loose white shirts, were upside down, walking on their hands across the cobbled yard from the stables. At the far end, Smith, a panama hat shading his eyes and the inevitable cigar between his teeth, was cheering them on with a slow handclap.

"It's the Carricks," Connie declared in exasperation. "As if last night at dinner wasn't enough! I didn't know where to look."

"They are jokers," Liese decided. "A very unusual couple. I think they want to shock everyone. Fringe theatre. But I am not shocked. I have seen many women dressed as men and men as women."

"All the same," Connie protested, "coming to *dinner* like that! In charades one might have accepted it."

Liese looked at her and sighed. Connie had missed the point, as ever. The Carricks had cross-dressed for a purpose: to start cross-seducing the others. Hal had been making subtle overtures to Smith, and Sabrina to Jennifer Yorke. Really it had been quite cleverly indecent. Reminded her of Berlin before the war.

# Flush

D I Mott was enjoying a late lie-in on Sunday morning when Yeadings' call came through. "Angus, there's been a development. Actually there are two, but I don't see yet how they connect. Can you come in?"

With new hope Mott threw on some clothes and legged it to the Superintendent's office, taking the stairs two at a time. The Boss had his back turned, slipping a new filter into the coffee machine. "On my desk," he said tersely.

Scribbled on the top sheet of a message-block was a note in Yeadings' squarish handwriting, headed with the date and timed 10.03.

*Consignment leaving Rotterdam by sea tomorrow Monday destination Isle of Sheppey ETA twenty-three hours. Weight and value unknown.*

"That's it?" Mott demanded. "If they know that much what happened to the rest?"

"Walter Merton rang me at home," Yeadings grunted. "That's all he's been sent. Complains of a difficult snout on the Dutch end, willing to take the money and run, but possibly hoping it's insufficient info for either Customs or us to get a full result. Thus living to grass another day. I'm not sure it's worth much. Merton's not happy himself."

"Isle of Sheppey," Mott considered. "A big area to cover, but there's only one real road off it, as I recall. That's the A249. I think it connects with the M20 at junction seven."

"I'm having maps sent up." Yeadings had switched on the coffee-maker and was waiting for the thing to burble. It struck him suddenly what kind of diversion it was. In his pipe-smoking

135

days hadn't he felt the same impatience for the tamped tobacco to draw with that comfortable, sucking sound? And according to Nan his pipe had been a substitute for the maternal breast. Did he make an instinctive back-to-the-womb retreat when faced with a teaser? God help Thames Valley force if that was the truth! He'd only meant to top up his caffeine level.

Mott was disposing his length on a hardbacked chair, legs outstretched. "And the other development? You said there were two."

"Yes. I rang the lab for any progress on that second lot of motorbike tracks. The results've just come through. The same tyres made both sets. Traffic's on to tracing the bike now.

"It seems there was a Masawaki ZX-7R in the rear yard of the Feathers on Tuesday night shortly after the car burned out. Could still have been parked there during our meeting. Then in the early hours of Thursday Z saw a bike being pushed away from the rear of Fraylings Court. When it was started up near the main gates it left some perfect tracks on the grass verge outside. Same tyres as at the burnt-out car: Dunlop 204s. So, if we're right about Fraylings being used to store the counterfeit banknotes, then Oliver Webb's body on the railway line and the cremated car driver's could be linked – the gang covering up with a torched flat and a torched car. I'm now pooling all info on both in the Incident Room."

"Assuming that the biker who stopped to watch the car burn was no innocent bystander?"

Yeadings shrugged. "That's the way I'd like it. It could be wishful thinking."

"You want me to visit the Feathers, check again whether anyone was seen leaving that bike or going off on it."

"And give them hell that they didn't come forward earlier. The pub wasn't missed out on house-to-house inquiries. If I find any uniform men were offered drinks there I'll see their licence gets revoked."

There was a knock at the door and a WPC handed in an armful of maps and coastal charts. Yeadings cleared his desk for them with a single sweep of one arm and Mott started to spread the sheets.

136

"It doesn't make sense," the Superintendent said after staring at the proposed area for the landing. "Rotterdam to the Medway, OK. Though I'd have thought the Hook was easier, because we're not talking big ships, are we? Then the Isle of Sheppey's all marshes and mud flats. As you say, there's just the one road to the mainland and Customs could close it off as easy as a paper bag. I get a sour whiff off that detail. It could be pure fiction. My nose tells me their informant is giving the right time but ensuring our reception committee's set up safely away from the real venue. Because he's got a part in the action and wants to save his own skin."

"So, not the east coast at all?"

"I wouldn't necessarily say that. I'm ready to accept the first part, which in any case we're not in a position to check on. If someone's making fools of us it will be about the delivery end."

He ran a finger over the chart. "Look, that dotted line is the Vlissingen car ferry's route to Sheerness. They'd not be far off that. When they showed up on radar they'd still look legit, making for the Medway mouth. Now where could they make to from there?"

"It has to be northwards. Towards the Thames estuary. We know there are regular runs for contraband in that general area, mainly drugs-smuggling, so there's no shortage of Customs activity with night equipment to draw on. But, given this new info, officers from there will be ordered down to Sheppey to keep watch, leaving their own patches wide open. They're skeleton-staffed just like us."

"So how far up-Thames have these beggars decided to go before off-loading on to the road? They could make it to Greenwich, or Chelsea for that matter. Any of a hundred drop-off points. We haven't a wax cat in hell's chance of hitting on the right one in advance."

Yeadings straightened from the desk and made for the coffee. He poured two mugs before giving his considered opinion. "They'll avoid central London: too much chance of hang-ups. The traffic stays solid all through the night.

"Let's consider it from our end. The fact that they intend

basing distribution as far west as our neck of the woods rather than on the Met's patch is significant. If they opt to come in by the M25 ring road, they can choose either direction and still reach South Bucks and have the stuff stashed before first light. That's one option."

"There's another?"

Yeadings pointed to the topmost map. "There's a small runway marked about two miles inland from Southend-on-Sea. I want to know about every aircraft that gets booked to fly out from that field from midnight tomorrow onwards. And if the airfield's shut down overnight I want to know of every pilot and aircraft usually there that's unaccountably not available then. And I want that information obtained with total discretion." He paused. "Now who do I know in the job down there?"

Essex Man, Mott thought. That doesn't sound too promising. But trust the Boss: he had tentacles that reached to the most unexpected quarters, and all manner of oddities who owed him a favour. "Suppose they do try an airlift, where are they likely to land?" he wondered aloud. Then, "Denham airfield," he answered himself.

"To park innocently beside the Thames Valley police chopper?" Yeadings asked. "That would be nicely ironic. But it needn't be a plane they use. A helicopter fitted with thermal imaging apparatus can drop anywhere at night, or hover for unloading. Anything we've got you can bet the opposition can afford twice over. Which tells me they'll make the drop as near their storage centre as possible, because by then the British team will have taken over and they'll be operating without observation from their Dutch suppliers."

"Is there something I've missed?" Mott queried.

Yeadings leaned back in his chair and grinned at his DI through the aromatic steam of his Italian coffee. "I've changed my mind about the Dutch squealer. He could have had no intention of fogging the issue. He could have leaked the delivery plans as far as he knew them; exactly as the principals over there had been informed. They are to lie off the Isle of Sheppey. Final landing instructions to be radioed to them on arrival at the given time. It's our villains at the UK end that are playing canny."

"Diverting them north-west to the Thames estuary at the last minute?"

"You don't sound entirely happy with that, Angus."

"I've done some sailing round there. It has drawbacks."

"Such as the currents off Shoeburyness, and the treacherous Chapman Sands? Have faith in the delivery men. They're Dutch, lad. Cheese, fairground organs and shipping. That's what they're about. You can count on it they'll have up-to-date charts and a competent pilot on board."

Mott put down his empty mug, still uncertain. He had a point to make and was in two minds about how to voice it. "Sir." He saw his mistake as Yeadings' mouth twitched. OK, so they both knew he only called the Boss that when he was being tactful. "We're assuming a lot there, sir." Dammit, he'd said it again.

"What you mean," Yeadings said with a lethal smile, "is that I've been talking a load of codswallop. And I'm leading you astray. I've nothing to back up my airy suppositions. That it?"

"Sir, with respect . . ."

Yeadings gave a suppressed whoop. "I knew one day you'd get round to that one. Come out with it, Angus. You think I'm off my trolley this time. Right, so you've time enough to get things set up. Go away and think over all we've just discussed. Work it out for yourself. Then make your own dispositions. On your head be it if you're wrong. On my head if I am. Can't offer you better than that."

Mott rose and made for the door. As he reached it Yeadings called, "What's Beaumont on at present?"

"He's looking into the man injured at Fraylings last night. Trying the hospital and then the Crown pub close by the Court. Hoping to pick something up without unnerving whoever we're looking for at Fraylings."

"Good. We'll have to think about back-up for Z. She hasn't come up with much yet, but the bike tracks must mean something. We have to take them seriously, especially in view of the proposed new delivery tomorrow night. Meanwhile, work on staff at the Feathers. Get that biker identified. He can't have vanished into thin air."

Mott paused in the doorway, catching up with what had floated into the back of his mind. "*Carver Ward*. He was there at the same time as us. Man with a colourful past. Could be he's taken to riding a bike?"

"Find out," Yeadings countered. "And don't overlook whoever was with him. Z saw two empty glasses. Ask about Ward's companion who left early."

Mott went downstairs more slowly than he'd come up. The Boss had been playing with him, leading him on in the guessing game. It wasn't his own concept of proper police practice, but he'd admit it often led to useful connections. OK, so there was logic to the sequence the ideas had run in, but Yeadings' conclusions about the drop were distinctly iffy. Too many equally valid options were overlooked. He could be dangerously persuasive, and today he'd been functioning in hunch mode, relying on the boasted intuition inherited from his old Welsh granny, the last of the Wise Women of Abergavenny.

One of these days, Mott vowed, he'd trace the old rascal's family back and expose him for a fraud.

Which idea at least had him grinning as he left the building on course to follow the bike trail at the Feathers.

Jane Pomeroy had exhausted all her anger by the time she got back to Fraylings by cab. At first most of it, Mrs Fellowes told Zyczynski, had been directed towards Pomeroy himself, helpless in his hospital bed, for being the object of an assault. But it was just her way of reacting to shock and she'd been weeping copiously in the embarrassed man's arms before she tenderly took leave of him. "There's no doubt in my mind," Cynthia said, "that she was terribly shaken and had no part at all in the attack."

Which left Z with the remaining east-wing characters in rooms one to five to choose among for his attacker. Dennis Hampton and Douglas Jeffries were no longer strong suspects. Which left the younger pair of show-off Carricks and the Dunnes, an oddly matched couple who weren't, in a legal sense, a couple at all.

It would be hard to find a more varied set of people. Hal and Sabrina Carrick were risk-takers and mischief-makers, well qualified to take part in illicit enterprises. Neither of them appeared to have any artistic motivation for joining the present group at Fraylings. So why were they here? She wished Beaumont would come up with more background on them. True, she hadn't considered them a priority, but that was because she'd brushed them off as lightweights. Now she wasn't so sure. Their offensive behaviour might well be a diversion to create just such an impression.

And then the Dunnes, Gerald and Pattie. How were they connected, unless it was in some commercial arrangement? She wasn't his secretary. Z had already seen a sample of her writing on a postcard left for posting in the hall. Two of the words had been scratched out and the spelling altered. One a correction; the other from 'sceanry' to 'scenary'. However low his opinion of modern education, a man of Gerald Dunne's impatience couldn't have tolerated a dyslexic scribe.

The postcard, showing the front elevation of Fraylings Court, had been addressed to a Ms May Fogarty at Merrieway House, in a street in west Reading, and bore an unpunctuated message of the 'having a lovely time wish you were here' kind. It was all Z had as a clue then, but it just might help to shed a light on what and who Pattie un-Dunne actually was.

Gerald himself was too self-absorbed to open up easily to others. It was only at poker that Z felt he made any outward effort, and then his play was reckless, almost desperate, as though he had to prove to himself that everything must go wrong for him. A depressive? Something a bit odd anyway. A sick man of some kind. In which case Pattie, scatty Pattie without an apparent care in the world, would be his minder.

With a sudden inspiration Z went to Connie Tinsley's office to borrow the phone book for Reading.

Fogarty was variously listed, but none of the names had the initial M. However, there was a Merryway (sic) House, and it was a private nursing home.

So was Ms Fogarty patient or nurse? Either way, mildly

141

dyslexic or not, Pattie apparently kept in touch with her. A colleague? Might even have worked at Merryway House herself at some time and now found private one-to-one care more profitable?

The more Z considered this, the more she believed the airy guesswork made good sense. Dunne didn't seem to care what others thought of him, so their posing as a married couple wouldn't be for social gloss. More likely it was to ensure that Pattie was with him overnight, to take care of him if anything went wrong.

And if she accepted this surmise, what difference did it make? Z asked herself. Was either of them the connection she was looking for; the one who attacked Pomeroy; the one responsible for storing and distribution of a fortune in false banknotes? She had to admit that the idea was pretty thin.

Connie Tinsley watched Miss Finnegan go out into the sunshine clutching her knitting bag. Such a helpful, kindly young woman. So sad what Joanna had confided to her last night: that the poor creature was a cancer victim. At first she'd thought it another of the child's wildly unlikely stories, but then she recalled there had been that special delivery from a chemist's in Reading; and Miss Finnegan had taken care to rest up since the wasp sting. Finally she'd come in to look at the Reading phone directory, and Connie – not nosey of course – just happened to see where she ran her finger down to on the page. She'd been looking up the number of a nursing home for incurables.

It would be terrible if anything happened to her here. Anything final. Connie determined that at the family's next tea-break she must warn them all to take special care – not to let Miss Finnegan over-exert herself; keep an eye on where she was all the time.

Joanna attached herself assiduously at lunch and Zyczynski foresaw an afternoon of her company. Since the child's probing conversation would probably distract her from present concerns she opted to join the sketching class.

"Are you sure you feel up to it?" Joanna asked anxiously,

padding behind and insisting on carrying her stool and painting satchel.

"I find it soothing," Z told her gently but with pointed meaning.. "Peaceful."

"Right. I'll see nobody pesters you."

They were painting at the farm again and it gave Z the excuse to walk about, ostensibly choosing fresh angles to sketch from. She paid particular attention to the electric cables slung between the outbuildings. It seemed the barns all had lights, and there were the usual conduits for leads to the byre's electric milking system. What she had not expected was a cable bypassing the bulkhead lamp at the farmhouse's front door and running into the lush honeysuckle foliage above. It was newish and unmarked. As recently acquired, she guessed, as the barely used equipment in the padlocked barn.

She settled her camp stool inside the porch and sketched until she felt secure from observation. Joanna, having doodled a while, had abandoned art for literature and was deep in the throes of composition some twenty yards away.

After a while Z stood to stretch, and ran her fingers into the foliage overhead. They touched metal and she groped deeper among the leaves. She felt her heart lurch as she realised what they had found. There was a steel-cased camera on a swivel-base and it was aimed towards the barn's doors.

If it had been switched on last night it must have caught her picking the padlock. Unless – as with roadway speed cameras – it cost too much to keep permanently loaded.

There was no way to know. She guessed the camera had been fixed there some weeks ago when the farm was first chosen for the counterfeit money's cache. Was it hoping too much that since then the leaves could have grown over the lens obscuring its view? At any rate now she could ensure that they did.

But the risk was already taken. Next time someone came to remove the film . . .

"Are you all right, Miss Finnegan?" Joanna's clear voice came as a shock.

She moved into the open. "Just stretching," she said easily. "I think I'll take a little walk. One gets rather stiff not moving for a while."

Joanna came too, sacrificing authorship for a stint of caring, and stayed limpet-like until called for junior supper at half-past six.

There were more minor shock waves to survive at dinner. The starter of liver pâté and cucumber salad was already on the table, but when Andy came in to remove their plates he brought someone with him.

"Listen, everyone, this is Charlie, who's new," Connie announced. "He's come to help us out."

And it was Beaumont, almost resplendent in white shirt, bow tie and a shiny striped waistcoat, which was two sizes too large and pulled in by the rear belt to make a puffball effect above a waiter's black trousers. Z choked into her napkin and took a desperate gulp of water.

"I can't remember what the rule is," Dennis Hampton said in an aside to her as he liberally buttered his bread roll, "which is doubtless due to my plebeian upbringing. But it's either that you can't have a butler unless you've already got a footman, or it's the other way about."

"I wouldn't know," Z murmured. "I just remember the frog footman in *Alice*. There was no butler mentioned there."

"Minted potatoes, madam?" Beaumont's wooden Pinocchio features were thrust abruptly between herself and Hampton as he flicked half a dozen of the things on top of her turkey slices.

"Thank you," she said faintly. "That's more than enough."

He didn't do badly for a beginner. Perhaps serving at table was no great challenge for a man with several conjuring tricks in his repertoire. And he had the convincing been-on-me-feet-all-day plod of a real waiter. Which would be no put-on if Mott had had him running in all directions and doubling because of her absence. Their respective positions now were more than unfair.

She spared him the curious glances of the other guests, noticing that Smith couldn't resist correcting his handling of the wine. The man had a talent for setting others' backs up. He could regret it before long.

After coffee (during which Zyczynski pictured the DS stripped down to his braces and scraping plates into a trash can) there was an early move towards poker. A cleaned-up Jolly was already hovering beside the salon window when she approached it with Hampton, Smith and Hal Carrick.

"Just the five of us?" Smith checked.

"Dunne's gone skulking to his room. Andy's on late shift in the kitchen," Carrick explained. "We'll have to round up some others. I'm surprised Tinsley doesn't play. Being a money man, after all."

"Is he?" Smith appeared startled. "Is he indeed?"

"M'm, City broker."

"I doubt," Hampton suggested, "that Connie would welcome her hard-won profits leaking so quickly back to us."

"Wives," Carrick said airily, shuffling cards like a pro, "are bottomless pits when it comes to money."

Which generalisation struck Z as unfair, at least in Connie's case. She saw Hampton's left eyebrow rise while Smith displayed a savage array of white teeth inside the black beard. Only Jolly didn't react. Perhaps he hadn't been lip-reading just then.

"I suppose," Z ventured, "you'd call Mr Pomeroy a money-man too?"

"What, branch manager of a high-street bank? Hardly." Carrick curled his lip. "Anyway, he's out of the action, it seems."

"Yes. Funny business, that." Dennis Hampton was keeping the subject rolling. "Who could have got so mad with him as to bop him one? He appeared such an affable fellow."

"A joke too far?" Smith suggested. "There's a limit to permissible jollity. Who's been sitting next to him at mealtimes?"

Jolly tittered. He must have picked up on the conversation again.

"But it wasn't an inside job, was it?" Carrick insinuated. "I overheard Tinsley complaining that the alarm system was switched off. Anyone could have got in. Maybe Old Pom had planned a secret assignation and the lady turned sour on him. He was in his nightgear, after all."

"So it was unlikely he meant to go out," Hampton considered.

"But whoever – er, bopped him might have meant him to go

out," Z said, daring them to conjecture further. "He could have been placed in the chairlift upstairs, where Sir James had left it. Then it was sent down with him unconscious in it. If the attacker hadn't been disturbed Mr Pomeroy might have been smuggled out of the house and disappeared."

"So who is this 'whoever'?" Smith challenged. "You were there, Miss Finnegan, as I understand. So you are prime suspect. Shame on you for taking advantage of a portly old gentleman like that. I had no idea you were so violent."

"Really, Mr Smith, that is a joke in very bad taste," she bridled.

"You all seem to know more about this than I do," Hampton complained. "The official version I heard was that Pomeroy was sleepwalking, fell and injured his head."

"The Tinsleys thought it better to tone things down rather," Z admitted. "So, how did you get to hear a different version, Mr Carrick?"

"The ambulance woke me and I came out of my room to see if I could do anything."

Lurking on the gallery to watch and eavesdrop, Z translated. Or was that a fiction to cover knowing too much of what actually happened, because he had been the attacker?

"Doubtless Pomeroy will bore us to distraction with the real facts," Smith said easily. "Once he gets to remember."

"Is he still unconscious then?" Z fished.

"Conscious, but unable to recall what happened, so the hospital informed me. When Carrick here told me at breakfast about the alleged attack, I rang through to ask after him."

How untypically caring of the man, Z thought. His concern would surely be for his own security and comfort, rather than any other's. Perhaps he was afraid of Press publicity if a crime had been committed. Or had he reservations about another visit from the police?

She glanced at Hampton who had conspicuously not joined in the last few surmises. He appeared thoughtful rather than concerned. Catching her eye, he shrugged. "What I missed! Too heavy a sleeper, I'm afraid."

Smith considered he'd closed the subject, picked up the five cards he'd been dealt and nodded across to Z. "Your lead."

She opened modestly on a pair of jacks, an ace kicker, a three of diamonds and a seven of spades. Jolly knocked, the others raised. She discarded the two low cards, drew another jack and a five of hearts. Now with three of a kind, she reminded herself there were no good hands, only good opportunities.

Three jacks, an ace and an unrelated five. With luck she could even hope for a Full House. Which of the two to discard? It didn't matter; she mustn't win. It wouldn't be expected of her. So what? She discarded both.

And picked up the fourth jack and a seven. This was heady stuff. A hand well worth raising on. And a sort of omen. The four jacks was what the plods called Yeadings' special team.

Steady, she warned herself. I'm not superstitious, but I won't take risks. Two of us undercover here now, so don't rock the boat. Don't disclose.

Conscious of the others waiting, watching, she grunted, folded her hand and threw the cards, face down, on the table, shrugged and complained, "This just isn't my game."

She was conscious of Jolly, next to her, staring; but he didn't challenge. She hoped she looked as disgusted as she felt.

Play continued in comparative silence, with Hampton pulling in the pot on a simple flush in clubs.

# Full House

Beaumont came bouncing into the Superintendent's office, his Pinocchio features transformed by a Cheshire Cat grin. Since he'd rung in that he was joining the staff at Fraylings and just dashing back for his gear, the DI and the Boss had come back in to hear him report.

Summoned twice to the nick on a supposedly free Sunday, Mott grumbled to himself. It wouldn't have been so bad except that, when he'd returned to the flat after the morning's session with Yeadings, Paula had been there, tired of waiting and unsympathetic to his sense of hard usage.

She had already devoured her half of the picnic she'd brought along and about two thirds of the drinks. But it hadn't made her more easily accessible. She'd wanted to go swimming and didn't see why he couldn't take her to the pool at Fraylings Court since he was running his sync-swim classes there twice a week.

It hadn't been an auspiciously happy reunion. He'd admitted he had other pressing things on his mind and he was still smarting from the sight of her in action in court. The gap between their professional attitudes had widened as he seethed over her twisted defence of the sort of rogue he'd sweat to build a solid case against. Still resentful, he didn't inquire how the case had gone, out of distaste for being told she had won.

For a while both of them carefully skirted the subject of her moving to Thames Valley but it finally loomed so that he couldn't resist suggesting once again that she move in with him and commute to her London Chambers. Several of her colleagues who lived farther out managed perfectly well.

And then she had been painfully frank.

"If it was only the travelling, I could do that," she admitted. "But it's the rest of the package I couldn't take on."

It rocked him. "Meaning living with me? I'm all right to spend the odd half-day or night with, but as a full-time prospect I'm not on? A semi-detached fiancé, but not a full-time lover? And don't give me that 'waiting till we're married line' because I've not noticed you're so reluctant over sex."

"It's not that exactly."

"So what *exactly* is it?"

"The way we are now I feel free to concentrate properly on my work, just as you can. I know that when we marry things will change and I'm prepared for that. We'll both have to compromise on a lot of things. There will be stresses I couldn't take on while I've such a heavy case-load. And by then I should be working locally.

"I admit it's a blow that Old Wheatears didn't take retirement as he'd planned, but it's only a matter of time. Our chance will come, but you agreed I can't abandon him while he's so down, Angus."

"You'd rather abandon me."

"I'm not doing that. I'm asking you to wait a little longer. And what's so wrong with the way things are now?"

He stopped himself in time from giving the answer which sprang to his mind: that the relationship was stagnating; perhaps had stagnated already, because this sort of grating argument was happening too often. Whichever way it was, he knew there had to be change, they needed to go on to something else.

"Come and live with me," he pleaded again. "If you think marriage is so stressful, try the halfway house first. Keep your freedom. See how we manage together."

"It wouldn't work. I know that. It's marriage or go on the way we are. Setting up house together would have its own kind of stresses. We'd make mistakes and there'd be nothing to hold us together. It won't be plain sailing when we're married, but then we shall have something to keep us in line."

"The shackles of vows: for better or worse, till death us do part," he said bitterly. "You make the prospect sound really inviting."

"Well, if you don't believe in taking those vows, why are we thinking of marriage at all?"

And that had been the dangerous brink they were hovering over when the call came from the Boss to go in to the office again. Mott had turned to her, his face a mask.

"Mr Yeadings?"

He didn't need to answer. She had picked up her swimming things, grimaced at the remains of their feast, waved a hand and left the flat.

Now, faced by the DS's beaming self-approval, he had to put him down. "Guess what," he invited witheringly on Beaumont's behalf.

"The mysterious B Smith . . ." Beaumont confided.

"Ah yes. Turns out to be a notorious Levantine financier called Obeidat. We'd got that far ourselves. Last night I tried the name Boulos on a broker friend in the city. Smith's a Brit by birth but married into a Lebanese family and took his father-in-law's surname."

Beaumont was only momentarily deflated, quick to pick up that that was all Mott had. "But he's not just Obeidat and Smith. There are more layers to this particular onion."

"So tell us."

"In English 'Boulos' translates into 'Paul'. And Smith is actually nearer the mark than any fancy Arab name. Born Paul Evans – and in the Welsh valleys aren't Evanses as common as our Smiths? The man has a sense of humour."

"A Welshman? That could account for his dark good looks," Yeadings said blandly, a quarter Welsh himself.

Beaumont had recovered his bounce. "Generations at the coalface accounting for the ingrained colour? Not a miner himself, though. He came from Powys, father a farm labourer, mother a maid at the castle until she married in her thirties; died when Paul was twelve."

"He's come a long way."

Mott had dried up, leaving it to the Boss to comment.

Beaumont went happily on. "Not quite the Richard Burton route to fame and fortune, though he has his share of acting ability. Seems able to fool himself as well as the others. Skivvied, then bartended at the local pub in his late teens and was sometimes called in by the castle to help serve at table when they'd a big occasion. Picked up some classy manners there. Caught the eye of a VIP guest. Wangled good references and eventually applied for an advertised post as trainee footman at Buckingham Palace. *Boom*! He had arrived on the London scene; nourished his delusions of grandeur in the uppest of markets."

Yeadings grunted approval of the background obtained. "The wires must have grown hot between here and central Wales."

"There's none so malicious as those who get left behind. But that's as much as they'd heard of his progress. At that point he disappeared from their ken, still a lissom, clean-shaven Ganymede using his own name."

"They're not exactly overpaid in the Royal Household," Yeadings said thoughtfully, "but there's a lot of standing around. I assume he kept his eyes and ears open, learned the right way to do everything."

A sudden horror struck him. "I hope you're not going to drag in any salacious scandals about the House of Windsor."

"So far as I could tell he remained discreet on that count. After three years' service he left for a more lucrative post at a gentlemen's club in St James's with plenty of back-handers."

"Ah," said Yeadings. "Arriving with an empty bankbook but a lot of accumulated experience of upper-class behaviour. Perfect training for a conman."

"He appeared to give satisfaction in his service there, was popular with the members, less so with other staff who thought he 'put on airs'. Could trot out an impressive imitation of Prince Charles, so he must have got his Welsh accent under control by then. But the trail ends there a bare two years after he arrived, when he suddenly gave notice."

"He'd been befriended by a member of this gentlemen's club who could further his career," Mott surmised. "That's the recognised pattern. A *Ganymede*, you said earlier. I assume you're being mealy-mouthed about a—"

"A Shakespearian term," Yeadings approved.

"S'right," Beaumont claimed, grinning. "Yes, one of those."

"If his new protector was part of mainstream West End life,"

Yeadings said heavily, "I'd expect his activities at that point to have leaked to us by now. At least his face would look familiar. So we must probably look for a country member. Living in some seclusion, would you say? Possibly a much older man who was starting to withdraw from active society."

"And wealthy," Mott said, "or giving up the fleshpots would hardly be worth Evans's while."

"Unless he was genuinely fond of his protector. After all, there'd been nothing too questionable in his conduct till then," Yeadings reminded them.

"We don't know, but I'd put my money on a wealthy patron too. He was biding his time," Beaumont backed the DI.

"Evans was ambitious. So a seriously wealthy lover, maybe a bit tottery, with no close family and not much longer to live," Mott insisted. "I'm asking, sir, for an order to examine lists of past members of the club."

Yeadings, who had seen this coming, made a lemon-sucking grimace. It meant a trip to Kidlington and a haggling session with the ACC Crime. Then, if successful, not only a balancing feat with the Met over acting on their patch, but every possible objection raised on the club's part to any breaching of their members' privacy.

"Leaving me with the sole decoration of the Order of the Lions' Den, plus egg on my chin if we've guessed wrong."

The other two were looking levelly at him. He sighed. Well, they were right. That's what being a superintendent was about after all.

Zyczynski abandoned the poker school at about twenty minutes after midnight and went straight upstairs to bed. As she had half expected, there was a visitor waiting for her and being dutifully entertained by a sleepy Mrs Fellowes.

"I could slip outside if you want to talk in private," the older woman offered.

"No need," Z assured her. "Tuck yourself up in bed. This will only be routine stuff; I guarantee we'll bore you to sleep in no time."

153

She turned to the other sergeant. "So how did you get in on the act here?"

"It was sheer luck," Beaumont explained as he took up a relaxed attitude at full length on the floor. "I was sniffing around at the local when the landlord took a call from the Tinsleys about getting more help in the house. He broadcast it to the blokes at the bar and I said I'd once been a waiter and wouldn't mind seeing how the other half lived. There was a bit of joshing and they pulled me in behind the bar. I did a couple of conjuring tricks and the landlord offered to speak up that I was a twisted sod but capable. So I turned up here and they took me on there and then. I've just been back since dinner to fetch some gear and report in."

"The Boss must think this end's serious if he's keeping two of us in."

"For good reason. Because we've just twenty-four hours before another delivery. News came through from Amsterdam. Angus is the proverbial headless chicken; can't be sure the Boss has read the signs right about where it's due to be landed."

Z listened while Beaumont put her in the picture. "Have you anything solid yet on any of the inmates?" he demanded at the end, before she could tell him of her discovery at the farm barn.

"Not really. Have you dug up any interesting background?"

Beaumont was positively purring. "Identities," he said crisply. "Well, apart from the phoney 'Smith' and the even more suspect Maeve Finnegan who hasn't a trace of the blarney about her . . ."

"Third generation Brit," Z claimed demurely. "We're very Bedfordshire by now."

"Well, apart, as I said, from those characters, it seems we have everyone by their right names and backgrounds."

So he was purring because there was nothing to report, a no-no for her to work on. She wouldn't put it past him to have saved some real peach for his own use, but there was no guessing whom it concerned.

"How about the Carricks?" she queried.

"Hal and Sabrina, as they claim. Surname's right for both." He grinned puckishly. "Not Mr and Mrs, though. They're siblings. Twins, in fact. Bit of a Roman holiday for them, flaunting their er . . ."

"Bizarre relationship. Quite." Z sounded at her most school-mistressy. She frowned, wishing she could decide whether their flaunting was to cover criminal interests or rewarding enough in itself. "And the Smiths?"

He hesitated just a second too long. This was it, she knew. He'd been holding out on Smith, hoping to pip her at the post. Why couldn't he just work in tandem instead of seeing her as his rival? But he was going to deliver now that she'd pressed him: he couldn't resist displaying his superior knowledge.

"Ah . . ." He was ponderously mimicking the Boss, even to the waggling of his eyebrows. Then suddenly he'd switched to the wooden puppet-face which he used to conceal real excitement. "I've put in some research on them. Got a lead from a plod who was here looking for the lost kids. He'd transferred from the Met's West End Central and he recognised the wife. Then I ferreted out the whole story. Do I begin at the beginning or work back from the present?"

"Whichever. Do it your own way."

"Right. He's married to Nadia all right. And her surname's Obeidat. He calls himself Boulos, which is Arabic for Paul. Started off as Paul Evans, a boyo of the valleys, look you. Changed to his Lebanese father-in-law's surname because the old man hadn't a son of his own and thought little of the fair sex beyond the obvious. Filthy rich from Mediterranean hotels, gaming clubs and a string of racehorses. Nice pa-in-law to inherit from, only it seems the old ogre won't hand in his chips. Rod of iron act, and wouldn't tolerate divorce, though he turns a blind eye to Boulos's bimbos. Gave him a little packet of European companies to play with and sat back to see what happened."

"And what happened?"

"Splashy success on the surface, but it could be overreach. There are whispers in the City that our man's shuffling the ledgers around, beating the auditors to it at the fifty-ninth minute of the eleventh hour. Angus had a word with an acquaintance in the SFO."

So this wasn't all Beaumont's unaided work. DI Mott had had a hand in it too. "Serious Fraud Office?" she picked up.

"Or Seriously Flawed Organisation: whichever you prefer. Anyway they're much on the defensive these days and nothing's considered serious under five million. The said acquaintance gulped at the name Obeidat and quickly started talking about growing dahlias. So we can take it that our 'Smith' is currently under covert investigation. Which could be a long-drawn business."

"And meanwhile he'd welcome any instant chance to boost the cashflow."

"It's a thought. He's a chameleon when it comes to adaptation. Quite a chequered career to date, playing all things to all men. Do you want the intervening CV?"

"I feel you're going to spill it anyway."

"Of course. You'll relish the fairy-tale bits."

"So, once upon a time there was this innocent young Welsh lad called . . ."

"Paul Evans. Well, he was a pretty youth and didn't fancy coal dust under his fingernails, nor cow dung if he'd followed his father. He went into service, waiting table for his betters. As indeed I find my humble self doing. But Paul had a taste for high-flying, so he answered an advert for a footman at the Palace. And I don't mean a dance hall. Buck House itself. So, in short, Paul put his charms about to obtain glowing testostero-monials from two local queens, blagged his way through the interviews and got the job. And hey presto, he was all set to pick up the upper-crust manners and toff-talk that would later take him to the top."

"And that was his route to happy-ever-after?"

"Not without a slip or two on the way. As Paul Evans he won himself a brief criminal record."

"Which you must have picked up from identifying the dabs on the tumbler your anonymous donor sent in from here. So what *is* his record?"

"Pimping in Soho while still at the gentlemen's club. Which was how a certain Jennifer Dodds came to be picked up by the Met, aged sixteen and very pregnant."

"You don't mean our Jennifer Yorke? You *do*! Well, she's a

good bit over sixteen now, so it wouldn't have been Clary she was carrying then. But it's interesting that she's caught up with her old pimp after all this time. Do you imagine she's blackmailing him; threatening to reveal all to Nadia?"

"If so, it could be dangerous for her. Especially if he hasn't the liquidity to satisfy any cash demands."

Z reflected on the little scene she'd watched along the terrace walk. "You're probably right about the danger. I'd say Smith's a very hard nut and holds the whip hand."

"Which leaves it to us to crack him." Beaumont gave an evil grin. "Fancy yourself as the Wicked Fairy, Z, spoiling his happy ending?"

She ignored the invitation. "He'd have the right dodgy background for the counterfeit dealer we're after, but it'll be difficult getting everything we want on him. Especially if the SFO are already setting up an inquiry."

"Nothing the boss can't handle. He's already seeing the brass about exposing some of Evans's missing years. If we find out who partnered him financially it just might lead to the Dutch connection."

Z sat for a moment thinking, then veered to another subject. "Has anyone come up with a reason for the attack on Philip Pomeroy?"

"Not yet. He says he can't remember what happened after he went along the corridor for a bath. His towel and washing things were still there. So I guess someone followed him in and slugged him."

Z nodded. "Then panicked? Sir James's chairlift would have been close by on the landing, so it was easy for the attacker to load Pomeroy in and send him downstairs. Whoever I glimpsed in the passage intended switching off the house alarms so he could get the injured man outside. Maybe he thought he'd killed him and had a body to dispose of."

"Just as well that you were up and about then, or our portly bank manager could have ended up as just such dead meat."

"Bank manager," Z considered. "Money again. Could his work have anything to do with the attack?"

157

"He's not our distributor," Beaumont said decidedly. "He manages quite an unimportant branch. He's too careful of his small-town reputation – pillar of the church, rotarian, bridge fanatic and to cap it all, this is the fifth such art course his wife has dragged him along to. There wouldn't be time left in his life for any skulduggery."

"So we can assume it was something personal that made our unknown attacker suddenly lash out? Pomeroy might tactlessly have touched a raw nerve, but I can't see him being intentionally offensive. Unless . . ."

"Unless what?"

"Nothing. But I'd be happier if we looked into everyone again for some outside connection with Pomeroy, however tenuous."

"It's a slim chance. And could be irrelevant to the main case."

"Slim chances are all we've had so far. Will you mention this to Angus, or shall I?"

"I will. You're only to get in touch in an emergency now, and then the Boss will take your call personally. I'm to be resident here on the job, but as it's a full house I'm lodging at the home farm. Which should guarantee me more privacy than you."

"Don't be too sure! You could be landing in the centre of the operation." And she told Beaumont about her nocturnal exploration.

"Wow!" he said quietly. "I thought the man there sounded surly when Mrs Tinsley rang through about accommodation."

"So watch out for yourself."

"The eye of the storm, isn't that it? Couldn't be anywhere safer. Anyway, I'd best scarper now and get my head down. It's heavy work being the Admirable Crichton."

Z looked out to ensure the corridor was empty, then sent Beaumont on his way. The temperature had dropped and she was glad to creep under her duvet, leaving him any further exploration for that night. Drifting into sleep she smiled, recalling his mention of a Full House. That was a good poker hand: a set of three and a pair, she thought muzzily, half-seeing the outline of cards in her hand.

She and Beaumont were the pair, equal-ranking as sergeants.

But in her mind another face, not her own, seemed to be forming alongside the DS's. It was gnomic, weathered, with its rough hair slicked down with water.

Jolly! she should have warned Beaumont that Jolly too was living at the farm. The DS wouldn't yet have caught up with the deaf-dumb gardener, having come straight in to serve table. And when the poker school met, Beaumont would have been busy clearing up in the kitchen.

Those two made the pair at the home farm then, she thought sleepily. And together with the trio back here – 'Smith', his wife Nadia and the spare woman Jennifer Yorke – made up the Full House.

Which excluded herself from the game. On the edge of dreaming she again looked muzzily at her hands and saw they were empty. She hadn't been dealt any cards at all.

She learned at breakfast that in the other sense Fraylings Court was no longer a full house because Jane Pomeroy was all set to leave, to be called for by a chauffeured car at the bank's expense and taken to the hospital to collect her husband. Then they would be driven home and their Rover picked up the following day.

Zyczynski accompanied her upstairs to help with the packing and lend a sympathetic ear. It seemed her last chance to get any information on the attack.

"I hope they're not sending your husband home too soon," she said. "Head injuries can be dodgy things. 'And he has amnesia too, I believe."

"They've done all the necessary tests," Mrs Pomeroy said stoutly. "No skull fracture or anything like that. Simply bad bruising and shock."

"So does he remember now what happened?"

"No. I'm afraid that's gone for good." She sounded more than definite, quite tight-lipped. Z, watching her in the wardrobe mirror, was almost sure that Pomeroy must have deliberately clammed up and Jane was furious at his obstinacy.

So, if he remembered who had attacked him, why wasn't he complaining loudly and levelling charges? Was it because the bank now knew of the incident and there were embarrassing circumstances? But what?

He'd been up to something he didn't want made public. But, whatever, it could have no connection with the counterfeit job because he was withdrawing from the scene just before the expected delivery.

Nevertheless the little mystery remained, irking Z because his attacker must be some person in the house still unidentified. Pomeroy, for all his surface affability, was hardly the type to make intimate advances to anyone he'd known for a mere ten days. So the connection must belong to the past. Mott had had the others' backgrounds checked and nothing of the sort had come to light.

"There's one good thing," Jane Pomeroy declared, ferociously zipping up a suitcase. "I'll be at home to supervise the laying of the patio. This was the only week they could do it, because the conservatory took longer than they'd promised."

"It sounds as though you're having major alterations," Zyczynski prompted.

"Well, it all takes time with a new house. Everything inside was done the way we wanted, but the gardens weren't laid. Now the front one's finished and the back's yet to be done. It'll be a real picture when it's complete."

Z almost held her breath. "I suppose that, as a bank manager, your husband has to move quite often."

Jane Pomeroy, looking unfamiliar in a serious linen suit, with the arty gear packed away, was in the bathroom applying lipstick. "Always on the trot," she called back ambiguously. "It's amazing how you can get used to pulling up your roots and planting them elsewhere. We've only been in Wells a little over six months."

"And where were you before?"

"Bristol," said Mrs Pomeroy, firmly pressing peach-powder on her sun-reddened nose. "I never really cared for it there. Seven years it was. This is going to be much nicer."

Bristol, Z noted. It rang a muffled bell. Surely Beaumont had spoken of Bristol in connection with one of the others?

160

# Four Jacks

E arly on Monday, as Superintendent Yeadings paused by the door to the Incident Room, he noted fresh activity among the murder squad. Six VDUs were simultaneously in use, and across the corridor four detective constables had phones clamped between jaw and shoulder, one gesticulating, the others scribbling furiously. They might be taking down today's shopping list dictated by the wife, but Yeadings thought not.

The previous evening he had appeared on television news with an appeal for information on a brown Volvo with its rear licence-plate missing. The programme had gone out nationwide and sightings were coming through by the handful, now being entered in the computer. It seemed there were more open-eyed drivers on the roads than he'd imagined.

One of the men phoning caught his eye, raised a hand, then continued scribbling. He grunted into the mouthpiece, tore off the top sheet and held it high. For some reason he really fancied this one.

Yeadings went across. He scanned the erratic writing: Manchester airport. Well, yes. He'd have preferred Heathrow, as being closer. But the date was right; the timing possible. And – glory be! – the driver had been seen lifting in a muffled invalid, loading his folded wheelchair into the boot.

*Got it!* Yeadings grunted his relief. So now they had a positive lead to the crashed Volvo. That one detail – the burnt-out frame of a wheelchair – had been deliberately kept from the Press.

The Office Manager was hovering to take the message sheet. "Run me off a copy," Yeadings told him. "I'll have this witness questioned by Manchester Met. And I want you to correlate any other sightings at any point between Manchester and the crash site. I think we can disregard all else.''

He needed to digest this fresh item. As ever, new info raised new questions. For a starter, if the Volvo had set out with a passenger in the back, why had only one body been found, and that in the driver's seat?

Somewhere *en route* the passenger had been dropped off. Decanted into another wheelchair? Or perhaps by then on his own two feet? Maybe someone who wasn't as frail as he'd earlier made out. Someone unseasonably muffled up. Anonymous, in fact; ready to take on another persona. And, seated in the rear, he'd have been in a position to control the man at the wheel.

There was just a chance that the 'invalid' had ended in the driving seat himself and it was the original driver missing. In which case it smacked of kidnap and possible murder.

But given a choice of the two scenarios, Yeadings plumped for the first. He didn't need the rising of short hairs on his neck to tell him that a connection with affairs at nearby Fraylings was a distinct possibility. He almost dared put a name to the missing passenger.

He stayed a moment to watch the message processed. He needed to contact Manchester Met now, then their Airport Immigration to get access to video film of passengers at Arrivals.

First he wanted to bounce ideas off his regular sounding-board, but the team was spread about. Back in the office which had been allocated to him he scowled at the three empty chairs across his desktop, frustrated. He snatched up the white phone and barked, "Find DI Mott. I want him here now."

Mott was already in the building. Yeadings swung round on him as he recognised his rap at the door. "Angus, remind me. What time did the man Smith arrive at Fraylings on Tuesday?"

"Early evening. He'd flown in from Honolulu, his wife said, and needed a kip in her room. I only saw him later, towards the end of our sync-swim class, down by the pool."

"I doubt it was Heathrow, nor Honolulu: Mr Smith appears to be an imaginative man. What's occupying you at present?"

"Checking tonight's set-up for this end."

"Good. Let me see the details before I make the call to Support Group."

Mott nodded. The gang hadn't hesitated to kill one Customs man. There'd be reason enough to make use of the Armed Response Vehicle.

"Talking of cars," Yeadings said casually, "we have a chance to identify the body in the burn-out. My TV appeal has brought in a lead to Manchester airport. I want you to ring them for a list of incoming flights that days from noon onwards with actual landing times and airports of origin. And see whether Manchester Met has anyone on the Misper list who meets the witness's description of the Volvo driver. Someone should have noticed by now that he's not around."

"Right." Mott hesitated, his weight on one foot. "D'you want the latest about the biker now?"

At the Boss's curt nod he turned back. "The girl with glasses who served us at the Feathers has been off with a broken wrist, so she was missed on the questioning. She's just back on duty and rang in a few minutes ago. She thinks she's the only one who could identify the biker. He'd put his visor up but kept his back to the room. Left the helmet on until he'd joined his mate in the corner by the hatch. She guessed he was shy of showing off his face because he had some bad scarring. It looked like recent cosmetic surgery which hadn't healed well. She took a good look because her dad's a fireman and he's had face repairs too."

"Further description?"

"Male, IC1, young. Teenage to twenty, five-eight, slender, big hands, probably light brown hair. Kept his eyes down, so no colour given."

"Standing over by the hatch?" Yeadings repeated thoughtfully. "Where Carver Ward was left with two empty glasses? Angus, we were there! Nearly eyeballed him ourselves."

"Barely missed him, I guess." Mott rubbed at his chin.

"Carver and Z's biker. So this could tie Carver Ward in with the car crash."

"We only know that this biker stopped to watch the car burning. There's nothing yet to show he was actively involved

163

in the crash. Then there's his sighting by Z at Fraylings. Are we to consider that a coincidence? Or must we consider both him and Ward as part of the counterfeit gang? Trouble is, I can't see Ward's hand in either of our killings. They're not in his line. He's simply a small-time mugger with a knife."

The DI considered it, recapping what they knew. "Body One: Oliver Webb was garrotted before being dumped for the train to run over. Body Two had extensive internal injuries and a broken neck consistent with the car crash, besides being charred beyond recognition. As a trigger there'd been a small incendiary device inside the car. It gives us two separate MOs. Carver could have given up knives for alternative skills. He's a savage enough bastard for anything and this time he could have been promised big money."

"He doesn't plan. There has to be someone running things with a smidgeon of imagination."

"Scarface in the skidlid?"

"I can't see Carver taking orders from a youngster."

"He's been away for quite a stretch," Mott reminded him. "He could feel he's losing his grip, so needs to work in harness. Anyway, we agreed there were signs of panic in the first killing. Whoever did it knew Webb was Customs, so he had to be silenced before he reported back. The mistake was removing his ID before they left him on the line, because they'd need instant identification in the Press, to be sure it was accepted as suicide. Patchy sort of planning, that."

But the Boss wasn't listening. Mott leaned forward to scan what he was writing. "What's that?"

Yeadings' biro tapped the word 'biker' and drew an arrow across to the words 'crashed car'. At an angle of forty-five degrees he drew another arrow from 'biker' to connect with 'Carver Ward', then a third from 'biker' to 'Jennifer Yorke'. "Right?" Yeadings demanded.

Mott grunted agreement so far and watched as the last arrow was extended and the Boss write in 'Clarissa Yorke'.

"Jennifer's little girl." Mott frowned. "So what?"

With a flourish Yeadings drew a curved arrow to connect the child's name back with 'biker'.

164

"You think the kid knew him?"

"Not by name. Whenever it was she saw him, he frightened her. Remember how the questioning went? The child hysterical after the adventure in the woods; confused and scared that she'd be in trouble for going off without permission. The mother insists, 'Tells us about the horrible, horrible man, Clary.' And what does confused little Clary come up with? A man with a face like rhubarb crumble."

"But there never were any men in the wood. The other child had made them up."

"That wasn't where Clary had seen him. But there *was* a 'horrible, horrible man' she couldn't forget from another occasion. Her mother's words triggered a nightmare memory. The sight of his face and whatever he'd been up to when she saw him had terrified the child and has haunted her since. Suppose the man had been with her mother, shouting at her, threatening, hurting her – and Clary was a witness to it? Is that too much to imagine? She's not a child to make things up like the other little girl does. And Z's pretty sure the biker was coming from the mother's room that night when she spotted him leaving by the garden. Clary hadn't been there then: she was upstairs with Joanna in the old nursery. Suppose Jennifer Yorke used the opportunity to contact the man and warn him to lie low because of what Clary had said. It's significant that neither hide nor hair of him has been seen since then."

Mott pulled up a chair and sat down heavily, staring at the diagram. "You need another arrow now from Jennifer Yorke to the man Smith," he said flatly. "We've got Z's observation that there's a personal link there. Probably of long standing."

"I get the feeling," Yeadings told him, "there should be a whole sunburst of arrows connecting Smith with everyone in the case. Despite how we discounted him earlier because he deliberately draws attention, we've no obvious alternative for the Mister Big running this counterfeit distribution. We're agreed that whoever is setting up the UK end must have considerable funds for buying the stuff in and paying everyone off. There's no one else we know of who could sufficiently impress the Dutch printers to take him on as a partner. You can be sure they've checked on his reputation and financial holdings, even if not as thoroughly as the SFO are presently doing."

Yeadings leaned back in his chair and fixed his DI with a steely gaze. "If that was Evans-Obeidat-Smith travelling from Manchester in the Volvo, I'd gamble that he had just visited father-in-law to tap his generosity. But, to be certain, we need a definite sighting of Smith in the Volvo before he reached Fraylings."

Mott nodded. "I'll look into it right away," he said tersely and left Yeadings to go on drawing whatever other arrows might occur to him.

Zyczynski watched the chauffeured car out of sight. Jane Pomeroy and her husband may well have been exiting the scene, but there was still that Bristol link to check on. She fetched her folding stool and sketch-pad and went off to find where Dizzy Crumm had set up the day's art class.

The students sat scattered half-way down the drive, working on a distant view of the house beyond a curving wall of glossy rhododendrons. Z waved back at Dennis Hampton's gesture of invitation but elected to settle down near where Dizzy was standing behind Douglas Jeffries' easel.

"Sorry I'm late," Z excused herself. "I've been seeing Mrs Pomeroy off."

"Yes, a pity," Dizzy said with vague regret. "That's two more defectors. Never mind, the rest of you are showing real progress. Look at Mr Jeffries here. He's been at this no more than half an hour. See what a difference when he works at speed? Loosens up completely."

Z went over to look. Poor Jeffries was embarrassed, blinking away behind his wire-rimmed spectacles. And Dizzy was right. His earlier, tightly constructed work, was transformed. The house and drive were neatly indicated, but the chosen foreground of brambles, partly unreeled barbed wire and an abandoned, upturned wheelbarrow were scribbled vigorously in with scratchy black strokes.

Z delivered the expected compliments, then settled herself

behind him and to his left, observing that when Dizzy walked away he sat slumped as though all the life had gone out of him. Life, or passion?

"Mrs Pomeroy is taking her husband back to Wells," she said conversationally, watching him.

"Yes?"

"Thank Heaven he's going to be all right now. His injuries aren't as bad as they seemed at first. And he doesn't want any bad publicity to reflect on the bank, so they intend forgetting all about it."

For a while she concentrated on her drawing. "That's a relief, isn't it?"

He turned in his chair but didn't look at her directly. "What do you mean?"

Z rubbed out a faulty pencil line, then looked up innocently. "I suppose you met him at his bank in Bristol?"

Jeffries fixed his sad gaze on her. For a long moment she thought he would deny it. Then his resistance crumbled, "Dolly did. I knew nothing about it until she'd got herself in too deep."

"A loan," Z hazarded.

His eyes drifted away. "If only she'd told me, I could have covered it somehow. He should never have listened to Dolly in the first place, but she was so enthusiastic. She didn't need to ask my permission. I had put the house in her name, you see; she used it as collateral and took out the loan ostensibly for an extension; said she needed an office to run home sales for a mail-order catalogue.

"I thought she was doing so well with the business, and I was glad because it meant a lot to her to have something of her own to run. She'd been really depressed up till then."

He shook his head. "She had me completely fooled. But a bank manager – he should have known the risks she'd be taking."

Jeffries stopped, reaching back in his mind. Zyczynski sensed that he was silently crying as he fought to get the words out. "Only . . . it was a disaster. Everyone – her friends, our neighbours – kept on ordering and ordering, just like Dolly herself;

and after the first few times, nobody was paying up. All along she was pretending it was a great success. Then suddenly . . . it crashed."

He crouched over his drawing-board, arms tight across his chest. "They said she – she'd taken the overdose soon after I left home that morning. When I got back . . . it was too late."

He brought one fist crashing down on the drawing-board and protested, "I never dreamt how deep in she was. Not until later. There were cupboards full of clothes and shoes and things for the house which I thought she was holding as stock for her customers. And all those demands. She should have told me . . ."

A familiar story, Z thought with compassion. Wild enthusiasm, overtaken by wilder despair. A bullish company that stimulated sales, thrived on its victims' mounting debts, and insufficiently monitored their actions. At the moment of truth, faced by ruin, how could the desperate woman admit what she'd done? She'd found an easier way out.

Z let a little silence build before asking, "You blamed Pomeroy for her death?"

"Who else? Dolly was beyond reason. Pomeroy was responsible."

And eventually Pomeroy might have begun to think so too, poor affable man. Wasn't it an admission of his own mistake that he refused to name Jeffries as his attacker? The police might try to follow the case up but if Pomeroy went on pleading amnesia it could never come to court. A sort of rough justice had been imposed. The account was balanced, provided that Jeffries didn't make a habit of confession.

And in blaming Pomeroy, Jeffries could shrug off any implicit guilt of his own. He needn't look too closely at his own role of uncaring husband. He had been negligent. Even if he couldn't diagnose his wife's mood swings as approaching manic depression, he should have known something was going very wrong. But he hadn't been close enough to her for that.

Zyczynski watched him now, methodically putting his things together, halting to stare at the sketch which had come out so

168

different from his normal studied precision. Finally he removed the drawing pins, folded the paper neatly in four and slid it into his trouser pocket.

He didn't look at Z again. She hardly existed for him. Just someone to hang his burden on. He walked steadily away with his art satchel, leaving the easel and stool behind.

Z sat on, restored to the outer world stirring around her. From mown hay drying out in the fields alongside there blew over her a peppery sweetness mixed with a bitter nettle scent and the dustiness of the gravel driveway. She heard persistent trilling as some small bird, unrecognisable to her town eyes, hovered high against an innocent sky.

The bird plummeted, the song stopped, and there was no other sound, as if the world was paralysed and her senses with it. Strangely she knew that this empty moment, and those few minutes before, would lodge in her memory for ever.

Then the world restarted and Dizzy was standing over her, shrewd-eyed. "Do I take it that Mr Jeffries has also abandoned us?"

She didn't accuse Z of being the cause, but the girl caught the same alerted look as in Jolly's eyes at something incautious she'd said or done at poker. It seemed she wasn't so good at deceit after all.

She felt suddenly deflated. If her cover was blown she might as well give up. Not just the present job here, but the Job itself: escape the pressures and the public mistrust, the delving into universal sleaze and the new, unwelcome rivalry with Beaumont; become a free woman switching off work at five, no longer suspicious of everyone around her.

The doubts hung on briefly before the police perspective was restored. She recalled with a mental click what she had seen before without properly registering. For the first time since he'd been here, Jeffries had appeared in public open-necked and without a tie. Now that he'd settled his imagined score with Pomeroy it seemed he'd released himself from more than one of his earlier constraints.

*     *     *

In the domestic quarters, while Andrew was re-stocking the supply cupboards, Beaumont divided his energies between polishing silver plate and entertaining Gayle with his edited, semifictional life story. As chores went, the first reminded the DS sourly of childhood abuses when pocket money had depended on keeping Granny's prized horse-brasses bright. Since Granny was the virago licensee of olde worlde premises in touristic Dorset it had seemed a lifetime's servitude to the boy.

Gayle, flush-faced, was unloading the ovens of outsized chicken and vegetable pies, and the kitchen filled with the savoury smell. "They're for tonight," she warned, slapping away Beaumont's hand as it automatically reached for a piece of broken crust.

"At home I'm allowed the uglies," he protested.

"Here we have no uglies."

"Except the temporary staff," Andrew called back. "You'd better count all the items, Gayle."

Beaumont muttered over his polishing rag. He'd be lucky ever to get a taste, due to Mott's message about tonight's scheduled operation. Although the catering pair ate before the family and guests, he was expected to fill up with leftovers between serving coffee and loading the dishwashers. And since he'd planned a minor accident to whisk him off after the dining-room main course, all he could hope for was a covert doggie bag.

Eight thirty p.m. was fixed for his meeting with Samways – Walter Merton's new contact from Customs – who would be waiting in his car outside the main gates. When he'd updated him on the suspect's movements he'd leave Samways to join the stake-out and get himself back to cover the home farm end.

It was lucky Zyczynski had spotted the camera focused on the barn door. During the previous night Beaumont had managed to fix it from the upper window, leaning out and opening the casing to flash his torch in and ruin whatever film it contained. If anyone thought to check on it before tonight's delivery they could assume it was faulty.

Mrs Barron at the farm had been quite pleasant, apologising

170

for not having a room prepared, but her husband was a surly
swine and clearly found him in the way. They hadn't met face to
face yet, but from his bedroom Beaumont had heard him
mouthing in the kitchen and shouting at the unseen child to
"Bloody shut up snivelling".

The only other presence living in at the farmhouse was an
elderly weirdo. They had met last night when the man came in
sweaty from the garden and smelling of horse. He had eaten in
the kitchen without a word to anyone, before going upstairs to
shower and make himself almost presentable for going out. No
one – certainly not Z – had thought to warn the DS that the man
was deaf and dumb.

At the door, before he left, he had given Beaumont a gap-
toothed grin and thrust under his nose a grubby notebook with
the word 'poaker' pencilled in capitals.

Beaumont had assumed it was the man's name, so he wrote
'Charlie Cooper' underneath and pointed to himself. This had
the man in stitches, slapping him on the back and *arf-arfing* like a
cartoon-film dog. Then he'd followed up with a sprightly char-
ade of dealing cards to an invisible table and fanning his own
hand in invitation.

With that Beaumont got the message, but he couldn't risk
tying himself up indefinitely. Besides he had other interests once
the house went quiet.

He had taken a nap first, then, towards two fifteen, while it
was still dark, he'd fixed the camera and taken a look for himself
at the interior of the padlocked barn. Forewarned by Z's report,
he made no attempt to go beyond the new agricultural plant and
open the roller doors. When he left he replaced the padlock
outside and, before re-entering the farmhouse, reported in briefly
on his mobile phone.

Immediately afterwards, he was confronted by a figure step-
ping out from a pool of shadow.

It was the deaf-dumb gardener. With a grin like a mouth-
organ, he was pulling out a bundle of banknotes to boast of his
success. Beaumont had no idea how long the man had been there
watching.

"Lucky you," he said drily, and the man nodded, almost slavering over the money.

Beaumont had given him a dismissive wave before heading for bed. Today, having cornered Z to question her, he now knew that the man was called Jolly, a Siddons family retainer almost worthy of the Munsters. And apparently a lip-reader.

# Joker in the Pack

The airport video film had been sent down by shuttle and a DC drove out to collect it. There were three tapes in all, but, following his hunch, Yeadings was concentrating on passengers from Middle East flights. Handicapped by having no Press shots of 'Smith' as 'Obeidat' to recognise him by, he was relying on Zyczynski's covert snapping of the guests at Fraylings Court.

Manchester Security had marked one sequence of film with a query. This showed several swarthy, bearded men in western business suits and a sprinkling of others in robes and kaffiyehs. One of these closely resembled a shot taken by Zyczynski; a half-profile of Smith, cigar in hand, gazing out from the upper terrace at Fraylings.

"That's our man," Mott decided, instantly freezing the film.

Yeadings nodded. "Could be. These are passengers from a Cyprus Air flight out of Larnaca. On the other hand . . ."

Mott waited, less sure now.

"If he bothered to disguise himself when he was driven off at Manchester, why not earlier? We need to get it blown up. I want to see the face detail."

Yeadings referred back to Z's snapshot. "M'm, I thought so. What we've got on film is a lookalike. See that right ear? It's not the same. Short of a Spock transformation kit, you can't really disguise an ear. They're all individual. But if this character is meant to distract anyone who's looking for Smith, then I guess the real man isn't far away. Can any of you recognise him in that group?"

The DCs crowded close behind Mott's shoulder as he restarted the film. Keen to identify the right one, they found that all those bearded Middle Eastern faces fell into two groups of indistinguishables: the fleshy and the hawkishly lean.

*Clare Curzon*

Yeadings sat back, grinning. "Try the tourists then."

Mott ran his eyes over a part of the moving queue who were hung about with oversized cabin bags, duty-free carriers, cameras and straw hats. After weeks of exposure to Mediterranean sun, their skin was darkened but their features Western. Most of the men were clean-shaven. The few beards were either designer stubble or Hemingway bushes. Ears, he reminded himself: the boss has this thing about ears.

"Hold it there," Mott suddenly exploded. Then, "I don't believe it," he said flatly.

"Bouncy as a beach ball, isn't he?" Yeadings grinned. "Taking refuge behind a load of false whiskers. Wonderful what a difference a bandana, round glasses and cheek pads can effect. That's Smith-Obeidat all right. So where does that get us?"

"So he lied about Honolulu," one DC complained.

"Or his wife did. She's his cover."

"If she knew he was to join her at Fraylings, why didn't she book a double?" a WPC wondered aloud and was overridden as others put their suggestions.

"Hang on. She has a point there," Mott cautioned. "Smith obviously knew where his wife was, but did she know as much about him? We understand they're semi-detached, just keeping up appearances to please her father, who controls the big money.

"Smith could have gone out to reassure him that things were still sweet on the marriage front and to keep the old man happy. It's just a short sea-trip from Beirut to East Cyprus, after all. Then he returns to the UK where someone has kept tabs for him on the wife's whereabouts, and the couple get together again. So this could all be about reconciliation: nothing to do with the Dutch connection."

"In which case why the elaborate precautions to remain anonymous? He has to be up to something shady. Like securing laundered funds for paying off the next delivery."

"Delusions of grandeur," someone suggested. "Like film stars in dark glasses."

"Maybe he got wind that the SFO were investigating his affairs, so he's being elusive. That could account for his paranoia."

174

"Or it was simply for personal security," Yeadings supplied when their suggestions dried up. "And considering what happened later to the Volvo, he probably had good reason to watch his back. Despite changing to a second disguise at the airport and taking to a wheelchair, somebody got wise to him. He was lucky to have been dropped off before the car crashed."

"Which disposed of the sole witness to where he'd gone to ground," Mott said grimly. "Too conveniently. I still think it could be Smith himself who left the incendiary behind as a calling card. If so, was the biker paid by him to follow and check that everything went to plan after Smith was dropped off? Or was he part of the opposition?"

The question hung on unanswered.

The crowded room went silent as Yeadings rose to face his extended murder squad. "This is our last general briefing before the delivery. It must be obvious to you all that we've little that's certain to work on. We've more questions than answers. Our principal for the counterfeit distribution could well be this man Smith-Obeidat. Or it could be someone we haven't yet seriously considered. But, whoever, we do have an ETA for the goods, a possible landing site and a final reception area.

"Timing requires we act immediately. If the combined operation isn't to be an almighty fiasco, flexibility is vital. With so many unknown factors, be prepared for instant changes of plan. You know your groups. Stay in touch with your unit leader. Accept direct orders only by established chain of command; but there's to be no open radio communication between you after ten p.m.: police and Customs frequencies can be too easily picked up offshore and you can bet the incoming lot will be on the alert for unusual activity down here. Armed Support Group will supply back-up as and when required, so I want no heroics from any of you. I'm counting you all out – *and back*. Understood?"

There was a mumble of assent and then Mott followed the Boss out to his office where he dropped into his chair, staring at the empty desktop. "I don't like it, Angus. We're too much in the dark. I've got this gut feeling . . ."

"Yes?"

"Someone's pulling wool over our eyes. There's a joker in the pack. Have we anything new in from Fraylings?"

Mott considered this a fraction of a second too long.

"Well? Spit it out, man. It's your play, but I need to know the whole game plan."

"Beaumont rang in. He confirms all that Z reported earlier, but he wants her kept out of the action."

Yeadings' furry black eyebrows shot up to his hairline. "That shouldn't really surprise us. They're in a photo finish for the next CID promotion."

"I don't think it's rivalry."

"He's suddenly overprotective? I thought we'd ironed out Beaumont's sexist prejudices."

"He's not happy. He thinks she's settled into her role too well and it's taken over."

"Z gone native? At Fraylings Court?" The boss was sardonically unconvinced.

"Not falling for the high life, no. But she's fraternising closely with the guests and family. He feels she's becoming too involved."

"Ah. On whose behalf?"

"He wasn't specific."

"And you never asked."

Mott saw himself losing face, but he was damned if he'd retreat and cancel orders already given. Unless, of course, the boss made a stand on this. He pushed further. "She seems to have lost confidence in herself. He's worried she might have declared her hand. It takes just one member of a small group like that to guess what she's there for and the whisper could spread. The whole operation would be endangered if personal pressure set her off at half-cock. Sir, we're not short of active bodies at this end. I'm holding her back at base on this one."

"Withdrawing her from Fraylings?"

"No. That could excite suspicion. She'll be all right, staying low where she is, until we've cleared the board."

Yeadings sat on, chin sunk on ample chest. Eventually he grunted. "It's your hand, Angus. Play it the way you think best. When it's over I'll have to speak to her. She'll need to know the

176

reason for being excluded from the action. Right, let's go over the main plan again."

He wasn't happy as he watched his DI gather his notes and set them in order. Mott wasn't normally sexist. Being engaged to a young woman barrister earning three times what he did, he seemed to accept that gender made little difference to performance. Yet now he'd let Beaumont, in a fit of spleen – probably at having to wait table on his fellow DS – put Zyczynski out of the action. And eventually out of a possible commendation.

Promotions took some earning in these days of tightly controlled budgets. He remembered well enough from his own experience: you could get stuck at DS level, however confident that you had the necessary drive to start giving a few orders as well as carrying them out.

When this case was over – successfully, he hoped – he would need to shake his team out, starting at the top. Maybe Mott accepted the accusation of Z's personal involvement because something in his own emotional life was a bit awry. Was his strained relationship with Paula giving him cause for doubt? If so, he shouldn't transfer his shaken faith on to Zyczynski. At the least he could have tackled Beaumont for a more specific complaint.

"Right then," said Mott, looking up and speaking from memory. "This is the way it should go."

Merton himself was commanding the dodgy offshore phase in a cleverly adapted fishing smack regarded by Customs as the seagoing equivalent of a Formula One Ferrari. Radio communication with the land would be sparse and by coded phrases regarding crew health and local shoals. Coastguards had been alerted between Herne Bay and Shoeburyness. Kent police were standing by on Sheppey with instructions to observe and report. Essex force were under the same orders for north of the Thames estuary. Every effort had been made to ensure there were no leaks, but the extent of the operation meant use of personnel unfamiliar to Thames Valley force, and so, regarded as doubly fallible.

"If it goes pear-shaped at the landing, the whole thing will blow. We shan't get a second chance," Mott said grimly.

"And I'll be hanged, drawn and quartered for budget-busting," Yeadings reminded him calmly. "Who's covering the airfield?"

"Essex force have a DS in Basildon who skydives. Makes me think policing there isn't dangerous enough. He's a familiar sight socialising at the airfield and it hasn't put anyone off bringing in personal contraband."

"This is something much bigger. We don't want them cancelling because of a wild card."

"He has instructions to act casual and drive away as soon as he has an inkling anything's afoot. He won't contact his own unit. They'll be watching him through infra-red on the outer rim."

"And passing on the good news—"

"To me directly, at this end. By phone."

"And if it's not the airfield after all, but they go overland or upriver?"

"It's up to Essex force to pass their movements on to us and the Met, once Merton informs them the stuff is heading elsewhere."

"And if, by chance, chummy gets wind of a reception party at any point?"

"There are provisions to cut them off with the stuff on them. But let's hope that won't happen, because it has to get through to us, so that we collar the big fish red-handed."

"Fish fingers I know of," Yeadings murmured, "but now fish *hands*? Right. If you're satisfied over co-ordination, let's discuss our slice of the action."

Mott went through it carefully, numbering the options, and Yeadings nodded at the end.

"You're not very happy, Boss?"

"You've covered the foreseeable outcome. Let's hope Customs are being equally discreet and won't jump the gun. Having wasted their man Webb on our patch, they need to watch their step. And murder outweighs smuggling, by any rules. Once the stuff is landed we should be shot of them, apart from one officer to be present at the arrests. See to it that he doesn't go back in a body-bag too."

Yeadings moved his weight heavily in his chair. "What still bugs me, Angus, is that second death. I don't see the need for it, and I'm

178

convinced it has significance. Was it simply a cold-blooded cover-up; part of Smith's paranoia? No, I can't see him knowingly travelling all that way with the fire-bomb for company. So was it meant for him? It can't have been a goodbye gift from his father-in-law, because when he got in the car he had no luggage. So is someone intent on taking over the operation from him?"

Mott considered the alternative. "There would have been time to break into the Volvo in the airport car park while the driver collected his 'invalid' passenger. Unless we have a random anonymous bomber, whoever planted the thing would have known Smith was to return in that car. So where did the leaked information come from? The driver, whom Smith appeared to trust? Or someone in the know from this end?"

"Apart from Julian Tinsley who spent all day in the city, none of the family or guests was missing from Fraylings that Tuesday. Uniform learned that from Sir James when they checked for witnesses to the car crash."

"How about the deaf-dumb gardener? Z thought he was suspiciously shrewd."

"Tuesday," Yeadings muttered, leafing through a mass of papers on the desk for Z's Fraylings diary. "Yes, I thought so. That day he was posing as model for the art class. Which lets him out."

"And we don't know whether he has wheels anyway."

Yeadings straightened suddenly. "No. But we know the elusive biker has. He stopped to watch the car burn. He could have been travelling behind all the way, waiting for that to happen. Might have contributed to the accident that sent the Volvo over the edge."

"Which triggered the device."

They sat digesting this idea until Yeadings rubbed a hand over his eyes and said, "So now we could have the death connected, however indirectly, with Jennifer Yorke, if it actually was her room Z saw him creeping away from."

"And Jennifer, we know, has no reason to love Smith. As Evans, he'd been her pimp when she was under age. Could she have arranged to get him killed and somehow it went wrong – he'd left the car before the device could go off?"

"Wouldn't the biker have known that, keeping on the Volvo's tail?"

"He couldn't get too close over such a distance. If he was hanging back he could have got lost in all those winding country lanes round Fraylings and missed the drop-off. When he did catch up he must have known they were near base, took a blind chance and manoeuvred the car off the road at a dangerous curve."

Yeadings smiled grimly. "If it did happen that way, Jennifer must have been pretty upset when Smith turned up there all in one piece. That could have been exactly what she and the biker were discussing in her room when Z overheard them.

"Angus, we haven't looked hard enough at that lady. She was pregnant at sixteen, wasn't she? So what is she now – thirty-eight? Forty? So the child, if it survived, would be in its early twenties. It's horribly late in the day, but I think we need to know if that baby was a boy. And, if so, what name he goes under."

The new man, Charlie, was dispensing pre-dinner drinks from a trolley on the terrace. He had to go down the stone steps to reach Zyczynski who sat apart, fanning cheeks over-exposed earlier to midday sun. "Your lager and lime, Miss Finnegan," Beaumont offered, rather overdoing his Jeeves stuff.

"I'd have preferred a Cinzano," Z muttered. "You should know by now. Anyway, what are my instructions?"

"You're to stay put. Every contingency's covered."

Z almost shouted at him. "Immobilised? Why, in God's name? Do you think I'm going to hide my head under the bedclothes and let you macho lot have all the action?"

"Boss's orders."

"Then he's gone soft!"

"Shut it. You're acting out of character. Take it up with him later if you want to question his judgement." Beaumont was already moving away.

"What else did the Boss say?"

Beaumont turned briefly back. "Just that Mott would ring my mobile at twelve-o-five a.m. Oh, and he wanted to know what luggage Smith brought."

Cold Hands

"None. Some new stuff was delivered later. I don't know how
much, but I could probably find out."

"You won't have any better luck than me. It seems no one
except Mrs Tinsley was about at the time, and I can't see you
asking her."

Nor could Z really. That sort of personal question about a
fellow guest would set Connie wondering. Not that she ever
allowed herself time for trivial chit-chat.

And now Beaumont had spent too long serving her drink. She
put on a good face. "Well, here's luck if I don't see you before-
hand. Break a leg, or whatever."

"Yes, miss," said Charlie stiffly, carrying his empty tray back
to deal with refills.

Z sat seething. Staying put was not on the cards. Or only so far
as she'd agree to remain on the Fraylings estate. By midnight
she'd be in hiding over by the home farm, ready to pick up on
Beaumont's final instructions. And that, she reminded herself,
would mean opting out of the nightly poker, with an invented
headache.

Joanna noticed that Miss Finnegan wasn't looking too chuffed.
In her condition maybe she shouldn't have sat so long out in the
sun earlier. It could upset whatever drugs she had to take. She
certainly looked more flushed than usual. Since everyone else
seemed so taken up with themselves she saw there was only
herself to watch and make sure Miss Finnegan was all right.

Because there were fewer to cater for tonight, a place had been
set for Joanna at the grown-ups' dinner table. This could provide
copy for the emerging novelist, so she was secretly pleased,
although it did mean sitting next to Clary's grumpy mother.
This evening there were two other people missing besides Mr
Pomeroy, and the settings had been moved closer. It took her a
little while to work out that as well as Mrs Pomeroy it was the
glum Mr Jeffries who'd gone missing.

Could they have eloped together? she imagined with relish, but
even to her it seemed over-the-top.

\* \* \*

181

Beaumont covertly slid his cuff back and took a peek at his watch. They were dawdling over their meal worse than ever this evening, going for second helpings and lots of lengthy badinage while they ate.

And it had been served late, partly due to a last-minute change of starter because the smoked salmon hadn't been delivered. So there were panic stations in the kitchen while cod from the freezer was thawed out and Gayle whipped up a béchamel sauce for *Morue aux Epinards à la Florentine*. And in fiddly individual portions! Why in the name of Escoffier couldn't she have simply grilled some half grapefruits and stuck a cherry on top?

By then the main-course carrots had overcooked and Andrew wouldn't have it said he'd ever served up mushy veg. So a new lot had to be prepared and sautéd. Only minutes of difference but, when you're pressed to get off early, every second counts.

Returning the entrée dishes to his serving-table Beaumont saw from the corner of his eyes a hand appear round the door which stood ajar. It was unquestionably Gayle's, and she'd be standing there ready to pass him the *Bombe Glacée aux Framboises*. He seized his chance.

He rushed forward as the door opened further, seemed badly to misjudge the distance and struck the edge squarely with full force. There was a horrified gasp all round the table as he dropped like a stone and lay unmoving.

Zyczynski sprang to her feet, then realised it should be none of her business and subsided. Dennis Hampton had joined a distressed Gayle and was bending over the still figure.

"Is anyone good at first aid?" he demanded. "I'm afraid he's out cold."

"Noem'noh," muttered Beaumont, struggling to prop himself on one elbow, with the other hand to his gashed temple which was dripping blood. "M'all righ'. Jus' need a li'l lie down for a minute."

"Is he drunk, do you think?" stage-whispered Sabrina Carrick with malicious delight.

Pattie Dunne trotted round to investigate. "I'll say you need a lie down," she agreed with Beaumont. "That was one hell of a thump." She pushed him flat again, slapped a linen napkin on the wound, helped herself to his wrist and began taking his pulse with professional competence.

"The man's a buffoon," muttered Dunne, tight-lipped.

Gayle had run in search of Connie Tinsley who took one look and fetched Julian to help her get Beaumont upstairs. He protested, but feebly.

"You can't go back to the farm," Connie insisted. "You're in no fit state. There's a sofa in my husband's dressing-room. You can rest there. But I'm not sure we shouldn't send you to hospital."

The little procession manoeuvred the sufferer out. Dizzy Crumm leaned across the table to Z, her eyes bright with meaning. "Now why do you suppose he chose to do that?" she purred.

"Sir." A grey-haired DC from the Incident Room staff shot into the corridor with a message sheet in his hand. There was no mistaking the light in his eyes. Something had made his day.

"I hope it's good news," Yeadings said encouragingly.

"The old leg injuries, sir. To the driver in the burnt-out car. I tried everywhere local but hospitals hadn't anyone with time to search back. The Path lab said something like a machete had been used. Sir, they've changed that to a panga – the sort used in Central Africa. I remembered then I'd actually seen a panga on a case like that in Slough when I was on the beat there fifteen years back. The victim's name was in my old case notes and I checked it with Wexham Park Hospital. They still had the X-rays from a paper their orthopaedic consultant had written. They confirmed the patient was a local heavy, name of George Manders. He's done time in Parkhurst since then for aggravated burglary and GBH. He's on file with a photograph."

"Manders." Yeadings extracted the grain, patiently enduring the chaff because of the DC's enthusiasm. He looked only a year or so off his pension, and this might prove the only story worth telling at his retirement party. "In Parkhurst, m'm."

"Shall I follow it up, sir?"

"Certainly. Find out where he's been staying, who he associated with inside. And put his photograph with the others on show. I'll get someone in to look at it. Good work, er . . ."

"Chandler, sir."

"Right, Chandler. I'll have a word with your DI tomorrow."

Over the phone Yeadings heard out the woman's protests. "We have a new set for you to look at," he persuaded. "If you do manage to recognise a face among these photographs, it could help us solve a very serious crime.

"I'm sending a taxi to collect you," he declared with finality. "Nobody will know you're helping the police unless you choose to tell them yourself. It will be with you in twenty minutes."

What else? he asked himself, replacing the receiver. Twiddle my thumbs, light a superstitious candle? No; leave it all to Mott and his minions. Go home to the family. Why train a good pack of hounds and insist on sniffing out the fox yourself?

All the same he'd give a lot to be out there waiting in the dark for the rush of adrenalin as the quarry came within reach.

He collected the summer raincoat which Nan had thrust on him that morning and went off to find a sympathetic WPC to take care of the woman who would be coming in. "She's a neighbour in the arson case," he explained to Betty Stroud when he'd cleared it with her inspector. "Rather reluctant and possibly afraid of repercussions. Assure her that, if it gets to an identity parade, she won't have to face the man herself. And give her a cup of tea while she looks through the new set of mug shots including Manders with a beard added."

In the car, halfway home, he remembered that, over a week ago, they'd planned a family outing to Brighton for today: a bucket, spade and shrimping-net operation. He'd been looking forward with glee to catching baby crabs among the seaweedy rocks at low tide: one of the unexpected pleasures at his age of being father to a toddler. Only it didn't take account of the Job.

By now Nan would have packed the kids in with a hamper and driven off without him.

So he'd grab a makeshift meal, then return to the grind. He'd not care to admit to Nan that when a case reached this stage there was really only one place he'd want to be, and little room in his mind for any other activity.

184

# Waiting Game

S itting on the third stair up and watching between the wrought-iron balusters, Joanna saw Miss Finnegan come out of the little salon. Mr Hampton followed her into the hall. "I hope you'll feel better soon," he said. "I shan't stay for a long session myself tonight. It's grown so oppressive. We must be in for a storm."

"I didn't want to break up the game," she apologised, sounding quite concerned.

"Don't worry. You won't put the addicts off, though Jolly doesn't seem to be turning up tonight. I'll look in on the kitchen. Maybe Andy will make up numbers."

Not likely, since Beaumont had walked out on the other staff, Z reckoned. There would be too much clearing up to do. But all she needed was ten minutes with Smith kept out of the way while she looked for his luggage which the boss had asked about. From the dining-room's french windows she'd seen Nadia settling on the terrace with a long iced drink and her even longer cigarette holder, which meant that their suite should be empty for a while.

At the top of the grand staircase the double doors to the family's apartments weren't locked. She went into the square foyer with its handsome glazed doors to either side. On the right she could look through and see horsey prints on the walls and Connie's riding crop on the leather settee. That sitting-room led to the Tinsleys' bedroom where she'd gone to wake them after finding Pomeroy unconscious. Beyond it would be Julian's dressing-room where Beaumont had been taken to lie down.

To her left the other sitting-room appeared more feminine,

185

with floral paintings, dainty china ornaments and swagged drapes; clearly designed to Liese's tastes. Apart from a couple of glossy magazines and a pair of dark spectacles on a side-table there was nothing to indicate the Smiths' tenancy. Z opened the door and went through. In the bedroom a maid had already turned down the coverlet on the king-size bed. Hanging from the glass-fronted wardrobe, which occupied the whole of one wall, were two empty hangers and two others with the day clothes which the Smiths had worn before dinner. Z rolled back the first door to find, below the row of dresses, a collection of high-fashion women's shoes and matching flight suitcases in apple-green neoprene. A second set was behind the next door, and these, suave black and apparently new, had to be the man's. Two were empty and the smallest held a jumble of underclothes, unworn and with the store's price labels still on them.

No clues there, Z decided. She wondered what the Boss had expected them to contain.

The remaining two wardrobes were locked and without keys. There was nothing to indicate whether it was the Smiths who had taken such precautions, or Sir James and Lady Siddons safe-guarding possessions too bulky to remove.

The dressing-table drawers contained only a woman's under-clothes, blouses, filmy scarves, jewellery and cosmetics, plus a small amount of white powder in a plastic envelope. Probably cocaine for personal use, Z guessed. Well, she shouldn't be surprised. There was a lot of that done among the well-off: the social snort to keep you on top of things.

She turned towards the tallboy against the opposite wall and caught the click of the sitting-room door opening. There were voices, a man's and a woman's.

The wardrobes were full. The bed swept low to the ground. There being nowhere to hide, she went forward into the room to confront the Smiths.

"I'm terrible sorry," she gushed. "I was looking for the poor man who got knocked out. I think he must be—"

"In the suite opposite," said Nadia. She sounded faintly amused but her face was expressionless. The strange, green eyes made Z feel somehow transparent. And then she saw that the man standing beyond Nadia was Beaumont himself.

"Thank you, miss," he said. "Would you tell Mrs Tinsley I'm feeling better now and I'm just leaving."

"Yes, of course. She was anxious to know if you needed anything."

There was a flicker of amusement in Beaumont's eyes now. Fortunately the woman's back was turned and she missed it, still disconcertingly centred on Z's every movement. She barely drew aside to allow Z to pass.

"Are you up to driving?"

"Fine, thanks. I've taken worse knocks at football." Beaumont was keeping up the pretence, providing her with back-up, but he looked really sick. Both knew that he had only a couple of hundred yards to go on foot; but there was no need to advertise that he lodged at the home farm. What Nadia didn't know she couldn't let slip to her husband. He mustn't be warned of an outsider possibly witnessing tonight's little drama.

"Right then. I'll leave you to it. Good-night, Mrs Smith."

Nadia merely smiled. She watched as first the schoolmistressy Miss Finnegan and then the stand-in butler in his ill-fitting uniform left by the double doors to go down the grand staircase. They parted in the hall without further conversation. Then she saw a shadowy little figure creep down behind and hesitate a moment before following the woman back into the lounge.

Nadia Obeidat went through to the bedroom, surveyed it for signs of interference, then opened the nearer wardrobe and reached for her outdoor shoes. These and a waterproof cape she rolled into a bundle and took to the open casement window. Directly below was a splendid ceanothus in full bloom. The bundle fell and spread softly like a second blossoming, black over the deep blue.

Samways was an unlikely-looking youngster with corn-coloured, razor-cut hair, a ring in his left earlobe and a full, rosebud mouth. Left too long on the nipple, Beaumont sourly condemned him, regretting that they must share responsibility for this end of the operation.

187

It bugged him how often now the specialists working with him looked little older than his own son. There was that thing people said about what kids the police looked nowadays, but that what really proved you were over the hill was when magistrates began looking young too. He hoped he'd make a higher grade before that stage set in.

Not that he'd been keen on the extra grind involved in promotion until just lately. Making sergeant had suited him fine and he was happy working under Angus Mott. But then Zyczynski had happened along and made it look too easy.

She was all right: he'd nothing against her, except that being a woman she had two advantages. Statistics had to show there was some kind of gender tolerance in the force, despite the rarity of female entrants. So you got negative discrimination. And then, again, there were aspects of the job where women always had the edge on the fellers: the tea and sympathy stuff, right up to the verge of sexual entrapment.

But if the day ever came when he was calling a woman Guv – someone who couldn't flex a bit of muscle and was likely to break down and cry when the going got hard, well . . .

He was conscious of the other man summing him up unfavourably. It was a pity about the gashed temple and rapidly swelling eye but he'd no intention of explaining he'd walked into a door more violently than he'd meant to. Bad enough to be going into action with a second lump like an egg under his hairline and a constant didgeridoo accompaniment in his ears. "I've had a word with your Mr Yeadings," Samways announced, walking right into it.

What he surely meant was that the Boss had taken him aside and given him a straight warning. Beaumont treated him to a long, po-faced stare. "Let's start," he suggested, "by comparing notes on the instructions we've been given. Then there'll be less excuse for a balls-up."

"After you," Samways offered coolly.

"Radio communication to start with," Beaumont said grimly. "What are you carrying?"

Samways slid his mobile from a pocket. "Just this."

"Well, switch it off. Or shall I heel it? From now on you take your orders only from me. No chat. I'll be on your tail all the time."

Samways' eyes slitted. The rosebud mouth had become a single thin line. "I'm Customs and Excise, copper. My case officer is Walter Merton and no other. We'll get that straight. And you can put your own mobile wherever it fits. Mine stays with me, accessible only to the department."

Superintendent Yeadings took the phone call from Nan with calm resignation. She would have been totting up the hours he'd actually slept over the past four days. Or at least the night-time hours he hadn't spent padding about the house trying to work things out. It was hard on her that his inclusion in the Brighton jaunt had gone to pot, but by now she knew the name of the game.

"Mike?" she opened.

"In person. I did call you at lunchtime but I got the machine. So I knew the seaside trip was on."

"And you chickened out of leaving a message. I guess that means you're glued to your office seat."

"For a while. Off and on. I dropped back earlier for a bite before you'd returned. I'm sorry about the missed outing. Did you have a good day?"

"Splendid. We're all quite tired, but I'll tell you our next plans. The children are staying up until you can look in to say good-night. I'm tired of reassuring them you haven't gone for good like Annabel's daddy."

"Who's Annabel?"

"She's a precocious teenager Sally met on her Saturday job at the garden centre. She's been bringing back horrific tales of dysfunctional family life."

Nan wasn't nagging. In fact there was a tinge of steely humour in her voice. But the message was there: come back or else.

"I'll see what I can manage. Sometime after eight."

"Mike, it's nine fifteen already."

*Clare Curzon*

"Is it? Bless my soul, you're right. I . . . OK. I'll not keep them waiting."

"We'll see." And Nan rang off.

There was a red light winking on the white phone. Yeadings lifted the receiver and another small piece of the current jigsaw fell into place. "Parkhurst prison? Good," he replied.

At last he felt ready to knock off, but first he must add another arrow to his earlier diagram. He reached for it from the desk's top drawer and smoothed it out. From Smith's name he now drew yet another line and wrote the name George Manders by the arrowhead.

Parkhurst, he considered. The two men had done time together way back, earned the same old school tie. And Smith (but still Evans then) had called on the connection after all these years and got Manders in to ferry him to Fraylings. So was that because he trusted him, or because the old lag was expendable?

And the neighbour had confirmed that it was Manders who, under the name of Collins, had rented the flat at Little Chalfont where Webb had probably met his death. Not that there'd be a murder case to bring against him now since he was dead himself.

Surely it had to be Smith who planted that device in the Volvo. Yet Yeadings was still uncertain where the biker fitted in. Especially since he could even have been Jennifer Yorke's grown-up son, kept in the dark from his half-sister Clary until one day she glimpsed him as 'Rhubarb Crumble'.

Out in the car park a little puff of hot wind tugged suggestively at the raincoat over his arm. He looked up to see dark castles and towers of cloud building. Nan, as so often, had been right about the weather breaking.

He should be home before the heavens opened, but it looked bad for the joint operation with Customs. Transport by sea, air and land, he considered. There was ample chance there for a screw-up on at least one leg of the delivery.

And it wouldn't be much fun for the drowned rats staked out at this end waiting for the deluge to upset the fine tuning of Mott's strategy.

\* \* \*

190

At Fraylings the rain began at a little after ten; a few heavy drops that spread into black circles as they struck the tarmac paths. They released a hundred fresh smells overlain until then by a patina of dry dust. A mean little whipping wind sprang up and momentarily opened the sky, exposing a full moon in tatters of dark cloud.

"Indigo," breathed Dizzy Crumm standing at her open window in rapture, her shawl flapping on her shoulders. She half closed her eyes and saw the sky of that instant printed static in her mind.

A scumbled wash of watery gamboge with plenty of Paynes grey and ultramarine dropped in, wet on wet, and then, when almost dry, an interrupted glaze of the same heavy colours mixed with big smudges of burnt umber. She had to get it down while it was still inspiring her. No time to stretch paper. She'd just tape some on a board and triple soak it with a sponge.

Rain was blowing in now in great gusts. She slammed the window shut and at once the glass was awash, as though she stood behind a waterfall. Perfect, perfect. She scuttled to fetch a table and set up her painting things, dimming the light until the white paper was no more than a pale glow against the dark. Her colour pans stood ready in their customary order. She could do it with her eyes shut, *alla prima*.

Beaumont swore out loud as the rain gusted against his window. That was all they needed. On a blustering westerly, the storm could reach the east coast just when the stuff was due to come ashore. And if conditions had been dicey on the North Sea crossing its arrival could be knocked way off schedule.

Out here it began to get light at four. Given a still overcast sky, say four thirty. They'd a lot to shift before then. Delay at sea must affect things at this end. They might not care to open up and put the stuff in store by daylight, when people were about the farm buildings. And after a long wet night, there'd be little suitable cover for the police reception committee lying in wait.

One thing was certain: nothing would be brought forward. So he'd get his thumping head down while there was a chance, take

191

the couple of painkillers Connie Tinsley had given him and hope to feel less of a dog in a couple of hours.

The only thing Rosemary Zyczynski knew for certain about tonight's operation was that Mott would be making coded contact with Beaumont at 12.05. And that was assuming that the DS wasn't deliberately misleading her. But the extra five minutes in the quoted time made it sound genuine, as though the DI would be expecting an earlier call on the stroke of midnight.

If she was to get a share of the action she must get to wherever Beaumont was and then latch on to the instructions he received. He wouldn't be far from the home farm, and with any sense he'd be keeping out of the rain for as long as he could. She decided to leave it as late as eleven thirty before she set out to find him.

Despite her practice at flitting about the house unseen, Joanna had fallen foul of her grandmother as she finally tracked Miss Finnegan to her room. "What are you doing up at this time of night?" Liese demanded over a pile of fresh bed-linen. "I thought you'd been settled down an hour back."

"I needed a drink," the girl said, scowling. "Anyway what are you doing here?"

"Looking for the Pomeroys' room. It was a double. Do you know where your mother put them?"

"Off the east corridor. But anyway they've left, both of them."

"I am aware of that," Liese purred. "Which is why I'm looking for their room. Since you're so wide awake you can come along and help me change their bed-linen. I'm surprised Connie hasn't had it done already. I have no intention of spending another night cooped up with your grandfather in a single room."

She marched ahead and Joanna fell in behind. Any diversion was welcome when she'd finished all the books the nursery had on offer. "It's raining cats and dogs," she said happily. "And it said on the radio we're going to have thunder."

"How very disagreeable. I detest storms. They're too much like the war."

"I love them. Maybe I'd have loved the war too."

"That is an idiotic thing to say. And why should it rain cats and dogs? The weather has nothing at all to do with animals."

Joanna grinned. The nice thing about talking with her grandmother was that the conversation always went off at such odd angles. "What would you do if it did? Rain cats and dogs, I mean."

"I should fervently pray that Connie didn't adopt the wretched things. We have enough bother with that pack of Westies she's breeding from. I suppose now it's turned so wet we shall have them under our feet in the kitchen all night."

"That shouldn't bother you," Joanna said pertly, "if you're tucked up comfortably in the Pomeroys' room. You only cook at night if you can't sleep and want to make Mummy feel guilty."

At eleven thirty the downpour was, if anything, heavier. Monsoon stuff, Z told herself. The raincoat she had brought to Fraylings was little more than shower-proof but was black and would help her melt into the dark. Or more likely dissolve.

Any earlier notion of concealing herself in the lee of the piggeries or among the fruit bushes behind the farm were definitely out. She would head straight for Beaumont's room – where with any sense he'd be keeping himself dry – and throw herself on his hospitality. He'd hardly turn out a dog on a night like this.

She thought, as she slid from the shadows at the top of the grand staircase, that she heard a low voice, then a door close followed by light footfalls. The sounds came from the east corridor ahead. She shrank back, changed her mind and made for the staff stairs at the rear. Rather than leave by the bolted conservatory door she would turn off the house alarms and go through the kitchen quarters into the walled garden.

The padded swing door at the end of the service passage gave an agonised shriek as she put her weight against it. For a second she hesitated, listening, then let it close behind her. She'd barely noticed the sound by day as staff came and went between kitchen and dining-room, but now the darkness amplified every creaking floorboard, every tinny *plank-plank* as a leaky hot-tap slowly dripped on a baking tray left to soak in the steel sink.

Outside, it was a bedlam of slashing rain and growling thunder. Overfed gutters splashed and gurgled. Puddles were uninterrupted lakes even on the gravel walks. Bushes tossed and bowed like gleaners in a film on rapid rewind.

There were times, Z thought, when the weather was total experience. There was just nothing else. Whatever had been happening to you was utterly wiped out. It was nearly like that now. She supposed battles had been lost because of nights like this. She just hoped it hadn't put off the delivery.

With her hair twisted up inside her baseball cap, the peak gave protection enough for her eyes. She could just make out her way ahead without using the flashlight. Water had already penetrated the shoulders of her raincoat and was trickling coldly down her back. Twice she'd thrown up a wave like a trial car at a ford, so her ski-pants were soaked to the knees. When I get to Beaumont, she promised herself, I'll strip off and shock him.

There were lights still on at the farmhouse, in the curtained kitchen, the hall and one of the bedrooms. A feebler glow through net curtains reminded her there was a child there who was probably given a night-light. With the other upstairs rooms she had a choice of five windows. Eliminating the bathroom and landing meant that Beaumont's room must be one of the two at the front, or the remaining rear one.

She couldn't risk guessing from outside, so her first slippery move was to climb up on the porch roof and get to work on the casement above it. Crouched precariously there among the scratchy stems of an Albertine rose and the insinuating tendrils of an ancient untrimmed clematis she battled for several minutes with the catch. Then a sizeable portion of the rotten woodwork came off with it, prised free by her Swiss army knife. 'Never go anywhere without it,' the Boss had once warned her, and she'd proved the wisdom of his advice more than once.

As last arrival, Beaumont would probably have been lodged at the back, she decided. A run of rather threadbare patterned carpet led past the stairhead to the rear where, in dim light suffused from the hall below, a once-white door displayed evidence of grubby hands. Above the rattlings of the house

194

buffeted by wind and rain she caught no sound as she laid an ear against the panels. Holding her breath she swung the door inwards and whipped round it to stand inside the room.

There was a steady sound of snoring. "Beaumont," she whispered urgently, moved towards where she guessed the sleeping figure lay, and kicked an empty bottle that rolled with a crash against a leg of the iron bedstead.

The man moaned softly and she heard him turn bodily on creaking springs. She bent more urgently over him. And it wasn't Beaumont.

She saw now why Jolly hadn't put in an appearance for poker tonight. He'd been on a binge. She would already have picked that up from the room's smell if she'd come in less impulsively. And she'd been lucky, because even if Jolly didn't have impaired hearing he was in no state now to be easily roused.

Maybe Beaumont was the same. It stood to reason that Barron, who leased the farm, was involved with the gang, being on the spot for delivery. Why else all that new, expensive agricultural gear out in the padlocked barn? It didn't match the stuff he'd been using up till now. He'd been paid a considerable retainer and one of his functions was to ensure that no intruders were free to witness what went on. He could certainly afford the odd bottle of booze to achieve that.

There was still the chance that Barron's wife was awake in one of the two remaining rooms. He'd sounded the macho sort who wouldn't want women meddling in his manly affairs. On the other hand she could hardly be unaware of her husband's sudden influx of cash. So was she in on the delivery, waiting downstairs with him for the stuff to arrive?

As if in answer, Z heard voices below as the kitchen door opened and the woman came out. She mounted the stairs alone while Z crouched in shadow against the far wall. If the woman turned left for the bathroom she was bound to be discovered.

But for some minutes Mrs Barron stayed rooting around in her room with the light on and the door ajar. Long enough for Z to slip by and into the last room, which must be Beaumont's.

He was stretched out on the bed, deep under, sleeping as

195

noisily as Jolly. Bending over him Z realised there was no alcohol on his breath, and of course there wouldn't be. The DS knew better than to drink on a stake-out.

So was it coma? The blow to his head had been heavy enough to cause concussion on a thin skull, and he'd looked really rocky when he left Fraylings two hours back. She listened to his stertorous breathing and was faced with a horrific dilemma. Fetching medical aid must blow the operation entirely. But if she left him as he was until daylight . . .

Then she saw the half-filled tumbler of water and guessed. Some Good Samaritan had offered him painkillers. He'd done an OD on codeine or some such.

She reached under his pillow and located his mobile. If Beaumont was out, she was most certainly in.

# Royal Flush

Midnight had Zyczynski sitting alert with her hand ready on the mobile. Five minutes passed and it stayed silent; fifteen minutes, twenty-seven. When it sounded she was startled, for all that it was muffled. She silenced it, withdrew it from under Beaumont's pillow and extended the aerial. 'Yes?' she invited.

There was a brief silence, but he'd recognised her voice; then, "Why you?" It wasn't Mott, but Yeadings himself.

"My friend's had a slight accident. He's having to lie down." It took an effort not to say 'Sir', and she'd no idea what codename he was using.

"Anything serious?"

"I think it can wait till morning."

"Right." The Boss's voice continued, light in tone: "When he's feeling more chipper he must pop in and see us. Tell him Maggie's had her baby. It was a bit dicey and took longer than we were expecting. But in the end they managed to avoid a Caesarean. Both doing well, as they say."

She thought she had the gist of it. "Boy or girl?"

"A lusty boy, just what we were all hoping for."

"Wonderful. Did they mention what he weighed?"

"They did, but I'm blowed if I can remember. Ten pounds, would it be? No, don't take my word on that. For all I know it could be twice that." He managed to sound the duffer male, totally out of his depth about such clinical details. And that was a man who could tell you his children's present height and weight to within the nearest half-inch or eight ounces.

"I'm so glad it's all come off well. We'll hope to see Maggie as soon as she can have visitors."

"Me too. Maybe a flying visit as soon as it's daylight. Thought you'd like to know. Any news your end?"

"Not really, except that it's raining. Quite flooded round here. Glad I'm not out on a night like this. I'm shacking up with my beau. Good excuse not to go home, eh?" She ended on a girlish giggle. Let him make what he would of that!

Yeadings wished her good-night, although it was morning, and broke the connection, leaving her to rerun in her mind all he had said.

He'd instantly realised she had no knowledge of the codes in use, so he'd improvised, making it simple for her. Maggie's baby was the Dutch delivery. A delayed business, which wasn't surprising in view of the weather. No Caesarean section: that meant no need then for Customs to intervene. Flying visit. So should she expect the stuff to be brought in by air? Landing could be dodgy with the countryside flooded, but at least the ground forces would hear its approach.

And the rest – the lusty boy, and the unlikely twenty pounds for its weight? Was that the guessed value or cubic capacity of the load? Twenty million in twenties or fifties? Yeadings had risked it, making sure she'd enough info to work on. What he hadn't given her was any idea of the instructions Beaumont was working to. And which it now looked as if she'd be taking over.

She slid the mobile back under the pillow and took another look at Beaumont. She tried shaking him by one shoulder but it had exactly zero effect. There were another three hours to first light and she doubted he'd be active by then.

Yeadings had promised himself – promised Nan really, by proxy – that once he'd taken over Mott's midnight check on Beaumont, he'd leave the rest to Angus, show he'd complete trust, and toddle off to bed with a nightcap. But talking with Zyczynski had made him uneasy. She'd not offered a real explanation for taking over at the farmhouse end, and Beaumont wouldn't have surrendered his mobile unless he was totally out of action.

She'd thought he'd be all right until morning. But Yeadings knew every nuance of Z's voice by now. She'd sounded unnaturally calm: so, anxious underneath. He'd have liked to send someone in to check on the situation. But with every passing minute the likelihood grew that the counterfeiters' reception plans were already being put into action and access to the farmhouse could be cut off. Under this heavy downpour it would be hard enough for the police party to take cover there on foot. They'd need to move their vehicles close to target, which made them liable to spotting from the air.

He sat hunched in the lounge at home, watching rain sheet solidly down the windows. When the hall phone rang it made him jump.

He rushed to it. "Yes?" he barked, ready for disaster.

But it was from the nick. At last they'd a lead on the biker. Name of Bernard Dodds. He'd been lodging in Chesham, garaging his bike in a lock-up near the station, but he'd left four days back, right after his landlady heard him phoning someone in Dundee. And she was peeved because he'd never paid her for the call.

"Ring Dundee Central," Yeadings ordered, and dictated a message for their CID. It could be a false trail, but one they'd have to follow, since it seemed Bernie-of-the-bike was certainly connected with the set-up at Fraylings.

Yeadings replaced the receiver with one twinge of regret: that the surname had been Dodds and not Evans. But he did have the satisfaction of knowing that his wild surmise had been spot on. Bernie was certainly Jennifer Yorke's son, with the same surname she'd been using when she'd been on the game for Evans in Soho.

Joanna had been held up by having to dump the used bed-linen in the laundry room and say a final good-night to her grandmother. So, although she'd glimpsed Miss Finnegan escaping down the back stairs in her black raincoat, she couldn't catch up with her inside the house. By the time she'd collected her own wellies and school waterproof there was no sign of her from the conservatory door.

The rain was pelting down. No one in their right mind would

choose to go walking on a night like this, would they? So perhaps Miss Finnegan was half-crazed with worry or something. Or else she'd decided to go for a drive because she couldn't sleep.

The quickest way out to where the cars were parked was through the kitchen garden. Joanna splashed her way across the waterlogged gravel and out by the gate in the wall. She could hear an engine ticking over but none of the cars had its headlights on, which seemed strange.

As her eyes grew adapted to the dark she saw one parked with its driver's door ajar and the dim inner light illuminating empty seats. Behind it, the hooded figure of the younger teacher was struggling with the window of another car parked across its tail. It looked as though she was reaching in to get something.

Then the second car began slowly to move in reverse. So the brake had been released and Miss Finnegan was pushing it to clear a way out.

Well, since she was so determined to go driving, she'd not change her mind if Joanna just suggested she should come back indoors. It would take time for her to calm down. The best thing would be to wait a while and then try persuasion. Meanwhile, there was room in the car's rear where Joanna would be sheltered from the rain. She opened the nearer door, slid in and closed it gently behind her. There was a woolly rug on the floor and she crouched down on it to wait.

Above the blustering rain she heard quick footsteps approaching and felt the car springs gently give as the driver got in. Gingerly the car eased out into the cleared space behind, turned and made for the main driveway.

Still there were no beams of light bouncing ahead to show the way, and Joanna knew that was stupid. Even the dashboard wasn't lit up. She considered whether she should point out how dangerous it could be. But she'd made critical remarks before about her mother's driving and had learnt it wasn't appreciated.

At least Miss Finnegan was going very slowly, the engine a subdued purr. And that was funny too, because when she had arrived at Fraylings, driven by her friend Mrs Fellowes, the little car had sounded quite different, almost tinny and somehow rougher.

Gradually the idea began to grow on Joanna that Miss Finnegan had made an awful mistake in the dark and let herself into the wrong car. She'd probably be upset when she realised what she'd done.

This was turning into more of an adventure than she'd expected when she'd defied being dismissed to bed. Granny Liese had said once that you can get past being tired. This was the case now. Joanna told herself she could easily last out till morning.

She could tell the point where they turned on to the main road. The car immediately speeded up, its tyres hissing on the wet, metalled surface. Joanna dared to peek between the seats and was reassured that the dashboard and the road ahead were now bright enough. So they weren't driving blind.

She stretched out more comfortably. It was cosy in here out of the rain, with the rhythmic *flunk-flunk* of the windscreen wipers muttering in a sort of foreign language but with familiar words floating unexpectedly in and out which she barely caught.

Joanna yawned, rubbed her cheek against the blankety warmth of the rug, snuggled up and relaxed.

DI Angus Mott cursed silently, wiping steam from the inside of the windscreen with his cuff. He lowered the window beside him and was slapped by a gust of heavy rain. It triggered a sudden memory of an autumn break spent with his bachelor uncle at Hastings.

The other kids had returned to school but he was recuperating from something – mumps or measles. There'd been no one left to play with, nothing to do in the quiet house; nothing interesting outdoors to compare with towering high seas whipping over the promenade.

He'd played a lone game of chicken, running between the mountainous breakers crashing across the tarmac. Once not making it, so that he was beaten to the ground and sucked, rolling over and over, back against the railings. He'd nearly gone through, to pitch sixteen feet down into the foaming, thrashing waves. He simply lay there, clinging on for dear life while successive torrents burst over him, flogged him and drenched him to the skin.

A drowned rat; between onslaughts he'd managed to scuttle safely away, once he'd finally gained strength and guts enough. The bruises on his back and ribs had lasted for days. He'd remembered them ever after as a child when he looked at the ornamental, iron-knobbed stanchions of the parade on subsequent seaside holidays.

Funny how the young had to take risks. There was that driving need to measure oneself against hardships. Maybe a purely male drive: girls seemed to have more sense of self-preservation. What was he then? Eight, nine? Early premonitions of testosterone. But in those days – not so very far back – there wasn't open talk of such things.

He turned up his collar now and was rewarded with a cold trickle inside his shirt. "You lot at the back, stop breathing, will you? I'm not risking running the blower."

There was a mumbled reply and the crackle of wrappings being removed from confectionery. A hairy hand came over Mott's shoulder with a chunk of slab chocolate in it. "Energy food," the DC assured him.

"Isn't that stuff supposed to make you bad-tempered?" his companion countered. "Bit of a risk in a cramped space like this, eh?"

Mott bit into the block, aware he was being got at. OK, so he'd been giving them a hard time, but this wasn't the moment to let up. This stake-out was built on uncertainties, and that was before the weather had joined in.

He had thought at first, good: full moon. We take up our positions early and just wait in cover. There'll be a clear sighting of how they make the delivery. If it's by light aircraft they'll have good landing conditions. While they're busy unloading we move in, surround the strip and grab them. On our signal, cars hidden out by the main road will block it at both ends and pick up anyone who gets through the net. Beaumont, together with

Merton's man, will cover everything back at the barn and pick up whoever arrives to take the stuff in.

Now this summer storm, building too rapidly from yesterday's sultry heat, had made a pig's arse out of the plan. The heavy rain obscured everything beyond a few yards distant. The only natural light came in brilliant flashes which would reveal the watchers as they moved in. Any saving grace existed in the gang suffering equal hardships (though for a shorter period) and if the torrent persisted they'd be keeping their heads well down.

On the other hand, although the first leg of the journey had succeeded despite delays, there was no guarantee that this end of the operation wouldn't be washed out and the stuff temporarily diverted elsewhere. Already parts of the lanes hereabouts were underwater and could soon be impassable. That would mean calling off the surveillance and holding the men ready without adequate rest until the villains chose to make a move when they thought fit.

"What wallies! We're on the wrong side," said the DC slumped beside him, almost echoing his thoughts. "And God knows we don't do it for perks."

On the wrong side, as Paula was. Yes, that still rankled. And perks she certainly had, earning high fees even as a junior at the bar. When eventually they got to putting down the deposit for a house, he could never match her pound for pound. And they'd started level, achieving the same class of the same law degree in the same year, first meeting at the presentation ceremony, seated by fate and the alphabet side by side, Musto next to Mott. If anything, he'd had the advantage then, salaried as a DC while she was still a debt-laden ex-student.

Life had looked a whole deal simpler in those balmy days of early love. He wished in some ways he could go back and start again. But not give up the Job. This was the right life for him, the right team, the right boss, the right necessary bursts of adrenalin. He wasn't the one who'd made the wrong choice that was steadily driving them apart.

There was a tapping at the window and a sodden PC appeared,

runnels of water streaming down his weathered face. "Note, sir," he mouthed, "from your Super, sir."

He produced a folded paper, miraculously dry, and thrust it through the narrow gap. Below the dashboard Mott switched on his pencil torch to read, and grunted.

"Expect a chopper," he told the others. "Let's hope it makes it here in one piece."

The rest of the message he kept to himself. He could see no reason why Nederhuis should be on board. His part was surely over, unless he was coming to make sure of a final payment.

"Do we let the poor sod in?" asked one of the DCs, eyeing the constable.

"No room," Mott said firmly.

"Nasty smell Uniformed have when they're wet, sort of dog's blanket stench," came an opinion from the rear. And they weren't exactly violets themselves, Mott thought grimly. He stole a glance at his watch. Two thirty-seven a.m. And still no permanent break in the clouds.

Boulos Obeidat regarded himself in the mirror over the kitchen sink. While he waited for the kettle to boil he examined the lines of his face: the calliper grooves from outer nostrils towards chin, lost in the stylishly trimmed black beard; the deepening ditches below the inscrutable eyes; the cavernous hollows below sharp cheekbones.

A handsomely villainous face, he decided. Assembled to play the Sheriff of Nottingham, Iago, or a wicked version of Suleiman ben Daoud. And what had it achieved for him?

Money, certainly. But money with steel strings attached. A wife discriminating men looked at twice, but who had no room for men in her life. Her lovemaking was mechanical, throwaway. Sometimes it struck him as contemptuous. Raised in a Middle Eastern house of women, how could she be otherwise? But at least she might act as if she were normal. The truth was, she had a lot of her father in her, and that fact made him uneasy.

For an instant he thought he saw his own father in the mirror, the brow more furrowed than his own smoothly supercilious one, the beard a mere growth of two or three days, whitish in parts like a scattering of dirty granulated sugar. He could almost smell the stench off the old man, of worked soil and sweaty, dung-spattered cows. The progenitor of Paul village-scruff Evans. At least he'd come a long way from that himself.

The kettle began to whistle and he stilled it; poured boiling water on the herbal mixture in his mug. With it steaming in his hand he rearranged his features again for the mirror and, satisfied, moved towards the door, snapped off the lights and steered himself towards bed.

Upstairs, in their superior suite, he found the lights on and the coverlet turned down, but Nadia wasn't there. Which was nothing new. Somewhere in the house there would be someone who'd taken her fancy, a man to humiliate or a woman to wrestle with. Maybe the two together if she'd gone to the Carricks. Well, he'd drink his tisane and wait for her to return. And then she should know who her father had sold her to.

He swallowed half the drink, grimacing at its bitterness, shed his clothes and showered, then refilled the mug from his private store of malt and drained the lot.

His head felt strangely heavy. His shoulders had a great weight on them. He reached towards the bed and only just made it there. The last thing he heard was the silvery chime of Lady Siddons' little Dresden clock in the sitting-room before he tipped forward into a deep well of blackness.

At three seventeen, the rain lessened. There was still thunder rumbling in the distance some seconds after paler flashes, but it seemed the storm had finally moved on. Furtive exits were made into neighbouring bushes, accompanied by muffled curses as shoes sank into boggy earth and trees dripped on faces upturned to scan the eastern sky.

Angus Mott took advantage of the less cramped space to spread his map over the passenger seat and check once again on the area he'd selected as most likely for the landing. It was an open field in the angle of two lanes, some mile and a half from the farmhouse, on a high point sloping gently to woodland which screened it on the south-west from the nearer village. It was among the trees there that the cars were hidden at present, but choosing cover was at cost of an uphill approach when – or if – the chopper put in an appearance.

Now that the rain had abated it was possible occasionally to hear traffic on the trunk road to Aylesbury but, elsewhere, there was a pervading silence. As zero hour approached, surely there should be some activity down near Fraylings, Mott reasoned. With his binoculars swinging from one shoulder he stepped warily out into the peaty mush and squelched his way through to the lower edge of the wood.

Less than half of the front elevation of Fraylings Court was visible through the field-glasses, but an unexpected number of windows showed lights. As he watched, the main door opened and three figures ran out with torches to pan about the upper terrace as if searching. Too openly to be connected with any clandestine business. It looked as if some crisis had broken.

That's all we need, he groaned inwardly. Fire engines and ambulances blaring and hooting through the middle of the operation. What in hell's name has gone wrong down there now?

No call had come from Beaumont, but maybe the Court was out of sight and earshot of wherever the DS was holed up. But if the search or whatever spread wider, maybe Beaumont could be discovered himself.

A diversion? he asked himself. Was Smith drawing attention away from the landing site, covering up any untoward noise of traffic there by causing a local hubbub? Yes, there were car lights now, down in the parking area, and torches moving among them. This was more than the storm's passing resulting in a universal passion for moonlight walking. Had the house flooded, or been struck by lightning?

He was aware then of a new sound, a rhythmic beating gradually overlaid by a metallic clatter. This would have to be the moment the chopper opted to appear.

He swung his binoculars up and refocused. The helicopter hovered undecided, swung in a semicircle towards the animated scene below, then veered away. Scared off? From up there,

Fraylings Court must look like a fairground. Hardly propitious for a nearby drop of something like twenty millions in dodgy sterling. The machine swung so low over the wood that he caught the crackle of radio and a shouted voice, but no words. Then it straightened, made again for the landing ground and disappeared behind the trees.

Caught off-site, Mott took to his heels, charging through the undergrowth like a bull elephant gone rogue, heedless of branches and brambles tearing at face and hands. His car, when he reached it, was abandoned. The Armed Response Vehicle stood silent with its doors open. Everyone was present on the job but himself. Hell's bells but someone should suffer if all the wheels came off. And that would most likely be himself, he knew, his heart pumping, breath soughing as he ran. He broke into the open.

The chopper had landed but the blades still slowly rotated. Beyond the ring of dark figures closing in he saw others, two or three, crouching under the down-draught. It was all in the timing now: could they unload before they got wind of a police presence? Was the pilot wary enough to sniff danger and lift the prize away from under their noses?

Towards the gate on the upper lane there was a sound of acceleration. He saw a car lurch into the space and start towards the group, then suddenly lodge fast. The engine roared impotently. Bogged down.

The figures by the chopper had no eyes for anything else now. They were all running to put their shoulders to shifting it out of the cart ruts. Mott risked stopping and slammed the field-glasses to his eyes. Beside the now idling chopper were the dark shapes of three large cartons such as removals firms used. So five more to come out. *Got 'em!* he panted, and slogged on.

Joanna awoke suddenly at the roar of the engine. She could feel the car slide sideways as Miss Finnegan tried to correct a skid. And then they lurched to a standstill, the roar rising to a desperate whine as the tyres spun helplessly in liquid mud.

A lot happened then in such quick succession that afterwards she had trouble remembering the sequence. But as people crowded round to help free the car she stared with shock at the back of Miss Finnegan's head. The dark hood had been thrown back to uncover a quite different wig. Not the mousey bird's-nest but a sleek bell of hair that shone gold in the fitful moonlight. Like Clary's mother's.

And of course that's who it was. Which explained why the car sounded different. The Yorkes had come in a blue BMW. The schoolteachers owned an old Ford Escort. Not only had she mistaken one woman for another, but she'd boobed on the cars too. That's what being sleepy did for you. And now, how was she going to explain her way out of this?

But it seemed that explanations were postponed for the present because a real fight had suddenly broken out round the car. Everywhere there were struggling figures and shouted warnings. Dozens of men in dark clothes and baseball caps with POLICE written on them surged in from nowhere.

Jennifer Yorke took advantage of the mêlée to crouch low and slide open her driver's door. But Joanna was ready, tugging the rug from under her and whipping it over the woman's head.

Then a brilliant light came on and the whole action froze. Someone was giving orders through a megaphone. People were actually being handcuffed, just like on TV. And round the outside of the group were some quite fearsome warriors with rifles levelled.

Lastly came Inspector Mott staggering into sight, enormous in black oilskins streaming water, and a fisherman's hat held on by elastic. Under it his face was wet with bloody scratches. Joanna had never seen a hero like him in any book she'd read. He was real cool, marvellous, towering over everyone and bellowing hoarsely like – like Captain Ahab defiant on his deck as he went after Moby Dick.

He opened the door and scowled in at Joanna. "What the hell," he demanded, "are you doing here?"

# Winner Collects

R ain was still pelting and thunder growling when DS Zyc-
zinski caught movement in the farmyard below. Behind
her Beaumont snored on. The muffled figure came stealthily on
foot – indistinguishable under a brimmed hat that could have
been a man's or woman's – attacked the barn's padlock with a
bunch of keys and went through.

No lights were switched on but Z could make out the beam of a
torch picking an eccentric path between the new farm plant as far
as the inner compartment. This having no windows, Z assumed
that, when all went dark again, the night visitor would be inside.

And from there on she had to play it by ear, having no access
to Beaumont's instructions.

She eased open the bedroom door and listened for the sounds
of the house. From the well of the staircase came the slow tick of
a longcase clock and the more distant hum of a refrigerator
barely audible above the outdoor noises of slopping gutters and
gurgling drains.

The stairs creaked as she went slowly down, alert for any
lightly sleeping dog beyond the open sitting-room door. In the
kitchen the only lights were the red dots on sockets for electric
cooker and fridge-freezer.

There was no key in the lock of the glass-panelled back door.
So, at last, here was someone who heeded the warnings of Crime
Prevention officers! But she hadn't far to look for the key. Two
identical ones, each on a ring with another, hung from a hook up
by the lintel. She helped herself to one ring, guessing that the
second key belonged to the padlock on the barn.

She checked the front windows of the farmhouse for lights

before running across the cobbles to the barn, and stayed there in shadow for some seconds waiting for any reaction she might have provoked.

Everything slumbered on as before, but at last some clouds were showing an edge of silver. The rain was easing up, the thunder more distant and with longer pauses between.

There was no need to use the second key. The padlock already hung from the loosened hasp. Old timbers creaked as she heaved on the door, making a space just wide enough to slip through.

Then it was a case of gingerly threading her way among the implements stacked in there, feeling for each lightly with her fingers before moving on. Like exploring a smoke-filled building in a fire precaution film she remembered. She slid each foot forward in contact with the floor to avoid kicking loose any ironmongery which could go clanging free and betray her presence.

In such total darkness there was no way of telling whether the inner barn doors were left open and the person she'd observed was waiting, listening for her approach.

When she judged she was halfway in she began to move obliquely, clawed her way round a tractor and found herself a little space to squat in between its high rear wheel and the stone outer-wall. And then again it was a case of waiting: how long there was no way of knowing because in here it was still as a tomb; no storm, no sound of traffic. If anyone arrived outside she would have no warning until the barn doors swung open.

Lady Siddons awoke to observe with considerable relief that she had been dozing atop a comfortable double bed in the redeemed room once given over to the Pomeroys. She hadn't meant to drop off when she was trying out the mattress but as one got older that sort of thing was liable to happen. Now it was more than time that she fetched poor James from his makeshift quarters in the library. On her royal progress downstairs she switched on each light as she passed, that being her custom.

Sir James, protesting only mildly at being woken for transport to a supposedly more comfortable bed, permitted himself to be trundled to the stairs and transferred to the chairlift. "This is very good of you, m'dear," he told Liese. "You shouldn't have gone to so much trouble."

"No trouble at all," she assured him stoutly. "In fact Joanna helped me get the room straight."

"At this time of night?" He looked at his watch in disbelief. "But it's gone three, m'dear. Is she still up?"

"I shouldn't think so. I sent her off to bed. Quite a while back, actually."

But when Liese had her husband tucked in safely, she felt a niggling doubt because she hadn't actually extracted a promise from her granddaughter that she was bedward bound. And the child must have been up to some mischief to be abroad at the hour that she was.

"Perhaps," Liese said in a burst of grandmotherly concern – or suspicion – "I'd better go and check on her."

The outcome was an alarm call to Joanna's parents and a panic searching of the entire public area of the house, with urgent whispers of her name which penetrated sleep more thoroughly than loud conversation would. Little knots of guests came out in their dressing gowns to inquire with varying degrees of concern what had happened.

"Not again?" was Hal Carrick's instant response when told that Joanna had gone missing.

"Kids," Dunne muttered with disgust.

"But she must be somewhere in the house," Pattie said with practicality. "She'd hardly have gone out on a night like this."

So the house was checked again, this time including the guests' bedrooms, while Liese bemoaned her own laxity and Sir James fumed at his enforced inactivity.

"I don't like it," Connie understated. "After that other time I was sure she would keep to our agreement. Something untoward has happened. I know it. Julian, get your boots on. We're going out to scour the grounds."

As the ring of dark figures closed in on the chopper, Nederhuis was the only one to catch their movements. He shouted to alert

211

the others, made a run for it and almost broke through to the trees. But two of the uniformed men headed him off and brought him down. Even rugger-tackled and winded, he put up a good fight. The chopper pilot and the other passenger had been more easily overcome. They were all arrested, handcuffed and dispatched in separate police cars for questioning at the local nick. Jennifer Yorke, protesting total innocence – she'd merely gone night-driving to settle a bad toothache – was overruled and instructed to drive her own BMW with a marksman crouching in the space Joanna had vacated.

If picking up Jennifer on the receiving end of the operation had been unexpected, that was nothing to Mott's shock at finding the stowaway in the car's rear.

Joanna hopefully expressed a fancy for travelling home in the Armed Response Vehicle, but its night's tasks were only half done. There was still no news of how many of the gang were awaiting delivery at the barn, and the ARV was to follow Jennifer's BMW in as she made the expected contact.

"I could comalonga you," Joanna offered her hero hopefully.

There was no alternative transport and Mott faced her with formidable wrath. "If you so much as show your face or I hear a peep out of you . . . Here, get in the back and lie flat."

It would mean he must keep to the perimeter of the action but he had no real choice. The girl climbed in beside the remaining DC and settled by his feet among a nest of crushed Sprite cans and sweetie papers.

A hefty police quartet rocked and heaved at the BMW, finally releasing it from its mud tracks with a uniformed driver at the wheel. Then Jennifer replaced him and the little cortège slowly moved off. She was still protesting that she'd seen the chopper losing height and thought it was going to crash. So she'd driven over to see what help she could give.

Mott tersely instructed her to save her breath and carry on as if with the delivery, issuing no specific directions, and she was unnerved enough automatically to take the lane that would bring her out by the farmhouse. When she realised she'd given herself away she protested no further, hoping that later she could claim she had co-operated and it would show her in a better light.

As they wound down towards the valley, the rain finally ceased, moonlight picking out the flooded edges of the lane and stretches of water in the lower fields. Mott ran the windows down and sniffed at the outer freshness.

They came on the Home Farm from the opposite end to Fraylings Court, but even before the car pulled up they could hear raised voices from the search party. Eight or nine figures broke out of the darkness and came running towards them, sweeping the farmyard with the beams from their torches. The headlights on Jennifer's car struck the scarecrow outline of Dizzy Crumm holding up a storm lantern like some grotesque parody of the Statue of Liberty.

"God, this is pure farce," Mott ground out. "Where's Beaumont? What's become of Smith's reception committee? How in hell can we pick out the villains in this mob?"

Jennifer was shaking as she braked. "I'm supposed to hoot," she told the marksman levelling his rifle behind her left ear.

"Hoot then."

She gave two light toots and waited. From the direction of the Court there came an instant unscripted answer as, yapping and panting, the entire Westies pack streamed into the hunt. Above the clamour Connie Tinsley made her dog-training voice heard, demanding, "Which of you idiots left the wall gate open?"

Mott groaned at thought of this final pantomime detail for his operational report.

Inside the barn Zyczynski stiffly eased herself upright and stared through the darkness towards the inner doors. She saw now they were rolled back and someone was coming through behind a powerful torch. While the light was still some yards off, Z moved, skirting the heavy tractor and lunging towards where she guessed the dark figure to be. But one knee caught the leaning shaft of a mattock and she pitched forward on her face among a clutter of tools.

As she fell, the wild swipe of the torch just missed her. She felt the wind of its passage and heard the other's gasp on losing balance. Z rolled sideways and reached out for the ankles. She got her fingers round one and then the other foot came stamping down to crush her hand. There was a second before the pain of broken bones hit her, but she was up on her knees again and with the other hand aimed a wild blow at crotch level. Her fist buried itself in the folds of a waterproof but the other staggered backwards, the torch arcing off and shattering on the concrete floor.

Then they were locked together, struggling, falling, rolling against the stacked ironmongery, filling the enclosed space with the clangour of grappling knights in armour.

Then there was dazzling light all around. "Right, that's enough!" and they were being pulled apart. Z wiped loose hair and blood from her eyes and gazed at her antagonist. Nadia Obeidat, savage as a cheetah, spat in her face.

Questioning was left to later in the day. The two women and three men were offered a rug and a hard bench in cells at the nick, coffee on arrival and breakfast at eight o'clock.

An hour later Mott began the taped interviews alongside Zyczynski – her left arm in a sling – no one having yet been charged.

Superintendent Yeadings, kept abreast of events, was still inquiring into Smith's part in the debacle and was mildly annoyed at learning that he'd spent the night in a drugged sleep while his wife got on with the active role.

"So it wasn't his set-up," he regretted to Mott later.

"No. The two women, for all they acted as bitter rivals, were in it together, with Nadia and Nederhuis planning the whole thing between them. Through his dabs, we've got more on him now from Interpol. It seems he and Nadia are an item; met some two years back, skiing in Switzerland.

"And Nederhuis is no Dutchman: yet another with an assumed name, originally Jiři Hrubeš. As a child he escaped from Czechoslovakia with his mother, when the Russians went back in, in '68. They settled in Germany and Jiři went to school there. He became a skilled jeweller, specialising in design engraving. Then it seems he bought an interest in the manufacture of quality paper. Put all that together and he had a recipe for printing his own money. The Düsseldorf police were looking for him about an issue of forged share certificates when he left the country. They hadn't yet discovered he was in the Netherlands under a new name. There he'd started counterfeiting US and British treasury notes. They've found the place he worked from, but the plates had disappeared.

"Nadia was to finance and organise distribution in the UK, and they'd planned other outlets in Europe and the Commonwealth. The stuff's good quality, as funny money goes. It was done on a big scale, to flood the market and make enough profit in one go to set them up nicely for life. And with Smith disposed of, Nadia would be free to marry Nederhuis whatever objections her father raised."

"So the incendiary and the car crash were intended for Evans-Obeidat?"

"But misfired, killing only Manders who was dispensible anyway and a big embarrassment after he'd been sussed by Webb who then had to be eliminated. I think the car business was intended to kill two birds with the one stone."

"So who placed the incendiary?"

"We should get confirmation on that when we get young Bernie Dodds brought down from Dundee. Although his mother would lie herself blue in the face to shift all the blame on to Nadia, I'm inclined to believe what she says about that. The Nadia-Jennifer alliance was based on no more than greed and a common loathing of Evans. Jennifer could never forget that he'd ruined her early life and left her as a minor to bring up Bernie on her own. There's an even chance of the young man being Evans's by-blow. Whether he intended killing his father or not he was certainly in on the currency scam."

"I find it hard to believe Evans was totally innocent of any part in this business. He's such a natural to fit the role of kingpin."

"Apparently not. Professor Martens has prepared a profile on him: his line is self-admiration. Narcissistic almost to psychotic level. He sees himself as a natural aristo, and has a gift for putting it across to other people. That's probably at the heart of Nadia's contempt for him, because she knows that on the strength of her father's money and name he was just so much hot air."

Yeadings nodded. "Like Æsop's frog – '*La grenouille qui vit un boeuf*'. In the end he's lucky to be still alive, not splatted as the frog was. By the way, what happened to that unlikely lad Customs sent to help with the arrests?"

Mott grinned. "After his disappointment in missing out on the action – thanks to Beaumont's Sleeping Beauty act and Z not knowing she should contact him – he's been awarded a consolation prize."

"That's nice," Yeadings said doubtfully.

"Yes. I've got him counting the funny money. Under supervision, of course. All eight cartons of it."

"Ah. Maybe I'll look in and thank him for his help, on my way to the hospital to see how Beaumont's faring. I gather he's still feeling pretty sick, with slight concussion."

On arrival in Thames Valley, Bernie Dodds wriggled on the hook over responsibility for the incendiary. Warned of a possible murder charge, he was at pains to explain his part in delivering it. His mother had asked him to hand it to Manders at the airport. It was gift-wrapped, he explained: a welcome-home present for Obeidat from his wife, with a covering note. He'd no idea it invited Evans to join her at Fraylings Court.

"Where she had no intention of his arriving. Otherwise, why hadn't she booked a double room?" Mott asked, discussing his evidence with Zyczynski as they took a break for coffee. "And she'd never warned Jennifer Yorke that Evans was likely to turn up. When they came face to face Jennifer nearly bolted. She said Bernie was simply to deliver the gift, then follow and watch where Evans went. That's what Nadia had ordered."

"So that he could carry back the story of a fatal crash."

"But after Evans read the note and told Manders where to head for, he left the package unopened. He says he fell asleep for most of the journey. It must have been a shock for Nadia when

216

he turned up alive and well. I'll bet she was working on some alternative surprise packet for him before she finally vanished into the sunset with her lover."

"What we're never likely to be sure about," Zyczynski regretted, "is why Bernie Dodds followed the Volvo so far. It seems unlikely he stuck to it so faithfully unless he expected something to happen. Why didn't he note the direction and scorch back at his normal speed? He says it was on instructions from his mother. And she says she took those orders from Nadia. But do we believe he's the innocent he claims to be?"

Mott reconsidered the written statement. "He had to refill his tank and so he lost the Volvo at one point, then picked it up after Evans had been dropped off. That much is true. We checked it with the garage he stopped at."

"But could he see whether the passenger was still inside when he zoomed past and drove the Volvo off the road, as Traffic division now believe?"

"Does it matter? We can still charge him with causing a death by dangerous driving, whoever was inside and whether he knew the crash would set off the device or not. It's up to the DPP to decide whether we've a case that will stick."

Mott stirred his coffee moodily.

"So what are the chances of convictions on the others, Guv?" Zyczynski asked. She had plastered pancake make-up on where Nadia's nails had raked her cheek, but could barely resist rubbing with her free hand at the healing scars.

"I doubt we'll get Nederhuis for more than the currency rap, because only Manders could tell us about Webb's murder, and he's dead himself. He probably had help: possibly Nederhuis, maybe Bernie or his friend Carver Ward. But there's nothing to prove it.

"Nadia will go down for the murder of Manders, with Jennifer and Bernie attesting against her to save their own skins. And they will face conspiracy charges on the counterfeiting. Not a bad result after all, considering. I just hope we don't get a woodentop prosecutor and some clever-kid defending counsel who rubbishes all our hard work."

"There's just one more important question, Guv," Z said doubtfully.

"What's that then?"

"When I put in for expenses, what chance I get back my losses at poker?"